DEATH
WE MEET AGAIN

A GRIM AWAKENING
NOVEL
BOOK THREE
MICHELLE GROSS

'TIL DEATH WE MEET AGAIN

Cover Artwork –© 2017 L.J. Anderson of Mayhem Cover Creations

BOOKS IN SERIES

'Til Fear Do Us Part

'Til Grim's Light

'Til Death We Meet Again

PROLOGUE

Somewhere in the makings of time…

God created man and, well, everything else. I don't have to go into detail since the truth itself was as old as the time it began. And most of you have heard of the name Lucifer at some point. An angel who plotted to overthrow Heaven and take his place as King. He failed and God, disappointed and upset with himself for never seeing the darkness—the ugliness beneath the beauty—in Lucifer, cast him out of the skies and into the deep, dark depths of the earth. All of the angels that had plotted with him were cast out as well, where they would then become known as demons. It was in the pit of darkness where they fell to their own wickedness. Over time, their offspring mutated and changed into something more fitting to the monsters they were on the inside, making them something entirely different than the angels they once were. That was how so many different demons came to be.

It was at that point in time where Lucifer became the King of the Underworld we all know him to be.

Satan, the Devil himself.

He was a darkness—a disease that could never be contained in the Underworld and it didn't take his wickedness long to spread. He sent demons into the human world. Everyone knew of God's love for the humans, so he found many ways to taint their hearts with bitter blackness.

And it worked.

So easily. So quickly.

Because humans were and still are vulnerable, so easily swayed.

Darkness grew and stretched in the realms of the human world. People died with the stains of their sins and could not be welcomed into Heaven. The balance was off, the souls of the wicked were among the living—there was no barrier between life and death, but that wasn't the only problem. Evil humans made evil spirits—poltergeists that prayed on the living. The sinners were left to do as they pleased even after death.

God's once perfect system was ruined by the very angel he cast out of Heaven.

And that was when he thought of me.

He created me from all the evil dead that still lingered on earth.

I was made from the vilest of mankind and demons alike. With the bones of fallen demons; I came to be. With my existence, the living and dead—the good and the evil—would have a balance.

In a moments time, I appeared on earth.

That *moment* was still engraved into my mind. I was nothing—I wouldn't even consider me a thing, yet I knew everything I needed to know. I knew what I was made for, what I was meant to do.

I was the shadow of death. People would later call me Death. And even later they would know me as the Grim Reaper. It was only natural that I took the names I were given since I had nothing when I came to be.

Not even human emotions. Only a purpose.

For the darkness I was made from, I was gifted with His light to balance my own darkness. The blue essence that hovered around and through my bones would be the only thing to tell me who I was created from. I would never know or speak to Him. The knowledge I needed was already there when I appeared on Earth.

And I did what I was made to do.

I wiped the evil from the lands. I sent the dead to Heaven or Hell. My existence made Satan furious. I was sending people down to his domain, disrupting his order. It didn't take him long though to find enjoyment out of those that were sent down to him. He came to love torturing and preying on any who were unfortunate enough to fall to him. But what did matter was that I took away any chance of him destroying the human world. Yes, he loathed the very sight of me, but he would never be able to get rid of me. I could be injured, but I could never die. As long as the life existed, so would I.

He did, however, create three powerful monsters called entities.

Fear. Harvest. Jackal.

I found out that I was also considered an entity, just not one made from Satan. I was different because of that reason, yet we were all the same: immortal.

I had never met Jackal or Harvest, sometimes I wondered if those two even existed but then I would hear stories or I would be there to take care of the aftermath of their havoc in body counts. Piles and piles of bodies.

Fear, on the other hand, sought out attention and fed on people's fears and weaknesses. He never stopped taking lives since the moment he was created which kept him on my radar.

...time passed and I lived a very, very long time. Only something that never should have happened, did. I began to develop... curiosity. And with curiosity came wonder. And there it was after centuries upon centuries of watching demons and humans alike, I developed actual feelings and emotions. I watched them eat. I watched them sleep, fight, and argue with one another but what gave me the most curiosity was the relationship between a man and a woman. They called it *love*. Only it was one of many versions of this so-called love. Foolish, absurd, it was. But nonetheless, I was drawn to it like a beacon in the darkness.   Then I came to realize my harsh reality and the pain that came with having human emotion. I would never know this love. It was impossible. I was a being made of bones. I had nothing to offer. I had no lips to kiss her. No flesh to keep her warm.

Then I heard something one night in the Underworld, beyond stupid it was... but I was desperate and just the thought of the whispers being true... I would try anything. The rumor was that of a merge between an entity and a demon. It was said that the entity Jackal had done just that and became one with a demon.

So, as crazy as it seemed, I found a demon and tried the merge. At first, I wasn't sure exactly how it was supposed to work and doubt ran through me as I gazed upon the demon. He smacked his lips, studying me with the kind of intent I recognized—greed, power— something most demons possessed. I ignored it though because I was desperate and trapped by my own desires.

I offered my hand, he took it, and I knew it began—the beginning of two becoming one. It wasn't what I expected or wanted. The moment our minds linked, I could feel how wrong my mistake had been. Evil poured through me; pettiness, darkness became my thoughts. It was a sickening moment, and I pulled away from him. This demon wasn't me. I could never be this sinister. I pushed him away and faded out of time to recollect myself. I realized it was wrong of me to have thoughts as I did. I was never meant for the things I craved. I thought I would never try again…

I lived for a very long time after that, doing the only thing I knew to do—my job. But then I felt it. No warning or clue what it was—I felt a pull in my chest like nothing I had felt before. I followed that bone-deep feeling as it brought me to the City of the Dead. Demons were chanting that I had come to merge with a demon, and then it clicked. I was here for that very reason.

He was here. I didn't know who or what he was, I just knew I had come for him. My other half. The end of my suffering. This emptiness.

I knew it was him that darted out from the crowd and into the circle where I stood. It was there where I became whole. Finally, I was no longer just the Grim Reaper; I was Killian.

And I finally lived. Really lived.

I discovered the touch of a woman. The caress of their skin beneath my fingertips. And I hadn't been wrong about them. They were jewels meant to be savored and with the blood of incubi coursing through me, I knew how to please them.

For the next two thousand years, the world grew larger. I could no longer keep up with dead or the living myself, so I created my own Reapers chosen from decent demons—those searching for a better life and purpose. I became something to these demons. Maybe they saw me as hope—an escape from their own darkness that begged to crawl out from each and every one of them.

I created a home on the outskirts of the Underworld. It grew overtime. Creatures and demons came to inhabit my land. I never once stopped any of them from doing so, and sometimes I wondered if somehow my own thoughts drove them to be here.

Like when every evil had reached it end, I could feel their presence against my skin and their every wrongdoing. It was what I felt every time something needed to die. You could say it was Heaven's way of giving me permission to eradicate something from the world.

And that was how I stumbled upon the dragons who were on the verge of extinction that were being hunted and killed by ogre demons. I descended every single one of the ogres and then afterwards, I offered the dragons my land in exchange that they would protect it and all that lived in it. They agreed and took over my skies.

I wasn't alone anymore but it wasn't enough...

I had yet to experience the one thing I wanted above all. Love. I had the company of women in the past, but nothing that ever made me want to keep them by my side to share everything with... to talk to and lay beside every night. I wondered if it even existed. I rubbed my chest every time I thought about it and knew that I wouldn't think of something so much if it wasn't real. Besides, I knew it existed because I had seen it enough times to know.

Maybe it was me. Maybe it was my fate to live alone, and what a terrible fate to have: to feel so lonely yet never feel a connection with anyone.

"Death," a soft, melodic voice whispered into the darkness of my room one night. I saw the light bouncing off her skin before I saw her as I turned. Angels were so beautiful it was terrifying and the light that bounced off their skin was hard to look at it was so bright. And they rarely left the skies. This would be only the second time I had ever seen one, and it was the same angel. The first time she came to visit me was when I merged with Killian. I smirked as I thought about it, guessing it was to see if the demon had tainted me.

"What do I owe this pleasure?" I asked the divine creature before me. She was a brunette. My eyes roamed over her body, but it was hard to make anything out because of the light radiating from her skin. Oh, right, I suppose the angels were right about the merge corrupting me because my incubus traits kicked in and I wondered if angels could have sex…

She made a sound in her throat and I lifted my eyes away from her chest—not like I could see it with all the light anyway. She was glaring at me with disapproval. "You may be Death, but I can still read your mind." I gave her my best smoldering look, and she merely flicked her hair from her shoulders in response. "I've come with news I think you would like to hear."

"Oh?" I arched my brow. When she made no hurry to continue, I motioned to her with my hands. "Go on."

"He knows what is in your heart, Death." By He, I knew she meant God.

I sighed. "There's a lot of things in that dark place, you've got to be more specific." My nerves were dancing along my skin, I was so curious and tried to play it off like I wasn't.

She gave me a pleasant smile. "A woman, Death; you have a lover."

I thought my heart was going to burst from my chest. I couldn't even explain the racing of my heart. I darted across the room toward her. "What do you mean?" I realized I was yelling at the angel, but I couldn't stop myself even if I tried. "Tell me!" The thought of having someone out there… someone to share every part of myself with… But then I stopped short, was love that easy? No, it wasn't. I had been with countless woman to know better. Love didn't just happen.

"Your thoughts are right. Love doesn't just happen. It's not easy, either, but it's there…between you and her. I can sense that connection waiting to bloom." I didn't like that she could read my thoughts.

I shook my head in aggravation. "Angel, you're not making any sense. If there's someone… if I have…" I kept pausing. "If she's to be with me, then where is she?"

She dropped her gaze. "She isn't born yet." I could only look at her. She gave me hope then turned around and snatched it back. She let out a deep sigh. "I do hate hearing your gloomy thoughts."

"Then stop listening," I interrupted her.

She closed her eyes. "Believe me, I would if I could. And no, Death, she isn't born yet but she will come to you in time. Wait and see."

I half-snarled, half-laughed, "You've told me what you wanted. Now go." I turned away from her.

I could tell that she was hesitant to leave things this way. "I only came to ease some of your loneliness," she replied softly. "To let you know it won't last forever."

"He made me to be lonely." I let the words fall from my lips before I can think of what I said.

"No, he brought you into this world, but you became who you are yourself. Nobody else, it's all you,

Killian, Grim Reaper." I couldn't hide my surprise as I turned back around to face her. I never thought I would hear an angel acknowledge me by Killian since that made me a part of the Underworld. "Have faith. Love will come." Her laughter mixed with her words. "And it's going to take you by surprise." The angel tilted her head as she smiled off into the distance almost if she knew the future herself.

She left me there to ponder that night and weeks and months after that. I even foolishly looked for someone that I knew wasn't born yet… until slowly the thought of her faded out of my thoughts completely. And the thought of love drifted through my thoughts less and less.

A thousand more years passed in the Underworld before I received a message from Heaven. A single note telling me that I had to protect the life of a human girl. Two other things were written on the letter. Her name and that she was the Vessel.

All I had to do was think of her name and I could find her—I am Death, after all. I could find anyone. It was the night before her eighteenth birthday, and I found her standing in line at a movie theater—a place where humans go to watch a bunch more humans on a giant screen, acting. I didn't get much out of the humans' way of entertainment, but I did occasionally find some of their movies… interesting.

I couldn't see her face because I was in the back of the line and she was closer toward the front. I knew it was her though, since I'm Death—maybe she was right about me being vain… but I'm getting ahead of myself.

Anyway… the first thing I noticed about her was she was small and way too jumpy. That was also when I noticed the ghost standing in line in front of her and she was staring at him… wait, she could see them? I immediately tossed my presence around in the room, so that the ghost would know that a Reaper was present. I could tell he sensed me because it didn't take him long to get gone.

I visibly saw her shoulders relax, and the guy next to her never stopped smiling—correction: the guy never stopped smiling at her. Even when she wasn't looking at him, he was always looking over and smiling at her. It made me realize I didn't know what I was even doing here. Or more like, why did I have to be here? Why not send an angel if she was so important? Were they too good to come down here themselves?

I rubbed my neck and didn't like how uncomfortable I felt. I stayed away from humans. Not that I disliked them… I just found them weak and often that mixed with greed and yeah, that made some no better than demons.

I walked around the theater not expecting anything to happen until finally, it did. I saved her the first time that night from a screamer—a fog-like looking creature that kept the soul of everything he killed—similar to what I could do with my scythe. She was crying out as she hunkered down on the toilet. She went silent when I stepped in front of the stall she was in. I walked away and left her there.

I didn't actually see her until the next night when Molly tried to kill her. That was how I figured out how much danger she was in. If the Vessel was as powerful as the rumors…then Fear could never get his hands on it.

But then I saw her… and every thought flew out the window. I was taken by her beauty. She was running out into the yard and she kept looking toward the house as she ran for the car. Her blonde hair was tied back as it bounced back and forth. I was wondering why the hell I was standing on her roof staring while her life was in danger.

Somehow, I regained some sense and jumped down when she was trying to get in the car. When she failed to open the car door, she twirled around and saw me. I noticed how long and delicate her legs were while she was running. Even with good height, I was a lot bigger than her, and I had no idea why I was taking notice of everything about her. I didn't touch her—I had my back toward her, but she fell back and hit the car as soon as she saw me.

You would think after I rescued her from Molly, she would show some appreciation, but instead, I had to grab her as she tried to run back inside. She kicked and wiggled in my hold, and I had to stop smiling before I turned her around to face me—because I was even freaking myself out. I mean, why the hell was I grinning like some idiot?

In the process of her fighting to get away from me, I let her fall onto gravel. I could see that she was afraid of me, but I needed her to turn around and face me as I talked. More like, I was compelled to see what she looked like. Her voice was distant and cold as she tried to hide her fear, but when she finally stood up and faced

19

me, she was anything but. Blue eyes peered up at me and the light of the moon gave them the effect of looking at diamonds.

While I loved her beauty, she feared me instantly. Her eyes, full of hatred, met mine as she backed toward the porch falling over, all the while shooing me away before she high-tailed it back into the house.

I could tell you I didn't fall for her that night, but I would be lying.

That was also when Melanie Rose became the bane of my existence.

Along with my growing want of her... My fear, distress, happiness, and life suddenly revolved around what happened to her.

I didn't realize what I felt for Melanie was what I had always hoped for until the night I offered my hand to her behind Deb's Diner. I wanted her to know me—not just know me—I wanted her to accept every part of me.

But I never thought she'd accept me… at least not all of me. She did though, and continued to show me her way of loving before I even realized she did.

And it never crossed my mind until she said to Fear, *"I'm Grim's Light."* Her skin looked more like gold as it glowed and when she pulled the scythe from her chest… I remembered what the angel had told me. *She's the one.*

She saved me that night when she pieced me back together.

My Love.

The one I fell for before I even knew I was meant to fall for her. That didn't matter, I would have made sure she was mine no matter what. The light she carried, it was a lot like angels. I smiled down at her... Did He bring me down a piece of Heaven?

I finally found her. This feeling, this moment was perfect. She was perfect. As I stared at her on the rooftop, the reality came into focus. She was human... fragile and the death in me could already see her death in the distant future.

It crushed me. Consumed me.

I couldn't lose her. Not ever.

Why would He bring her to me if I could not keep her for eternity?

CHAPTER ONE
Molly

I kept a safe distance from Fear once we were back in his cave. Grim got away from him again, and Melanie—the Vessel that was suddenly not the Vessel. What the hell? So, everyone had been wrong and I didn't even understand what that made her now, but those two did a number on Fear and he was pissed. It didn't matter that he was severely injured, every demon, chair, or table in his path was being destroyed.

I ducked my head just as he threw a demon he had been sleeping with for asking if he was okay... I had liked Rick and as I raised my head back up and turned my body enough so that I could see his now lifeless body resting on the stone floor... I wished I hadn't.

I closed my eyes for a second and wondered when it would be me that would perish under Fear's wrath. I was a ghost and yes, Fear did give me something extra to go with it... which explained my red eyes, but... I could still be destroyed.

I opened them back up and faced him again. His tail moved wildly behind him as he growled in frustration. "He doesn't know what he's talking about! I won't die, I can never die!" He sounded delirious as he spoke.

My heart jumped once, twice, doubling more and more as I watched him. I hated him, but he could give me what I wanted. Was having a grown body so important? I found myself asking that question more and more… but I couldn't go back now. I was just as vile as him now—the things I have already done to get this far…

Grim spoke of his death… if it was true then I needed to make sure he gave me what I wanted before that happened.

"Fear." I finally spoke. He didn't hear me. He was too caught up in his own rage to care. Why did Grim make him this way? Why did he want to be Grim so bad? And why didn't Fear care that Marcus wanted more than just him? Was Fear incapable of thinking for himself? Or did he want to be Grim as well? "Fear," I said louder this time.

He whipped his head around to face me. A female demon took that as a chance to scatter out of his path. The other demons that were near were too terrified to move. When I saw the unmasked madness on his face, I wavered, but Grim's words hadn't only upset him, it did me as well. I wanted to be a grown woman before I lost the chance! "My body. You keep telling me—"

"Body?" he cut me off and the cold, detached tone told me I should have kept my mouth shut. I was already taking a step back as he walked forward. He brought his hand over his wound. "Please do not tell me you are bringing up your need to be an actual woman." I looked down quickly. I hated to show weakness, but it was better to be docile and afraid in front of him then to show any sort of strength—that got you killed with him. But I was more angry than scared. He kept telling me to do this, and this, and this, and this before he'd give me what I wanted and I started to realize he was pulling me along. "Look at me, Molly." He was in front of me now and I looked up. He was pointing toward the sword wound. "Do you think I have time to worry about what you want?" He leered down at me, then his hands were in my hair and he pulled me up off the ground that way. "I don't know, Molly, you've done an awful shit job of everything lately... maybe I should just get rid of you. You've failed me every time when it came to handling Melanie." In my head, I was thinking that he was no different. He had failed every time when it came to Grim or Melanie.

I didn't speak, but I did show my defiance in the way I met his eyes. I wouldn't show him any fear. Even if I didn't want to die. Even if I wanted to look like more than a child... I knew I should have never taken his offer so long ago, but my own wants always came first.

He watched me several silent seconds before throwing me across the cave. I tumbled a time or two on the ground before I got back up and looked at him.

He was still looking down at me even from this distance. Like he was better than me. The scariest thing in the way that felt was if it were true. That I was no better than the monster that made me into one.

"You're lucky." I waited to hear the thing he said every time he spared me my life. "If it weren't for Fear, I would have killed you a long time ago."

Those words, I never understood them. He spoke like he wasn't Fear. Regardless, for whatever reasons, he always kept me around and I'd continue to do what he asked until I got what I wanted.

CHAPTER TWO
Melanie

I gripped Killian's hand as he faded us into his home—the one in my world. I was glad to finally get away from the Underworld but worried all the same. My face must have shown a reflection of the way I was feeling because he tugged on my hand and made me look up.

"Ryan's safe, you saw one of the Reapers take him back to my place." Right before we had left, some of Killian's Reapers showed up and he convinced me it was best that Ryan stayed at his place. He was still under Fear's control, and it would be a lot harder for Fear to get to him if he was there. It didn't make me feel better about it, though. I had a lot of guilt when I thought of Ryan.

Killian had somehow managed to get me some clothes to change into since I had been wearing nothing but panties underneath his cloak. During the time he had been talking to the Reapers, I put them on before giving the cloak back to him.

Yes, it had been an eventful night.

I tried to smile but it turned into a sigh. "He's not going to like waking up there... I think I should go and stay with him."

He tilted my chin up. "I think you should go home and rest." He pulled me closer and I reluctantly went into his arms. It had felt so good to tell him I loved him on the rooftop, but now all my worries were back. "Melanie, he's been through a lot and I think more than anything he'd want a chance to figure out what's happening to him before you…" he trailed off, but I already understood what he meant.

I pressed my nose into his chest and wrapped my arms around him. Killian was no boy. I breathed him in and thought of every sin I wanted to commit with him. My own thoughts made me think of what he did to me in the alley during the Human Festival. He placed his chin on the top of my head. "You confess your love to me not even an hour ago, and already you can't keep your hands off me."

I groaned at his conceited comment. "Fine, I'll move." When I went to pull away, he wouldn't let me, and I grinned into his chest before looking up at him.

He was gazing down at me with a smile. I traced his lips with my eyes and I contemplated kissing him until I was distracted by his sigh. It wasn't the pleasant sort of sigh I wanted to hear, though. It was the kind I hated. The kind that reminded me of everything that was wrong. My smile vanished as I lowered my head. That was when I noticed the state the house was in… The place was a mess from when Molly brought the wolf demons here. "You should probably use your handy powers about now and clean this place up," I told him just as I caught a whiff of something… I stepped away from Killian and tipped my nose in the air. "Is that the smell of chili?"

As I walked down the hallway, the hole in the wall began to vanish along with the mess. "I told you time moves differently here than it does in the Underworld," he said and I remembered, but as I hurried into the kitchen and touched the pot on the stove I was still amazed. It was still a little warm.

"I spent three days at your place…"

"It's only been a couple of hours at most here," he added. I turned around and almost bumped into him. I hadn't realized he was right behind me. He had a sly grin on his face and I was sure he was enjoying my curiosity about the difference in time, but I needed confirmation. I hurried away from him and went to search for my phone. I was pretty sure I had left it in the living room and found it on the floor next to the couch. When I picked it up, I flopped down on the couch. The date was exactly as when we left a few days ago. The only difference was a few hours in time and it was dark. It had still been daylight when we had left.

"That's amazing," I said looking at my phone.

He followed me into the living room and stood in front of me. There was a crooked tilt on his lips as he smiled at me. "When will you stop making sure of everything and just believe me when I tell you something."

"I believed you when you told me, but it's still weird that the time is so different."

"After everything you've been through and witnessed, the time is what you're most amazed about?" He cracked another grin my way.

I laughed and let my head fall back against the couch and closed my eyes. Since I used the power again on the rooftop, my entire body ached and there was a pounding in my head. I wouldn't tell Killian because he didn't agree with me using the power but if I hadn't, who knew what would have happened.

As bad as I wanted to go check on Ryan, I knew Killian was right. I needed to rest. Now that I was sitting down, it felt even worse. I heard him move above me, but I was so focused on my headache that I didn't bother to open my eyes. "How are you feeling?" he asked me.

I raised my head slightly and opened my eyes. "I'm fine, why?" Of course, we both knew I was lying.

He exhaled before bending down over me. He brought his hand up to my face and lifted it enough so that I was gazing into his eyes as he leaned over me. "Don't lie to me. You used a lot of your power earlier."

I grabbed his hand that was on my cheek. "Killian… what am I, really?" My tone was serious—desperate even. I searched his eyes for an answer.

The room was quiet and the draw of breath that escaped his mouth branded a place in my memory. Not because it was sexy or deep, but because it was a new type of intimacy I wanted to share with him. Being in a quiet place, in an empty room with him as we talked about things that held meaning. When would he give me more of him? When would he share some of the burdens he carried with me?

"You mean, you make that bold statement earlier and declared yourself as Grim's Light to Fear and don't even know what that meant?"

Now that he put it that way, I laughed shyly and was glad that the light in the living room was off to hide the rise in color on my cheeks. The hallway light was enough to see most of his face as he loomed over me. "Yeah, now that I think about it, it was kind of embarrassing." We laughed together, and it became another brand on my heart that I never wanted to forget.

"We know you're human, but I don't know what else you are," he admitted. His eyes lowered to my lips as he spoke, "But I think it's safe to say we didn't cross paths by accident."

As his mouth drew closer, I silently thanked the reason I was born to be with him. And I hoped that the *me* in my dreams hadn't been lying when she told me that I was his light. For whatever reason, I just wanted to be with him.

Only, he didn't kiss me and leaned back up. "Come on, I'll take you home."

I pretended to pout as he walked me to the car and opened the door for me. I got in and leaned my head against the car door after buckling up. *Tylenol, here I come,* I thought.

We drove in silence and I found myself thinking of Ryan. He only ever loved me and look where that love got him. I knew everything that happened to him was my fault, but just like his love made him selfless, mine made me selfish. I went straight into Killian's arms despite it all. That was why I would find a way to save him from Fear.

The drive was short and we were soon pulling into my driveway. I unbuckled my seatbelt. "Melanie." I looked over at him. He leaned back into the seat and suddenly he was thrusting his hips up in the air so that he could get something from his pocket. My eyes zeroed in on his crotch. My face heated and I grabbed my neck and looked away. I thought that things would go back to normal now that Killian's incubus impulses were under control, but it wasn't. My mind always steered in that direction. I blamed it on the books I read.

His hand left his pocket and moved it in front of my face. Something shiny dangled from his fingers. "I've been meaning to give it to you for a while but never could find the right opportunity." I looked down at the necklace in his hand. I touched the white skull on the necklace and smiled. I also noticed that there were two, but the second necklace had no skull on it.

"Why two?" I asked.

"Do you not like it?" I could tell that he was waiting for a different reaction from me.

"No, it's beautiful. I love it." I smiled at him as I took the necklace with the skull from his hand. The white of the skull was like nothing I had seen before. It almost seemed magical and knowing him, it probably was. "Is the other one for you?"

He nodded. "Yeah, it's actually more than a necklace." I looked up. "Remember the demon I killed from the lake?" I nodded. I could never forget that night. That was the night he showed me what he did as the Grim Reaper. "I made your necklace from the pearl I took from her. Pearls can be very powerful if you use them right, so I had a witch turn it into a protective charm. Even when I'm not with you, this will keep you safe in my place."

I knew the mood was romantic, but I couldn't stop myself from being me. "I was beginning to worry you were taking me home, so that I could be kidnapped by some demon and you wouldn't have to protect me anymore." I was joking, but it had crossed my mind that I wouldn't be safe if he left me here alone.

His eyes darkened and my belly dropped with both worry and anticipation. "I'll put it on you." He took the necklace from my hand. I leaned over the gear shift and scooped my hair up off my neck. The shirt he gave me on the rooftop was super baggy and I knew he could see my breasts if he wanted to. My heart jumped along with the blush on my cheeks. It wasn't like he hadn't seen them already.

He didn't miss the way I was acting—the increase in my breath and the way I watched his eyes to observe where they might roam. He didn't say anything as he brought the necklace up to my neck, but my skin spoke for the both of us when it tingled and broke out into goosebumps when his hand grazed my neck.

The necklace felt cool against my warm skin. His eyes finally lowered to the necklace, but it didn't take them long to stray toward the X on my chest. I covered it instinctively. I lived with it so long, and it came naturally for me to hide it. There was something terrifying in the way his eyes darkened the longer he looked at it along with the way he tightened his jaw. He moved my hand away so he could look at it. He rubbed his thumb across it roughly.

"This is an eyesore." I lowered my gaze from his. I hated the mark even more than he did. "Melanie, I won't let anyone take your life away from you. I won't let anyone take you. Ever." Killian had the perfect balance of light and dark; one minute he was gentle and the next he seemed just as dangerous as the demons he was keeping me from.

I wanted him to be right but Fear couldn't be killed yet Grim kept speaking like he would soon die... which was it? So instead, I changed the subject and smiled slightly. "Let me put yours on you."

"I can put it on," he told me, but I was already taking the necklace out of his hand. I raised up from my seat, and that put me even further onto the gear shift. For someone so old and experienced, I took pleasure in the way I could catch him off guard. I brushed my cheek across his as I put on the necklace. I could see his Adam's apple move slightly, and I knew why. My breasts were in his face—yes, on purpose.

"What's wrong?" I moved back when the necklace was on but only enough that I was inches from his face.

And I knew I gave myself away because his eyes fell over me knowingly. "Melanie, if I didn't know better

I would think that you had them in my face to get a reaction." When I tried to look away, he grabbed me by the chin and wouldn't let me go. His hand trailed up my arm, across my collarbone before going into my hair. The tightening in my stomach was strong enough that I felt the need all the way down to my toes. I kissed him before he could kiss me. It was only enough to brush our lips together and it was over. Then he pulled me back in for the real one. Our mouths bumped and slid apart, the sound of our breathing and our tongues meeting were the only things I could hear. My stomach was so wound up, I felt like combusting but then he was pulling back away from me. "It's okay to slow down, Love. I'm not going anywhere and neither are you."

His words peeled back a layer I thought I kept hidden. I was scared. I was scared of losing to Fear. I was scared of dying and being stuck in the Underworld with Fear. I was terrified of what might happen to Ryan if we didn't do something. And most of all, I was terrified of not knowing what it felt like to love Killian before I lost the chance to.

"I'm not," I sounded defensive as I slid back over into my seat. "Don't you like kissing me? Or now that your incubus voodoo is under control, you no longer want to kiss me?"

He sighed. "Melanie…"

"What, Killian? I don't get it. After everything we did—you did to me earlier while we were in the Underworld…"

"Yes, Melanie, I feel bloody terrific that I gave you your first orgasm in a filthy alley in the Underworld where humans were being killed and without a choice of what happened to them," he said sarcastically.

My chest tightened and I knew I had to get out of this car. I jumped out and slammed the door shut before he got a chance to stop me. *Please don't cry, please don't cry,* I told myself as I hurried up the steps. I couldn't walk into the house crying because Alex or Mom would ask why.

But, I felt so horrible. So, so, ashamed. What happened between Killian and I had been beyond amazing, but it didn't change the fact that it happened at the wrong place. At the wrong time. And I was exposed in front of all those demons in just my panties and Ryan had seen me that way too.

The humiliation would never end.

I stopped at the door and took a deep breath, recollecting my thoughts before I walked in. I was surprised to see a smile on Mom's face as she stepped into the hallway. For a moment, just the sight of her after three days was enough to make me forget about what I had been so upset about. The way my life was lately I wasn't sure if I'd live to see her smile—or Alex complaining about something normal—or Tess telling me another one of her crazy stories.

But that smile of hers vanished as her eyes lowered. Oh, crap. I was wearing a different outfit than the one I had left in. "Melanie." Her voice was intimidating, and now I knew how Killian felt when he came over.

"Yes, Mom?"

"Why are you wearing different clothes than what you left in?" It felt ridiculous. I spent the last three days wondering if I'd ever see her again and if I'd even survive to come home. Yet, I get interrogated the moment I was home. I giggled. "And why is this funny?" she asked as she crossed her arms over her chest.

"Nothing, just thanks. I kind of needed that." I shrugged my shoulders at her, and she looked at me like I had lost my mind.

"You didn't answer my question."

"Mom!" I groaned as I moved toward the kitchen. "Trust in your daughter. Besides, you're the one that told me to have fun before I left but NOTHING happened." Not exactly nothing… I started searching through the cabinets. "Oh, but he's my boyfriend now, I think." I did storm out of the car on him… "Where's the Tylenol? I have a headache."

She went to the cabinet I had just looked in and handed them to me. "You think?" She gave me another funny look. I grabbed a water and took the Tylenol. She finally sighed. "Well, if he plans to get serious, he should probably think about coming over for dinner sometime."

Killian? Mom? Alex? All together at the dinner table…

I gave her a quick hug. At least she was starting to accept him. "I will ask him." I saw Alex eavesdropping from the hallway. "I'm going upstairs." Alex hurried away as I went upstairs. "I saw you, Alex."

I shut my door as soon as I entered my room and came face to face with my boyfriend. I couldn't even look at him. I could feel the shame creeping across my face. "I have a few words to the girl in front of me who thinks I'm not interested in her." He started to walk forward and I stepped back every time he did until he had me against the door. He placed his elbow above my head as he towered over me. "To the beautiful girl who suddenly feels ashamed of what he did to her earlier because of the way her idiot boyfriend—of only a couple of hours, I might add—worded what he meant wrong." I started crying. Oh, God, did I cry. "When I said those things, Melanie, I wasn't being harsh to you but myself. I don't regret what we did in the alley, but I do feel guilty that as a man, as a demon, and as the Grim Reaper I followed along with Fear's games so that I could get a chance to merge again. And for you making that happen, you will have no idea what that meant for me. I won't ever regret having my hands on you, I just would have preferred it to be anywhere but there." He wiped away my tears.

After I cried to my heart's content, I let him carry me to bed before he left to check on Ryan.

CHAPTER THREE
Melanie

I was up before my alarm clock went off. It was Sunday, so I didn't have to worry about going to school. I had satisfying sleep but the moment I opened my eyes my uneasiness grew. I slept a whole night here in the human world… just how long would that be in the Underworld? The more I thought about it, the guiltier I felt for not waiting for Ryan to wake up before I left.

I knew Killian had a point that I needed to give him some space. Things had been awkward between us in the Underworld. He had been shackled by Fear to get a reaction from me… and the fact that he was the charred demon that was always trying to kill me was even worse.

While waiting for Killian to come get me, I went downstairs to get a glass of milk. Everyone was still asleep so I was quiet until I flipped on the kitchen light and felt my soul leave my body. Sitting at the table was a man flipping through my mom's cookbook. He looked over at me and did a chin lift in greeting.

What the—

"Honey, what's wrong?" Mom came staggering out of her bedroom barely awake. She looked at me then into the kitchen. Her eyes scanned the room and moved right over him before she looked at me again. "What is it?" Then she grabbed her chest. "Please don't tell me it was a rat?"

He wasn't a ghost. The more I studied him, the more he looked like a Reaper! The dark clothing and calm nature. Was he here to keep watch? "Uhhh…"

"Grim sent me here to protect you and your family," he finally told me. "But pay no mind to me, go about your business." How the heck was I supposed to ignore someone that was sitting in our kitchen? Then he flipped to the next page in the cookbook and Mom's eyes shot open like she was suddenly out of her drowsy state.

"Did you see that?" she asked me while still staring at the cookbook on the table.

I ran to the table and snatched the cookbook off the table and glared at the Reaper before putting it back in the cabinet. "No, what was it?"

She looked up to the ceiling fan before shaking her head. "Nothing. Just still trying to wake up, I guess." As she walked to the coffee pot, I shot him another glare and mouthed, "Stop touching things!"

"Mom, it's too early. I'm going back to bed." I told her quickly and ran back upstairs to wait and yell at my boyfriend for not telling me he put a Reaper in the house with us. Luckily said boyfriend faded into my sight right as I stepped into the room and shut the door. "I expected to see a loving face when I arrived here, why do you look like you might want to murder me?"

"Why didn't you tell me you got a Reaper to stay in the house with us?" I whisper-yelled at him.

"Oh, Miles," he said nonchalantly.

"Yes, Miles," I muttered in a ridiculously stupid manner. "He scared the crap out of me, and you should have seen Mom's face when he flipped a page in her cookbook while he sat at the table."

He looked so serious for a second… only a second before he became a boyish looking man with a shit-eating grin. "Oh, I would have loved to see that." He leaned close. "I bet it was funny."

"Oh my God, it was not—" But I was already laughing at his goofy grin. "Okay, maybe a little." Then I slapped his shoulder and tried to get serious. "But seriously, this ain't funny. I don't want him going around picking up stuff and moving them around. Mom will lose her mind and let's not forget, I have a lot of experience when it comes to thinking you're going crazy… it is not fun!"

He covered his smile with his hand. "I'm sorry, you've been through a lot." I squinted my eyes at him… he didn't look sorry at all. "You ready to go see Ryan?" he asked me. I nodded quickly. He tilted his head at me. "Dial down the enthusiasm; I know he means a lot to you, but you are with *me*."

He grabbed my arm before I got a chance to say anything and faded us to his home.

————

I didn't know what I expected to happen when I spoke to Ryan but I never expected him to smile as soon as he saw me—the laid back, easy-going Ryan sort of smile I'd seen half my life.

"Melanie." His smile was confident, sure of himself—hiding how he really felt—as he walked over and wrapped me in a hug. "Why do you look like someone stole your lunch?" He ended the hug so that he could say it to my face.

"Don't do that." I pushed him away and felt my anxiety crawling up my stomach like a disease.

"Do what?" He feigned ignorance. Now that I was actually looking at him, I could see the dark circles, the lack of sleep, the droop in his shoulders… it was all clear. Ryan was just very good at making me think he was okay.

"Ryan…" I didn't even know what to say. "After everything you've been through…"

"Oh, you mean the fact that I turn into a monster that wants to kill you?" he said with ease, so much so that I was caught off guard.

I shook my head at him. "Ryan, that wasn't you."

He sighed. "Yeah, I know but it is me." He stepped away from me. "All I ever wanted was to keep you safe and somehow I ended up being one of the monsters that tried to kill you." Ryan looked to Killian who never spoke a word as he watched us.

I walked a couple steps to get to him. I grabbed his shoulders and made him look at me. "Ryan, how can you still worry about me right now?" My voice was soft and the lump in my throat was getting worse. "Ryan, you died and now Fear turned you into a demon… Be mad. Get angry! But, please start thinking of yourself instead of me!"

"What kind of guy do you think I am, Melanie?" This time he was the one grabbing my shoulders. "I've loved you for too damn long and it's hard for me to stop worrying about you." He sounded so earnest it broke my heart.

"Ryan…" I whispered. "I won't let Fear take any more from you. We will figure out a way to get rid of the demon he created inside you." *And save your afterlife. And hopefully keep me from falling into his hands as well.*

"Melanie… this demon, it's too powerful… When it takes over, I truly become something else and I can't control myself." I watched him shudder.

"That's why we have to keep you from Fear." He laughed at me.

"That doesn't matter, he doesn't have to be around for him to control me. If he wanted me, I would have already changed… He's waiting for something, Melanie, he's sick and twisted. I know he's just waiting, and I can't stand not knowing when it's going to happen to me again." Ryan looked scared. Truly afraid.

"Ryan, what happened to you during the time you were with him?"

"Grim, we have a problem." We all turned to a new voice in the room. Killian turned his head last. He made sure he met my eyes before he looked away.

"I'll give you guys a minute," Killian told me as he walked away with the Reaper. I wanted to follow him, but he never left me an invitation to.

"Melanie." I turned back to Ryan. "He'll be back."

I shrugged my shoulders. "I know." I prepared my nerves from what I was about to say next. "About Killian…"

"You guys are together. I already know."

I arched my eyebrow at him. "You do?"

He groaned. "Grim told me."

"He did?" I couldn't keep my surprise hidden.

He nodded. "Oh yeah. After he found out I wasn't emotionally damaged from what I went through with Fear, he made sure to bring up the fact. Loud and clear."

I brought my hands to my cheeks. "I'm sorry, I wanted to be the one that told you—"

"Don't worry, competition won't hurt me." He gave me a lopsided grin.

"Ryan, I'm already with him."

"That doesn't matter to me. Until I lose myself to Fear completely I will go after the things I want… and you've always been the only thing I've ever wanted." My stomach bottomed out. How was I supposed to respond to that? "Come on, let's go. Grim might not be so interesting himself, but he does have a pretty nice home."

———

Ryan pushed open the front doors of Grim's castle and led us outside. I took a deep breath as I looked at the view. It would never stop amazing me how a place could look so magical. I watched him as he looked around. "Is this your first time stepping outside the castle?" I asked him.

"Not since..." He let his voice die out. Why did I ask stupid things? Now I was picturing him chained to a tree and I was sure he was doing the same thing.

I cleared my throat. "So, do you want to see the dragons?" I looked over at him with a smile.

He didn't look surprised to hear there were dragons. He continued to look around. "This place is... something else."

"It's beautiful," I told him.

"It's not what I've pictured the Grim Reaper's place to look like. I mean, the place has a darkness to it. Even now the sky looks too dark to be considered daylight yet... it's also full of color and life."

"It's enchanting," I muttered another comment as I eyed the place like it was my favorite ice cream flavor: cookies and cream.

"If you say so," he grunted in response, but I could tell by the look on his face that he was mesmerized like I was.

"Sky!" I yelled.

"What the hell?" Ryan looked at me. "Who's Sky?"

"A friend," I told him. "And I was the one that gave her that name," I added proudly.

It took a few minutes for her to become visible in the sky. When she did, she was like a star in the orange colored sky. She called to me, it was a piercing echo that lasted several seconds. She dropped down in front of us and tucked her wings to her sides. "How's Rixen?" I rubbed her neck.

Her head lifted to the sky and I looked up to see the dragon leader soaring above us. "Glad to see he's okay."

"She's beautiful," he mumbled next to me, transfixed by the beauty that was Sky. At his words, Sky eyes shifted to him and growled. Her nostrils flared, teeth bared, as she hunkered down and eyed Ryan. He brought his hands up and took a step back, not wanting to upset her, but she only grew more agitated. What few times I got to spend with Sky since coming here, I knew she was very docile and gentle compared to the other dragons. Why was she being so hostile with Ryan?

"Hey, Sky." I moved closer, guiding my hands in front of her to take her attention away from him. "What's wrong?"

I could keep pretending I didn't know why she was acting this way, but one glance at Ryan's haunted face and I knew he understood, too. "It's him, isn't it? She can sense *him* in me."

"Sky, he's not our enemy." Now I was desperate to make her understand, Ryan *needed* her to understand. Rixen roared in the sky. His tail swayed as he watched

45

us, I didn't know what he might do if he thought Sky was in danger. "Please, calm down, you're making Rixen anxious." I placed my hands against her snout and tried to soothe her. She took the opportunity to put my wrist in her mouth just so that she could jerk me to her side. She kept me close as she watched Ryan.

His face was worse than a man of defeat. It was the look of someone that had nothing left.

"Sky!" I stepped right back in front of her.

"Don't force her to understand," Ryan told me from behind. "She should know to fear me so that if I ever become the demon again she would know to stop me."

Sky was no longer growling and I knew she was trying to figure out what Ryan meant. "Fear made him something he's not… just to hurt me because he's someone I care about." Her eyes darted back and forth between Ryan and me, and it was so plain to see that she was having her own inner turmoil with her instincts. That gave me hope. She wanted to believe me. "We're gonna save him, so I need you to watch over him like you do me. I'm sure Grim will keep him safe here."

"He's safest here, but Fear can still get to him." I turned in the direction of Killian's voice and saw him standing a few feet behind Ryan. "He died with Fear's mark. No matter where I take him, Fear will eventually be able to get to him. It's the rule of the mark." There was that awful pang in my chest, the combination of a volcano erupting and the drop of despair pitting against every 'hope' you want to believe. "Ryan, have you felt him lately?" he asked Ryan.

"No," he shook his head.

"Nothing at all?" Killian asked again.

"Nothing besides dreams of being the demon... and going after Melanie." He lowered his head and wouldn't meet my eyes. I wanted to reach out to him and tell him that none of what happened while he was the charred demon was his fault, but I knew nothing I could say would ease what he must be feeling.

I felt out of place and disconnected with everything. I thought the more I knew about why Fear did what he did to me, things would feel different. The only thing that was different was my best friend dying and being controlled by a demon Fear placed inside him. How much more would Ryan have to suffer before I could finally save him?

"The demon is feeding you memories as a means to break you," Killian told him. "He knows you trying to kill Melanie will break you quicker than he ever could." Did I hear a hint of praise in his voice toward Ryan?

I used the chance to turn toward Sky while Ryan was focused on Killian's words. I moved my face in front of hers and grabbed hold of her. "Sky, please. Look at him. Do you really see someone you should fear?" Her huge, beaded blue eyes fell on Ryan again. "Because all I see is a tortured soul that's in this mess because of me."

Sky took a deep sigh and pulled away from me. I looked back and saw Killian staring at me. I couldn't decipher the look on his face. And maybe, just maybe, that look was because he couldn't decipher me either.

Our stare down was over when we noticed Sky inching toward Ryan. He didn't even notice at first. When he lifted his head and saw her, he froze. Rixen roared down at us, but he didn't sound angry... more like he wanted his presence known.

Ryan was too terrified of scaring her to even move. She moved closer, and closer, until she waited for him to make the next move. And he finally did. He brought his hand to the place between her eyes where he rubbed her down to her snout. She moved her face closer for him, even closing her eyes and showing trust.

I was smiling long before Ryan looked over at me in amazement.

———

Once we were back inside, Ryan met my eyes. "When you speak to Tess, tell her that I moved on from this world and that I'm sorry I chose to leave before saying goodbye." My throat tightened. "I don't ever want her to know the truth." With those words, he disappeared into another room and I didn't stop him.

"Come on, there's a room I want to show you," I looked to Killian just as he grabbed my hand. My chest grew warm as well as my stomach, but I felt guilty for the way I felt. "Melanie." He was tense and I could tell he wanted to say something as his hand tightened around mine.

He didn't say anything else, instead, he led me up one of the stairways by the hand. We were quiet and I took those silent seconds to recollect my thoughts. We passed two bedrooms before we stopped at a closed door. This door was different than the others, it had a rocky appearance and something was engraved into the door, but I had no clue what because I didn't even know what language it was.

He held a key out to me as he released my hand. "What?" I asked him.

He grinned because Killian always took delight in my confusion. That was to be expected from someone as vain as him. He took enjoyment in his regard for himself and what he knew that others did not. But, that wasn't entirely true, I knew he had a protective nature and a big heart, and I mostly liked calling him vain just because he was too good to be true sometimes.

I would continue to unravel the things that made Killian who he was and discover just who it was that I fell in love with.

"Stop grinning and just tell me, so that we can both grin about it together," I nagged at him.

"Just think of something you want and unlock the door with the key."

He placed the key in my hand. "Huh?" He laughed and I couldn't help but smile. What was he so excited to show me?

"Always with the questions," he told me. "Just think of something—anything. Just make sure it's something you like."

I squinted my eyes at him before turning to the door. Something I liked... I sighed. It was hard to think of something in this situation. I didn't even know what was going to happen.

Oh, I got one!

Ice cream cake!

I unlocked the door and opened it. This place was much more than an ice cream shop. There was ice cream everywhere. There was a bar filled with ice cream cakes on the right and a row of ice cream machines lined up beside the bar. Ice cream was being made in the back of the room with... was that a robot? My mouth finally opened. "Oh my God." There was even a couch made from ice cream! Everything was cold and yummy looking.

Killian laughed beside me. "Is ice cream the only thing you thought of?"

"Technically, I thought of ice cream cake," I clarified and he didn't seem impressed. "What? You said to think of some*thing* and I did."

He shook his head at me. "You need a better imagination than that, Love, if you plan to use my key." His key? I arched my eyebrow at him as he reached for the key. "Here, let me show you how to properly use it."

I moved my hand away so that he couldn't take it from me. "No, I'll try again." We stepped out of the room and shut it back.

Here I go all over again as I studied the key in my hand. Hmm.

Oh, I got a good one!

I stuck the key in again and opened the door. Food paradise! Only this time I did better. One side of the room was dedicated to nothing but chicken being rotated on racks. The other side was a replica of the restaurant Happy Days and I drooled as the mechanic female made a milkshake. She placed a cheeseburger and fries next to the milkshake. "That would be for me," I told him as I hurried into the room, but I took one look at the chicken again and stopped. Mashed potatoes… rolls…and all kinds of sides that could be added with the chicken. I looked to the cheeseburger again. "Man, this is a hard decision," I mumbled to myself, chewing on my bottom lip.

I could hear the grin in his voice as he moved behind me. "I'm starting to see a pattern here. Are you hungry?"

"Yeah, I didn't get to eat anything because the Reaper sitting at our kitchen table scared the life out of me this morning." I went for the milkshake and grabbed it before going to the other side of the room to eat the chicken.

Killian joined me on a barstool as I ate. He was watching me with a smile. "Earlier," I started. "Did the Reaper have something to tell you about Fear?"

He leaned forward in his seat with a sigh. "I don't know yet."

I gave him a confused frown. I sat my fork down. "This room is magical and all… I get it, this is your way to get me to relax, but what happens now?"

He tucked a piece of hair that had fallen out of my ponytail behind my ear. "Can't you let me take care of everything?"

He already knew the answer to that. "I want this all to be over." He reached out for my hand. "Will he try to merge with Grim again?" I asked.

He shook his head. "Whatever you did to me on that rooftop was permanent. There's no separating going on anymore, thanks to you." He squeezed my hand, and I gave him a small smile.

"I don't even know what the heck I did on the rooftop," I admitted sheepishly. "Just whenever I use the power, things become clear and I automatically know what to do… I only knew I didn't want to lose you."

Neither of us had brought up the fact that I would die and he would lose me one day since we left that rooftop, but right now, it felt like it was hanging in the air between us.

"I'm not going anywhere." His eyes held that dark intensity as his thumb rubbed across mine. "You're here with me, but your mind's not. It's clear by the expression on your face."

"I am," I told him quickly. "It's just… will this with Fear ever be over, and if it does end, what will happen between us?"

"Marcus will die by my hands, it's only a matter of when it's going to happen. When he dies, your ties with Fear should end as well."

"And Ryan, too?"

He dropped his gaze from mine for a second, but it was enough to frighten me. "Okay, I'm going to tell you what's going to happen. When this is all over with, you will be by my side whenever you want and the same applies to when I want you—so don't look to be getting away from me. And as for dealing with Fear, that makes our time together short right now, so when we are alone, forget everything else." I felt my face getting hot, and I hoped I wasn't red in the face. Any sort of emotion I felt showed on my face way too easily.

Large hands snaked around my waist and pulled me close. "I want you to promise me to leave your worries behind when we're alone."

"I'll try," I whispered, although it was never hard when his hands were on me.

He sighed. "There's something else you want to ask, right?" He could read me too well.

"What will happen to Ryan once this is all over?"

His hand was tangled in my ponytail. I stood between his legs while he sat hugging me. "That's up to Ryan." His voice was low.

"What does that mean?" I searched his handsome face for an answer.

"He's different."

"What do you mean?" There was an edge to my voice. "But we're going to save him. Right?"

"What are you expecting to happen to him?" He countered my question with another question.

"Is there something I don't know?"

"Grim," Lincoln's voice drifted from the doorway. We both turned. Only the front of his body was visible at the door, the rest of his horse body was hidden in the hallway. "I didn't want to interrupt... okay, maybe I didn't mind since it's so fun to get the little human riled up, but the Reapers are back." I glared at his words.

"What did they find?" I backed away so that he could stand.

"Ten more portal chips have already gone missing since you last spoke to them," Lincoln told him, and Killian's eyes pinched together in aggravation.

"What's a portal chip?" I interrupted.

"I'm the only person that can fade out of time to get to another place. With that being said, any demon that wants to enter the human world or travel to a different place in the Underworld needs one, and only certain demons are allowed to have the chips because if the wrong demons get a hold of them then your world would be in trouble," Killian answered.

"But I've seen Molly, and Fear, as well as Vengeance, disappear like you do." I frowned and his eyes lit up with a smile. Why was he always smiling every time I asked a question?

"In the human world, Molly can disappear a certain distance away without a portal chip just because she is a ghost. Fear and Vengeance use portal chips even though you never see them use it. The day Molly opened a portal for you to go to Fear's, she was using one and she uses one every time she's in the Underworld."

I nodded with my mouth open in a big giant O.

Killian looked back to Lincoln after answering my question. "Have they found out if Fear is the one taking them?" Killian asked and Lincoln shook his head. "I'm guessing there's still no signs of Molly, either? Fear has his own eyes and ears in the Underworld, we are bound to find someone that can give us answers."

CHAPTER FOUR
Melanie

After Lincoln dropped the news of more portals being stolen, Killian decided to take me home. I didn't get to say goodbye to Ryan before I left and knew a day spent here could measure out as weeks being gone there…

It was still morning back home—more like a few minutes were all that passed while I was gone and I was already ready for a nap.

But I had to see Tess and tell her what Ryan had told me to say…

I waited a few hours before driving over to her place to give her time to sleep. It was after noon when I arrived and knocked on the door when I saw that her parents were home. Which was weird if you knew them because her dad, Dan, was always away on business and her mom, Linda—well I didn't even know how she managed to stay gone all the time.

Dan answered the door and it was extremely awkward because I hardly knew him even after all the years I've been friends with Ryan and Tess. "Hey, Melanie, it's good to see you," he told me, and I smiled stupidly.

"Hi, Dan. I'm here to see Tess." I mentally slapped myself because, *of course,* I was here to see her.

"Hey, Melanie," Linda joined in on the meet-and-greet at their door.

"Melanie!" Tess yelled from her room. I slipped off my shoes and hurried to her bedroom. I shut the door as soon as I was inside and gave her a look that spoke volumes. "I know, I'm scared, too," she told me. We knew each other so long that we understood each other's facial expressions.

"I can't believe your parents are both home at the same time," I admitted.

Her sandy brown hair was matted to her face and she was still lying in bed. She looked like a raccoon with the eyeliner caked underneath her eye. She raised up with a sigh. "You saved me from having to put up with those two any longer!"

"Huh?" I flopped down on the bed and couldn't suppress my grin.

"They've been wanting to take me out and do stuff, ya know, go out and hang and be a family." By the look on her face and sound in her voice, you would think that meant the end of the world. Which only explained how dysfunctional her family had been for her and Ryan all their lives. "It's weirding me out."

I only shook my head and laughed in response. "So, where's Ryan? He needs to know what kind of crap I'm going through with our parents?"

My smile dropped and we were already at the conversation that I dreaded. "Ryan's not coming back, Tess," I forced myself to look her straight in the eyes.

I watched her face morph into surprise, followed by hurt. "What do you mean?"

I squeezed my hands together. "I mean; he's moved on from this world. I don't think he wanted to stay a ghost any longer," I told her what Ryan wanted her to know even when my heart wanted me not to lie. But if I spoke the truth and she found out what happened to him because of me... she would never forgive me.

She was clearly upset, but her next expression surprised me. She almost looked relieved. "Did he even say goodbye before he... I'm disappointed that he didn't tell me—well, tell me through you before he left. But this is a good thing, right? We always talked about how ghosts weren't meant to roam with the living, that they needed to move on."

My eyes were watering, and I knew I was on the verge of tears so I quickly wiped them away. "Yeah, that is what we always said. And I think Ryan would have told you goodbye if he had gotten the chance but maybe when it's time, it's time," I cleared my throat and looked down at my hands.

"My brother... he was a good guy, right? That's why it hurts so much for us to let him go." Her tears finally fell and with hers, came mine. She cried, I cried for her and for Ryan and the fact that they lost each other because of the mess that came with knowing me. I moved over the bed to hug her.

"Boohoo, what will I ever do without my brother," I recognized that patronizing voice and turned around quickly. Penny stood in her blacked-out getup with an amusing grin.

"What?" The word tumbled from my mouth before I remembered that only I could see her. I couldn't stop myself from glaring at her, though.

"Why are you surprised to see me?" She smiled as she stepped around in the room. "Grim has me watching over that *thing* next to you. Do you realize how hard it is to deal with her?" she let out an exhausted sigh.

"What is it?" Tess asked me.

"Nothing…" I stumbled with my words. I tried to ignore Penny since she must be here to watch over Tess. I'd admit that I disliked Penny entirely on the fact that she had slept with Killian, but she didn't try to make me like her either…

Crap, my insecurities were bubbling up, and I didn't even know how to handle them. Why would he put Penny somewhere where I would run into her? I looked her way again, and she was still standing there with a smirk. Her and those dang busty boobs and… UGH!

"Have you talked to Mike at all?" I asked Tess because I cared and I needed to ignore my own growing insecurities and focus on someone else's.

"He's been calling nonstop, but I still haven't answered." She glanced at her phone on the pillow.

"You're gonna have to eventually hear him out." Because Vengeance was to blame, not Mike.

"I know," she said quickly. "I'm just scared."

I understood all too well. "I also have something to tell you." She looked up and waited for me to go on. "I'm dating Killian."

Penny snorted next to us, and I tried to ignore the trickling of fear crawling up my throat by the way she was acting.

I waited for Tess to get mad but for now, the only thing that blew up were the size of her eyes. "I guess it's kind of not surprising since he picked you up after school the other day, but I thought you hated him. What happened?" She didn't seem upset, just curious, and I sighed in relief.

But I didn't want to discuss Killian with Penny around. "He's amazing," I started out. "I just misjudged him when I first met him… well, he did act like a prick at first, but I didn't act any better." I grinned as I thought about how we first met.

"Melanie, you're grinning like an idiot," Tess told me, but I didn't miss the grin on her face either.

I stayed and hung out with Tess a while longer before going home. Penny followed me outside, and I scowled at her as soon as we were alone. "Are you really here to watch over Tess?"

She sighed. "Yeah, remember Grim did send me to watch over your mom and brother during the time you were staying at his place, but now he has me watching over Tess in case Fear goes after her because of you or her brother." She couldn't help but add, "He didn't want me staying over at your place now that you were going to be there."

I got in my car and drove off because I couldn't even think of one smart remark.

———

Night came and the house had a chill to it. Once Alex fell asleep, I decided to take nice, hot bath. Mom had already left for work.

The water was relaxing but not enough to take my mind off of Penny. I slid my body further down into the tub when my phone went off.

I had to get out of the warmth of the water and wipe off my hands before grabbing the phone from the sink. I hurried back to the water with a pleasant sigh as my toes dipped back into the water. It was Killian.

What are you doing right now?

Even though I knew it was him, I still pretended not to know.

Who is this??

I sunk into the water and held the phone at a safe distance from it as I waited for him to reply.

Ur Lover. The handsome hero. That guy you are always thinking about.

My snort echoed in the bathroom as I tried to hold in my smile.

Killian?

Does that ? imply that you have more than 1 lover?

How are you even texting me right now?

Always with the questions… who do you think I am?

You can't see me, but I'm doing a major eye roll right now. Ur so vain!

Oh, I can see you.

If I hadn't been already burning up from the water, I definitely was at the thought of him watching me. I raised up slowly in the tub and looked around.

I don't see you.

I texted him and when no reply came, I was disappointed. I decided it was time to get out, I was baking and on the verge of passing out. I patted myself down with my towel before tying it around my body.

I tiptoed to my room because I was positive I would see Killian in my room. Only he wasn't. When I crept into my room, it was empty and I dropped my shoulders in disappointment. I walked to the bed where my clothes lay and let the towel fall to the floor. It was at that moment the sound of a book being closed filled the room. I jumped and looked behind me and saw Killian standing before me with a closed book in his hand, holding it in the air like he had made the sound on purpose. A devilish grin descended upon his face.

My nerves were already shot from the noise, but now the sight of him devouring me with his eyes kicked me into overdrive. I panicked, covering myself quickly. "Turn around!" I hissed.

"Sorry." He didn't look sorry.

"No, you're not. You did it on purpose." I puffed my cheeks out at him.

"I thought I had made it clear already that I was no gentleman." But he did finally turn around, and I waited several seconds to make sure he wasn't going to turn back around before I hurried to put my clothes on. "I came at the right moment. I thought you'd be happy to see me."

"Don't pretend you've been here this whole time." I grabbed his shoulder and forced him to face me. Of course, that grin was still plastered on his face. And of course, I wasn't really upset with him.

"Why do you get all hidden on me when I get here? It's not like I haven't already seen you before, and if I recall, you were putting those beautiful tits in my face on purpose last night." My heart rate increased and I thought about turning away so that he couldn't see my face. "I also remember you were trying to get me all riled up while we were trying to watch a movie together a few days ago…"

"That's wasn't entirely me," I stammered and told a big, fat lie. I could always tell when he was affecting me with his incubus voodoo and when he wasn't… I just wanted him. I still wanted him, but now I was caught off guard and had no clue how to handle the feelings he was giving me.

My stomach tightened with anticipation and I tried to look away, but his hand was already holding my chin up. He lowered his face to mine. "Whatever you say," he whispered into my ear and goosebumps took over my skin. My nipples were visible in the white t-shirt I wore and the heat that entered my stomach was already dipping between my legs.

His hand left my chin and slowly slid down my neck onto my chest where he stopped at my breasts.

Touch me, go on. I waited with anticipation. I wanted him. I craved him.

"Melanie." I let my head lean closer to his neck as he breathed into my ear, but he pulled back. "Should I make you beg and get all needy on me before I finally touch you again?" I was thrown off by his question and looked him in the eye. Darkness played out in them. "You did make things difficult for me when I was an incubus demon knowing that I didn't want to take advantage of you. You did what you wanted anyway. I was trying to be a good demon around you, but you kept on and on and on—"

I jerked away from him, but he snatched my hands and threw me onto my bed. I bounced, and the springs creaked under my weight. "What are you doing?"

"Teasing you, Love. I want to see what reactions I can get you to make."

I covered my face with my hands to hide my embarrassment. "Come here." I uncovered my eyes to see him offering his hand out to me, and I took it. He pulled me up from the bed and wrapped his arms around me.

"I want to get to know you more," I breathed into his chest. I wanted to know him more than any other woman did. "Not just emotionally, but physically… I want to *know* you, Killian. I have no experience with relationships or—"

"Where is this coming from? You were never bothered about it before." He looked down at me.

"Why didn't you tell me that Penny was watching over Tess?" I asked quickly and looked up to see a slight smile on his face.

"So, it's Penny." He moved to the bed and sat down pulling me into his lap. My shorts were more like underwear and I was self-conscious of every part of me. His hands gripped my legs as he held all my weight. "Are you upset that I didn't tell you that Penny would be there or are you upset because I've slept with Penny in the past?" My stomach clammed up at his words, and I shrugged my shoulders. I hoped my face didn't look as sick as I felt.

"Look at me," he told me and I did. Pleading dark-brown eyes stared back at me. "I can't change my past, I've lived alone for a very long time, Melanie, and I've done a lot of things, but I was still lonely." I tilted my head toward him and waited for him to continue. "If I could pull my heart from my chest and let you see and feel what I've felt all these centuries—the loneliness that's always been there, the yearning that has consumed me to find someone to love… then you'd understand that I've never once loved anyone until the day I met you."

He grabbed my hand and placed it on his chest and I felt the rhythm of his heartbeat thump against my palm. "In the few weeks I've known you, I've discovered pain and heartbreak, fear and worry—so many new things, all because of my love for you."

I dropped my head against his shoulder and he breathed deeply. "I'm embarrassed, with everything that we've been through and still going through, I've done nothing but stress about your relationship with Penny since I saw her."

"Penny is a Reaper, a good one at that, but that's it." He touched our foreheads together and I closed my eyes and drank in this moment. "You know, you don't have to be apart from me, not if you don't want to be." I opened my eyes and I hoped his hearing wasn't good enough to hear the increase in my heart rate. Was he hinting at me staying with him—at his castle?

With our foreheads still touching, his breath quickened, and so did mine. I could feel his breaths against my face as we drew closer. "What about you?" Our lips drew closer.

"I want you by my side. Always."

We kissed.

Softly. Slowly.

But it was so much more than that. It had my heart exploding in my chest, unmasked desire became us—we parted our lips only enough to get air into our lungs. My hands were immediately underneath his t-shirt, tracing the hard ridges of his stomach. I realized this was the first time I was actually touching him—he always seemed to be the one touching me.

He was so much bigger than me—strong, sexy. He knew how to take me over the edge before bringing me back down with gentleness.

"Killian," I moaned now that his mouth was trailing down my chin and neck.

"What is it?" I was glad to hear that I wasn't the only one breathless.

"Aren't you going to touch me?" My head fell back but my hands were still all over him.

He kissed my neck as he spoke. "Here, turn around and straddle me." But he was already positioning me around to face him and placed my legs at his hips and the first thing I felt was his hard length pressing against me. The passion burning my insides became chaos, unrelenting and all-consuming for what he offered.

His hands took hold of my butt forcefully and held me firm against him. I grabbed his face and pulled him in for another kiss. He held me there against his erection as if to foretell what would soon come.

"You're so—" He pushed me onto the bed. "What the hell?" I turned to see what he was looking at. Three ghosts stood in my room looking at me. "If you're coming to me, I can automatically assume you all are ready to part from this world?" Killian stood up.

"You." One pointed to me. "Save us!"

That was all they said before they started moving toward me. Killian became Grim and his scythe materialized in his hand and the portal to Heaven opened, and he threw one into the bright light. The Reaper that had been staying at my house walked through the door and knocked another one in as soon as he entered.

"No, bring me—" The ghost didn't get to finish what she was saying to me before Grim pushed her into the light and it disappeared.

"What was that?" the Reaper, Miles, asked him.

Grim's essence was no longer his normal shade of blue, but black. He changed back into Killian and his brows were pinched together in frustration. Or confusion, I wasn't sure.

"She was trying to say something to me," I mentioned. "You should have let her speak before sending her."

"They came for her despite sensing we were here?" Miles sounded surprised.

"Just what were they trying to do?" Killian seemed to be asking himself that question. "And, why did it take you so long to get up here?" He turned on the Reaper. "If I had not been here, they could have gotten to her before you even entered the room."

"I only let my guard down because I knew you were here," he replied.

"Remember you did give me the necklace as well," I tried to ease some of Killian's agitation.

He ran his hands through his hair. "You can head back downstairs," he told Miles, and he simply nodded. "If you sense anything unusual going on in this house, you better move regardless if I'm here or not."

"It won't happen again."

Once he was gone, Killian turned toward me. He walked over to the bed and placed his hands on each side of me and kissed me. "I don't want to leave you, but I have to figure out what Fear's got planned. It's making my fucking skin crawl."

"What's been going on?" I asked him. "Did you figure out if it was Fear taking the portal chips?"

He placed a kiss on my forehead. "I'll figure it out. I don't want you to worry about anything."

I sighed. "That's not how this works." His eyes met mine and I told myself not to get lost in them. "When will you start sharing things with me? I want to know the good and bad. I want to carry whatever burdens we have and face them together."

A smile touched his lips. "You're amazing, you know that?" I shook my head at him. "I don't know yet. We still can't find Fear or Molly. I'm more worried that we won't find them at all at this point, not until he wants to be found. He's scared. He doesn't want to accept that his death's coming, yet he's smart enough to hide away and prepare, but no matter what he does, Death can't be stopped."

"Will it all be over when he dies?" The thought sounded amazing, and it was becoming a question I kept asking him and myself.

He looked down. "Marcus is the one that will die, and even though I'm sure he's the reason you are marked, Fear's still an entity and we have no clue which one is thinking what when it comes to your mark." He stared at my t-shirt, the spot on my chest where the X was. "There could be another way…"

"What is it?" I asked quickly.

He shook his head and raised up. "It's not something I'd want to—forget I said it. I'll come and get you after school tomorrow, okay?"

And he was gone, just like that.

CHAPTER FIVE
Melanie

It was early—too early to be feeling the guilt that I did as I looked down at Haley's leg in a cast. She bullied me growing up and I disliked her for it, but I didn't mean to break her ankle.

Only I must have or it wouldn't have happened.

Haley's ankle was the least of my problems, though.

"God, it's gotten cold quick the last few days." Tess rubbed her arms as she sat next to me in class. It was cold since it was October, but I didn't think that was why this room was freezing. I looked around. Ghosts were everywhere.

Ever since they came to my bedroom last night, they just kept showing up. So many that Miles called for backup. Not that they were dangerous—his words, not mine, but they didn't have a clue what they wanted with me.

"Save me, bring me back," a lot of them would cry. So, apparently, these ghosts thought I could bring them back from the dead. Which was making this school day extremely difficult. The few ghosts that normally roamed the school were enough to distract me from the living, now they were all over the place! I couldn't concentrate.

"This human cannot bring you back to life. Us Reapers, are here to protect her because she can't do anything." Then there was that. I turned my head to Penny talking to one of the ghosts and glared.

"My daughter needs me!" the ghost lady cried, and Penny sighed. "I have to come back!"

"In you go," Penny gave the ghost a push toward the light. The ghost tried latching onto my desk and I jerked back. The desk skidded and the whole class turned on me. Penny shoved her into the light. "Who's next?" she called around to the other ghosts.

"We just want her to bring us back," another ghost spoke.

"Is everything okay, Ms. Rose?" Mr. Stevens asked me.

No, the number of ghosts in the room double the amount of the living and for some reason, they think I can bring them back to life! I leaned over my desk and placed my hand over my chin awkwardly. "Yup, I thought I saw a spider."

Some in the room laughed, and Mr. Stevens looked at me unamused. I looked over to Tess and she had her face partially covered with her hand as she shook her head at me.

"Not so fast!" Miles yelled as one of the ghosts tried to make a run for me. I ducked my head just as he grabbed a hold of him and threw him into the light. When I looked up, Tess's expression was murderous.

I was in total ghost mode, and she hated when that happened.

This was going to be a long day.

———

I picked Alex up from school and took us home. Ghosts were waiting in my yard. I closed my eyes and sighed as I turned off the engine.

This entire day had exhausted me.

I had been so preoccupied with the ghosts and Reapers that I forgot to ask Tess about Mike. Hopefully, I would remember tomorrow. She did manage to tell me about a Halloween dance the school was having—or maybe she was talking about a party she was wanting me to go to? Okay, so I couldn't concentrate on everything she was trying to tell me at lunch.

A Reaper had stayed with Alex and one with Mom today. Miles had filled me in, and it put me at ease to know that Killian was taking every precaution to protect my family. Miles was already slipping out of my car and ascending them all to Heaven. Thankfully, I parted ways with Penny when she went home with Tess.

"I wonder if Mom has something cooked?" Alex wondered as he stepped outside blissfully unaware of the craziness going on around us.

"She's probably still in bed," I told him as we headed inside. I weirdly maneuvered around the yard just to get inside, earning me a few strange looks from Alex.

"So," Alex started as we stepped inside the house. "I can't believe this guy actually likes you," he said, and I was too stunned to answer at first so I glared instead.

"I'm offended." We took our shoes off at the door. "Are you trying to say I'm not likeable 'cause I happen to find me extremely lovable," I informed my kid brother.

He snorted. "I only meant that he seems all bad and dangerous while you are…"

"I'm what?"

"Innocent?" he offered then sighed. "Good? That's it, you're too good for him."

I smiled at him. "Are you worried about me?"

"Someone has to look out for you, obviously, this guy might not be a good person, and you have a bad judge of character. Besides, now that Ryan is gone someone has too."

I watched him walk through the hallway and disappear into the kitchen. I followed after him. He was standing in the fridge getting something to drink when I grabbed his shoulders and turned him around. "Alex, no one is ever gonna take Ryan's place. He will always be the guy that was there for me first—my best friend." I could tell that this conversation was making him uncomfortable. He was only seven, and he was too young when Dad died to actually know how it felt to lose someone he loved. He had been close with Ryan, he enjoyed when he came to visit because Ryan would always play video games with him. "We miss him, but you can't hold that against Killian. You and Mom don't even know him."

"He knows that, Melanie," Mom stepped into the kitchen with us. She still wore her pajamas and a bad case of bedhead.

Now that I was talking about Ryan, I turned toward Mom and couldn't stop the words from tumbling out of my mouth. "You don't think I feel guilty about Ryan? I wanted to be with Killian despite the fact that Ryan was buried last week!" I wiped my face and went on, "I can't change my feelings, not when I finally feel so connected with someone."

Mom didn't say anything, instead, she walked across the kitchen to hug me. The feeling her arms gave me were foreign—we lacked physical contact for so long and grew distant since Fear marked me when I was nine. But when I breathed in the familiar scent of her, I realized how many nights I had wanted her to do this when I was too terrified to fall asleep.

"You don't have to explain yourself. We can't control where our feelings lead us." She patted my back.

Ghosts were walking right through the walls into the kitchen. My eyes widened as Alex went right through one. Was Miles still outside taking care of the ones in the yard?

"I swear this house is so cold lately... we must have a bad draft coming in from somewhere," Mom mumbled, and I stepped out of her arms to rub my eyes. I hadn't cried, but my eyes had that itchy-watery feel to them.

"It is cold, but it's October, Mom," Alex added.

There was a knock on the door. "It's probably Killian," I told them quickly.

"I'll get it," Alex said then looked at me. "Don't worry, Sis, I'm going to give him a chance." I watched him take off into the hallway, and Mom took one look at what she was wearing and her face turned ashen.

"Alex!" Mom yelled before taking off into the hallway with him. "Do not open that door until I've made it into my bedroom!" I stood in the kitchen smiling.

I heard Alex open the door. I heard Killian greet him, and Alex told him to come in. "She's the one!" a young boy ghost told another.

"Bring us back to life please!" another screamed.

I stepped back slowly. "I can't bring you back to life," I whispered.

"She told me that all I had to do was jump into you and it will bring me back," the young boy informed me. That was ridiculous, and I wondered why the ghosts even believed such a lie!

"That will only let you possess my body, that won't bring you back." I backed on up. "Who told you to that?"

"You'd try anything if you were dead like us." One of the ghosts launched at me.

In this moment, I was missing the voice inside my head and the strength she gave me. Why wasn't my power reacting or helping me like it always did before?

I brought my arms out in front of me, but before the ghost could get close, the necklace reacted. Blue light moved in front of me and created a barrier. The ghost screamed as it was dissolved into the light.

The others were hesitant now, but another ghost went ahead and attacked. He dissolved just like the first.

"What are you doing?" Alex asked me as he stared at my ridiculous pose. Killian's eyes were leveled on the ghosts. Their eyes lit up with fear of him, yet none of them made a move to leave.

"May I use your bathroom?" Killian asked but before either of us could reply, he was walking off in the direction of the bathroom. When he walked back in the room as Grim, I realized he had gone and switched to get rid of them.

"Did he already leave?" Mom sounded breathless as she arrived back in the kitchen looking more presentable.

Great. Perfect. Alex and Mom were both in the room while Grim was waving a giant scythe around in our kitchen to scare the life out of some ghosts. Only they weren't running, so he opened the passage for them and started forcing them all in the light.

"He went to the bathroom," Alex answered Mom's question.

"I should probably make us some food," Mom said, and a ghost ran in her direction. It wasn't going to try to possess her to get away from Grim, was he?

He was! "Woah!" I screamed just as Grim jerked him by the shirt before he could.

"Jesus, Melanie!" Mom was holding her chest as she gave me a confused look.

Right, I yelled. "Woah!" I tried to toss my hands in the air with enthusiasm. "Woah. Yeah. I think that's a good idea."

Kill me now. Alex was looking at me like I had grown two heads.

Mom was grabbing something out of the fridge when Grim took care of the last one. For now, anyway. He stepped into the hallway and walked back in as Killian. "I hope it's okay that I came over," Killian said to Mom.

She was putting stuff together on the stove and smiled back at him. "No, you're fine. Give me a second and I'll have some food ready. Are you okay with cheeseburgers? It's the quickest thing I've got to make."

"I'll eat anything," he replied grabbing his belly.

She looked him up and down. "I'd reckon your parents must have fed you good growing up, you're a big boy."

He looked down at the ground. Mom's words made me realize I didn't know how he grew up in the

Underworld. "Actually, my mom abandoned me long before I even knew what a parent was…"

Everyone was quiet, and I looked at the man I loved. What kind of life had he lived before he became Grim? And what was Grim before he became Killian? So much I cared to know.

"I'm so sorry, I didn't mean—"

"It's okay, I didn't say it to make you feel bad. I shouldn't have said it," he told her quickly, shaking his head.

I walked over and grabbed his hand. "Don't say that." Mom tossed her hand up in the air at him. "I want to get to know the man my daughter is dating."

"So," Alex piped in. "Do you like video games?"

"Sure. What do you play Xbox? PS4?" I looked at him surprised.

"Xbox!" Alex replied excitedly. "Do you play Black Ops 3?"

Killian nodded. "Yep."

"Me too," Alex really couldn't contain his excitement now, but I could tell he was getting too into the conversation, so he added another, "Me too," that was calmer.

I smiled. This was going better than I expected.

"Seems you two have something in common." Mom turned to smile at them.

The Reaper that was outside slipped into the kitchen with us. "I took care of the ones outside," he told Killian.

A few minutes later and Mom was making Killian a burger while Alex and I had to get our own. "This is a great burger, Tina," he praised Mom and she hid her smile by turning around.

"Yeah, Mom's a great cook," I helped along with buttering her up.

Only she knew what we were doing because she turned back around and arched an eyebrow our way. We all sat at the table together. "Don't think I don't know you two are trying to butter me up," she told us, and I grinned sheepishly at Killian who looked worried that he had ruined his chances.

"Your daughter is very precious to me and I plan to prove it," Killian was dead serious and Mom burst out laughing. It didn't take long for Alex and me to join her. Killian was completely lost as he looked at us.

"She means a lot to me as well," Mom coughed and straightened back up.

We stayed a little longer before leaving. Alex asked Killian if he wanted to play a game together and that was when I knew we had to leave or we'd be stuck here all day. Once we were in his car, I said, "I didn't know you played video games."

"I don't. Ryan gave me some advice."

I felt my forehead wrinkle up. "Ryan did?"

"Gotta' take this car back to my place before we go to my other place." Killian gave a strange look. "If that makes any sense."

"Makes total sense."

I watched him as he drove and kept remembering what he had said about his mom. I desperately wanted to ask him about it, but I didn't know if I could. "Um, Killian..." I tried.

"There's something we have to talk about when we get to the castle." He was looking ahead as he spoke. There was no smile on his face, just a blank expression as he drove. It made my stomach tighten.

"What is it?" Only he didn't answer me.

———

Ryan was waiting for us in the ballroom when we faded into the castle. That ominous feeling in my stomach got worse. I looked to Killian. "What is it?" Did I really want to know? Ryan wouldn't meet my eyes. Killian didn't answer. "Has Fear done something? Or have you figured out what's going on with the ghosts and portal chips?" I asked him.

"Come on." Killian led me to another room I had yet to be in. It was full of old furniture that reminded me of my grandma's house before she passed away when I was little. There was also a grandfather clock that actually worked.

Tick-tock, tick-tock. The sound was loud in the quiet room.

Killian forced me to sit on one of the couches. Ryan sat across from us. "We can save Ryan from Fear," Killian spoke first.

I smiled. "Really?" I was the only one smiling and it dropped fast. "Will you guys stop and tell me already."

"I have to die," Ryan said and met my eyes.

"You're already dead." I tried to shake off the uneasy feeling.

"It's not his body we are talking about," Killian told me. I turned to face him next to me. "His soul, Melanie." That didn't expect me to believe that, did they? "His body died long ago, but his soul... it's not his anymore." He placed his hand on my leg.

"You already knew, didn't you?" My voice was small, unsteady but my heart... it beat wild and furiously.

"It's not something I wanted you to know and I didn't want to tell you now, either," Ryan said with a sigh. I didn't even know how to respond.

"He had Fear's mark when he died. He wouldn't even have an actual body right now if it wasn't for what Fear did to him, he'd be a ghost or he would have already moved on... but that can never happen."

"What does that mean exactly?" I wasn't looking at either of them. I kept my eyes on the ground as the coldness spread through me.

"Grim has to destroy my soul," Ryan answered what I didn't actually want to hear.

"There's no coming back from that. He will completely cease to exist."

I ignored Killian's words and stood. Then the dam burst and I couldn't contain how I reacted any longer. "No," I mumbled. "No, I refuse to believe that's the only way to save him."

"This is why I didn't want to tell you," Ryan said quietly.

"She needed to know," Killian told him.

I wouldn't lift my head, but I heard Ryan step in front of me. "Melanie," he pleaded. "I'd rather not exist at all before I become something that wants to kill you."

I knew, believe me. I understood his reasoning completely. He didn't want to be a monster. He didn't want to hurt me. But I was the girl—the reason he became this way.

I lifted my gaze and shook my head violently. "Let me ask you both something. If I died and belonged to Fear and like you said, the only way to save me was to destroy my soul, would you?" Ryan looked down and even Killian wouldn't meet my eyes. "That's what I thought." I looked back to Ryan. "We don't know what will actually happen when he finally kills Marcus. It could end everything."

"Or it could solve nothing." Killian moved next to me.

I met his intense gaze with my own. "Then, I'll never have a shot at life, either, right?" His jaw hardened as he glared at me. I could stand here and have at it with him all day if that was what it took.

Ryan forced me to look away from Killian by pulling at my shoulders. He looked miserable. "It's gonna come sooner rather than later... that moment." His words became a whisper, "When you have to let me go."

CHAPTER SIX
Melanie

I wished there was a way to tell the future. A way I could look ahead and know that everything was going to be okay. If I was going to be okay. If Ryan would pass on to Heaven. If Killian and I would last like I desperately wanted.

But there wasn't and I was stuck living every second of each day, wondering if it was okay to even hope for something happy in my future.

I ran out of the castle to get a few minutes by myself. Sky laid beside me with her huge head resting on my legs. I rubbed her head and it was nice. Relaxing even. I didn't speak to her. I felt perfectly at ease not saying anything.

She must have felt the same way because she purred in contentment.

It wasn't just Ryan's situation that was bugging me… since I pulled the scythe from my chest and put Killian and Grim back together, the voice had gone silent. What did that mean? Was she gone now that I knew she was a part of me?

Should I be worried that I still didn't know what I was? Even Killian didn't have an answer. I knew I was connected to him somehow but that was it.

Light… Grim's Light… Just what had I meant when I spoke the words so confidently.

I lifted Sky's head from my legs and stood up. Maybe I should just try it and see. I stepped closer to the giant tree that was in front of me. I brought my arms out and tried to concentrate on the power like I always did before. Sorry tree, but I needed a target. I thought of pain and aimed my palm at the tree.

Nothing.

I tried reaching into my chest. I couldn't.

I placed my hands over my face and sighed. Was I not motivated enough?

"May I ask what you're doing?"

Killian was leaning against a tree. His expression was blank, so I supposed we were still at odds. Sky was next to me rolling around on her back like a playful kitten until she noticed the mood and flew off.

I decided to ignore him and headed into the woods. "We don't have time for your childish games," he called from somewhere behind me. I picked up the pace and felt my cheeks getting warm.

Seriously, what was I doing?

Why did I always go seeking attention in the strangest ways when it came to him? A branch snapped to my left and I stopped. My nerves were a tangled mess. I looked back to see if he was there.

Oh, God. What did I do? I started something he would finish. The thought was terrifying as it was thrilling. Adrenaline rushed through my veins. "Killian." It was best to play nice.

The woods were dark once you got inside despite the glow of the trees. I could hear the dragons flying above me but couldn't see any of them because of the leaves on the trees.

"Why walk away from me when we could be spending this time together?" He laughed, but I couldn't tell what direction it was coming from. "You know… with you in my arms." He was behind me, his words in my ears. His mouth was close and his hands were sliding over my jacket.

I closed my eyes. "I walked away because we are at odds when it comes to Ryan." I let him turn me around so we faced each other. My eyes were open now, so it wasn't my fault that I got lost in the depths of his.

"That's true, but I thought I had made it clear that when we are alone, nothing else matters." He placed a hand against my back and pulled me close. In the process, the darkness came and I knew we had faded.

When the light brought us back, we were standing next to a small drop off embedded in the ground. It looked to be about ten feet, but there was a man-made path that led down... I gasped. It was a small pond, if you'd call it that. Pink, purple, and green vines hung down the hill and hung over into the water. The water itself glowed like everything else and everything was visible underneath.

"It's beautiful," I mumbled, and he took my hand and started down the path.

"Come on, let's get in," he said.

I moved my hand away from his and stopped on the path. "Right now?"

He looked back at me and nodded. "Yeah, why do you think I brought us here?" He looked downright mischievous right about now!

"We don't have anything to swim in." I had my suspicions about what his plan was and it had my heart about to beat right out of my chest.

"How about we leave our clothes on the bank and skinny dip?" His smile was impossible... impossible not to fall for. "Or you can just swim in your panties and bra if you're afraid of being naked around me... afraid of losing those virtues of yours? Don't worry, it's safe for now."

My face and neck were on fire, and I had to look away from him. "Your face is red, Love." He let out a husky laugh and I turned back to see him walking on down. My stomach fluttered at the sound of his laugh.

His shirt was the first thing to go. He started unbuttoning his pants and I covered my eyes up, then uncovered them because let's face it—I couldn't make up my mind. "What are you doing?" I knew exactly what he was doing, I just didn't know how to react.

"I told you I came down here to get in the water. I'm not leaving my clothes on." He turned around and looked at me. "Do you want me to relax you with some of my incubus charm?" he asked.

"Don't even think about it," I warned him.

He laughed again. "Relax, Melanie, I would never do that to you. I would never have in the first place if I could have controlled it. Honestly, though," he grinned at me, "Let's face it, I have no need for it. Look at the way you're staring at me."

I rolled my eyes at him. If I could help it, I really needed to stop boosting his ego. "Get over—" My words were lost when he slid down his jeans.

I knew his butt would be perfection, but so help me, I would not have been able to stop staring at his backside if my life had depended on it. He looked back again to make sure he had my attention (Oh, he did!) before stepping into the water until nothing but his head was visible.

His handsome smile reflected off the glow of the water as he smiled up at me. "Come on and get in!"

Then I knew this was another brand on my heart that I wanted to keep forever. Killian looked so at ease that all my worries could wait, too.

He splashed some water at me that never reached. He was grinning like we didn't have a worry in the world. He looked so carefree, so open, and breathtaking, I loved it. "What are you waiting for? It's not like I haven't seen most of you already…"

I smirked, feeling brave and much like the girl that took on the Human Festival. I wanted to give him a taste of his own medicine. "Turn around and give me some privacy," I told him.

He arched his eyebrows but otherwise listened and turned around. I hurriedly took off my clothes and laid them in a pile. I stepped into the water—it was warm, soft even. It rippled and moved around me as I swam toward Killian. His back was still turned and my heart pounded against my ribcage. I was nervous, yet excited.

I took hold of his shoulders—even his back was intimidating as I placed my lips against his neck. His muscles moved beneath my fingertips, but he made no move to turn around. He was respecting my words even now…

I slid my hands across his shoulders, down his arm, admiring everything. I kissed his neck again as my arms slid beneath his and wrapped around him. He groaned when my naked breasts pressed against his back and the sound went straight to the pit of my stomach where the heat dipped in between my thighs.

"Fuck, Melanie you're not wearing any clothes?" His voice was raw.

"You're the one that wanted us to be naked," I whispered as I slid my hands across his ripped stomach.

"Yeah, but I didn't think," he stopped talking and went still, "Melanie, why is your heart about to fly out of your chest?"

So he felt that? It was because of what I planned to do next. Before I chickened out, I slid my hands down his stomach and grabbed a hold of his erection. He sucked in a breath and my stomach contracted with a wave of heat and fear. I held him with both hands and even that left so much more…

He placed his hands over mine. "Why do you go and do something that's going to scare you away from what I plan to do to you?" He sounded hoarse. How could he sense my worry about his size? "May I turn around to you now?" I didn't speak, but I nodded against his neck.

He moved my hands and arms away so that he could turn and soon I was staring into his dark eyes. "You're too nervous to be making the first move," he told me. He never tried to look down into the water to see me naked, instead, he took my arms and placed them around his neck and pulled me close. It was impossible to ignore the hard length of him present between us, though.

"Maybe that's not such a good idea either," he said and pulled away from me again.

"I'm nervous, Killian, but that doesn't mean that I don't want you to touch me," I told him.

"I wasn't pulling away because of that, I'm pulling away because I can't think of anything else but your body pressed against me and believe it or not, that's not why I brought you here."

"It isn't?" I smiled.

He laughed. "No, I want you to relax." I arched an eyebrow and he sighed. "Relax. Float around or something."

"Why? I'd look ridiculous floating around naked."

"No, you wouldn't."

"Then, you float around."

He grinned sheepishly. "I can't for obvious reasons." He motioned his eyes to his hard-on through the water. I didn't dare look, but I laughed so hard it became a snort. "Cute," he whispered, then we became quiet. I moved my legs to keep myself afloat while I watched him. "Okay, obviously I wasn't thinking this through when I said for us to swim naked. Let's go somewhere else and talk." He started to move away and I leaned over his back to keep him from doing so.

"It's okay, we can talk right here." He looked back at me and smiled.

"I really can't complain when you're all pressed against me, now can I?" I shook my head 'no' in agreement.

"Am I allowed to ask about your past?"

"Yes, not that it's anything much to talk about," he replied.

I wrapped my arms around his neck as he swam around. "Is it true what you said about your mom?"

He was quiet for a bit. "It is. She left me to die. A group of sisters found me and kept me. They were witches."

"So, they took you in and became your family?"

He snorted. "No, they knew exactly what kind of baby I was and kept me for the very purpose of profiting from me when I grew older."

My heart sunk with suspicion. "What do you mean?"

He leaned his head back and touched my hair with his hand. "I want to tell you everything you want to know about me, yet at the same time, I don't want you to see me any differently than the man I am today." I placed my hand over his and brought it to my mouth to kiss it. "But, you already have an idea of what they wanted me for, right?"

I nodded and he dropped his hand. "At the age of thirteen, I started needing sex to sustain myself. It wasn't an everyday need, at that point I only needed it once a month. That was when the witches informed me that I had to repay all that they had done for me, so they sold me to the highest bidder every month." I placed my hand against his chest and felt the rhythm of his heartbeat. "I tried to escape, but once I was caught trying they started locking me away until it was time. But every year I grew older, my needs grew worse and knowing that I had no choice, I was bid on more often." He laughed sadly. "They made a fortune off me."

I moved my hand around in the water before bringing my hand up to rub his face and neck. The water trailed off his skin and I noticed that he had a five o'clock shadow today. "You were so young..." My chest caved just thinking of a younger Killian being locked up and caged; used. "What happened? How did you manage to escape?"

"Marcus was the one that freed me."

"Marcus did?" I asked surprised. It made sense, though. Killian had always seemed so reluctant to believe what kind of monster he was until recently...

"Yeah, he killed them all." He shook his head. "Now that I think back, I should have been wary of his actions even back then, but I was so glad that I had gotten out of that place—I was twenty when he killed them and I didn't even know why he did it. I left with him that day and had thought of him as a friend since, but Marcus constantly caused problems and had terrible mood swings. It was chaotic staying close to him, he was constantly doing things I didn't understand, yet... I could never leave his side, not when I felt like I owed him my respect and gratitude."

"I was thirty the day Grim came for me. Marcus tried to take Grim even then—he didn't care that Grim was about to merge with me. I kept making excuses for him when deep down I knew the truth. He never actually rescued me, I just happened to be saved when he brutally murdered the witches—I don't even know why he did it, not that they didn't deserve it, but he never had sympathy for life. I only let myself see what I wanted when it came to him."

"Not everyone's meant to be saved. At least Marcus got one thing right when he saved you from them, but he's a monster himself. A terrifying one."

He turned around to face me. "I lived those ten years before I met Grim getting by as an incubus demon and a lot of that time was spent seeing him do things that I shouldn't have let happen."

"He saved you from that horrid place. I can imagine it was very conflicting to decide what was right and wrong when it came to him. Not to mention, everything you went through..."

He smiled at me and traced his thumb over my collarbone. Pinpricks broke out across my skin. For sharing his difficult past with me only made me realize what made him the protective man he was today. I could never judge him for something he had no control over. I would love him for everything that he lived through. "Is it because you've been through your own amount of turmoil growing up that you understand me so well?" he asked me.

I met his eyes. "Let's just say I know what it's like to feel judged when you have no control over what gets thrown your way. My parents never believed me growing up, you know even with this mark, they thought I had carved it on myself. I was placed in therapy and for a long time, Killian, I really believed that I might be crazy. Ryan and Tess, they believed me and I don't think I would have made it through those years without them." I gave him a goofy smile. "I guess it just makes it easier to understand what makes a person when you know what they've experienced and conquered to get where they are."

"I want to save him," he told me. "Ryan, I mean. I don't want you to carry that weight on your shoulders if something doesn't work the way you want it to. I will ask around and see if there's another way but don't get your hopes up. Ultimately, the choice comes down to what Ryan chooses. To become a monster or disappear as himself."

I hid my face in his shoulder and hugged him. It wasn't exactly what I wanted to hear, but it was enough.

I lifted my head up and was close to kissing him when a paper fell next to me. I looked up. "Um, Killian." I tapped his shoulder and he looked up with me. Papers began to fall all around us landing into the water. It wasn't just around us, though. As far as I could see, the papers were falling everywhere.

"Yeah, I see it." He picked one up from the water.

Come All Demons,

The time has come for us to take what should have always been ours. The human world. We don't have to hide beneath their world anymore. Humans are nothing but prey.

I think it's finally time to show them we exist and what better way than on the day they pretend to be us. Let's show them how wicked monsters really are on their Halloween.

When the day comes, I will open a portal for all those that wish to cross.

FEAR

Killian crumbled the paper in his hand. "I think it's safe to say we know he's behind the missing portal chips."

And Fear's games continued.

CHAPTER SEVEN
Melanie

Killian carried me out of the water and placed me on my feet where we stood in silence as we put on our clothes. It would have been great if he had brought us something to dry off with. My jeans refused to go up my wet legs. I grunted in frustration.

"Having trouble?" he asked as he raised back up. Of course, he would already have his clothes on. His dark shirt clung against his wet skin and I marveled at him.

"Whose bright idea was this again?" I told him as I tried to shimmy into my jeans.

He laughed. "Here." He stuck out his hand and a towel materialized. I stopped wiggling and glared at him.

"Are you serious? My clothes are already wet."

The towel disappeared and his smirk appeared. He did nothing but look at me, but the water on me started to bead up and fall off me and my clothes. I looked to him when I could finally slide up my jeans. "Why didn't you just do that to begin with?" He didn't care to show off the things he could do when we first met, but now he was greedy with it.

"To make you ask questions," was his answer.

He faded us back into the castle where things were strangely chaotic. Lincoln was in the ballroom along with a few Reapers. Their expressions were grim and Killian tensed beside me. "We were about to come looking for you," Lincoln said to Killian.

I stared at all the papers lying around. Fear wanted us to know what he was up to, that much was obvious. "Have you found where Fear's hiding?" Killian asked.

Lincoln shook his head. "No, but we did find him." He turned his head and two Reapers were holding a man by the arms behind him. They shoved him to his knees and he glared up at Killian. He looked… normal. Although, it did look like he took a good beating from the Reapers before we got here.

"Lycanthrope," Killian spoke to him. So, he was a werewolf? I looked back at him. "What does he have to do with Fear?"

"We caught him stealing portal chips," one of the Reapers told him. Killian nodded and stepped toward him.

"You have no idea what he has planned," the werewolf spat.

Killian dropped down on one knee in front of him and picked up a piece of paper from the floor. "Actually, I do. Fear's already made what he plans to do very public." The werewolf laughed. "The problem is finding him; he must have some pretty good help to even hide the scent of his death from me. I'll bet you know exactly where he's hiding since you are delivering the chips to him."

The werewolf snorted. "Whatever you say," was all he offered.

"You do realize you're going to die. The moment you chose to help Fear, you sealed your fate and your death is now at my fingertips." Killian stretched his hand out and it became skeletal. I never seen him partially become Grim before. The first time he had changed in front of me, one of his hands was the first thing that changed, but he had been holding himself back from changing. "And I must decide whether I want to send you to Satan's Flames—you know what to expect there—or…" His scythe materialized in his hand. "Trap your soul inside my scythe with the rest of the souls I've collected since I came to be. Which sounds better? Endless suffering and agony or endless battles with demons much worse than you?"

The werewolf's cocky smile faded a few seconds before he finally regained his composure. He jerked his shoulders away from the Reapers that were holding him in place. "I. Don't. Care." Killian smiled at his answer.

Something didn't feel right about this. I studied the werewolf. He didn't look afraid at all. Was he that okay with dying for Fear?

Listen to your instinct.

I was so stunned—relieved—happy to hear the voice that seconds were lost. I looked back to Killian and the werewolf—he was smiling. Killian was standing up now, holding his scythe at the werewolf's head. He almost looked like he expected Killian to take his life.

The X set my skin on my fire. I covered it with my hand and yelled, "Wait, Killian!"

It wasn't too late. Killian turned back and smiled. "You sensed it, too?"

What did he sense? I just got some bad vibes and knew something bad was about to happen.

"Why aren't you killing him?" Lincoln asked as he studied me curiously.

"He's been spelled, but I have no clue what kind of spell." He looked back at the werewolf who looked annoyed that we figured it out. "And since he's at ease with dying, my opinion is that it doesn't activate until he dies."

Lincoln nodded just as all hell broke loose. The werewolf growled and swung the two Reapers at his sides backward but instead of attacking anybody, he just grinned and lengthened his fingernails.

"Killian!" But this time we were too late. The werewolf looked up to Killian with a sinister smile right before he ripped his own heart out. Where his body fell, darkness flooded in and we all went sailing backwards from the force of it.

I hit both my elbows trying to brace my fall and the pain shot up my arms. Killian was the only one that hadn't been blown back by it. He covered his face with his arm as he looked at the opening. "This was his plan!" Killian yelled as he became Grim. Demons piled out of the darkened passage. These were beasts, similar to the wolf demons, only a lot bigger. They stood on two legs and their legs weren't bent backwards like the rat-looking wolf demons. Their eyes were all a golden color. "Take Melanie! We don't know what Fear's after!" he told Lincoln. I stood up. Three went after Killian and his scythe morphed into a sword. He took down one as another one grabbed him—he faded in the werewolf's grip and reappeared behind him. Another jumped him.

I looked over at the stairway. One of them was sniffing around and then he looked up. My heart raced. "Come on, I have to get you out of here." Lincoln tried to pull me by the arm, but I jerked away. The werewolf that was sniffing must have caught the scent of what he was looking for. He started up the stairway.

"Ryan!" I screamed. "They're after Ryan!" I took off running for the stairs.

"Melanie, wait!" Killian practically growled at me, but he was too busy to stop me. Lincoln called my name behind me. I took the stairs across from the one the werewolf was going up. He noticed me running up them and growled. He climbed onto the bannister and jumped. I ducked just as he landed behind me on the stairs, but I kept going up.

A heard a familiar painful cry as I made it to the second floor. When I turned for the hallway, Ryan was already there on his knees. He saw me and looked up. "Go, Melanie!" His eyes were fading out, turning solid white. I ran to him anyway and grabbed him by the shoulder and lifted him to his feet. I hissed and let go of him. He was blistering hot.

Now that I was close enough, I could smell burning flesh and smoke steaming from every part of his body. He howled in pain. The werewolf growled in front of us. "Fight it, Ryan! We can't stay here." I grabbed his shirt and pulled him with me.

"I can't!" He didn't sound like himself. "Go, Melanie, I can feel him…"

"Listen to him, Melanie!" Lincoln lunged for the werewolf. The werewolf slung him against the wall like the centaur weighed nothing.

"Melanie, get away from him." Lincoln managed to get the werewolf on the ground but two more were closing in behind him.

Ryan went up in flames. He fell to the ground screaming and thrashing. I couldn't look away until the charred demon was standing back up in his place. I stepped away slowly, but his eyes turned on me. Saliva dripped out of his lips as he hissed at me.

He took a step toward me and the necklace reacted. He flew backward into Lincoln and the three werewolves. Lincoln was clearly outnumbered and he didn't even have a weapon. The charred demon was already coming back toward me.

Grim was suddenly in front of me slicing the charred demon's chest open with his sword. He stumbled back. "Grim!"

"He can't be killed in this form," Grim told me. I knew that but it was still Ryan.

"Lincoln!" I was surprised to see Penny. She took down two of the werewolves at once with two thin, red swords and tossed one to Lincoln. He caught it and killed the one that had been giving him trouble.

"We have to get that portal closed or they'll keep coming," Grim stated as he waited for the charred demon to attack again. His white eyes traveled over me and he seemed to be deciding something.

Instead of attacking, he started running. When Lincoln tried to stop him, he slammed him against the wall. Penny stepped in front of him and swung her blade and missed. He backhanded her and it was enough to land her on the floor. Once he was at the bannister, he jumped down to the first floor.

"He's going to try to leave through the portal," I told Grim. "We can't let Fear get his hands on him again!"

Grim faded and Penny disappeared right after him. I didn't have time to check on Lincoln. I ran for the stairs. If he was really trying to leave, I had to find a way to stop him. Just running this much already had me feeling sluggish, and I didn't understand why my powers weren't trying to help me somehow. If I could do what I did during the Human Festival, it wouldn't be so hard to help.

As I hurried down the steps, I could see that the ballroom was flooded with demons. Grim was after the charred demon. He was running for the portal, and Grim slung him backward. He faded and reappeared behind the charred demon and held him back. I thought he might be trying to knock him out but it didn't seem to be working. The charred demon got ahold of Grim's cloak and slung him off.

Another Reaper stepped in his place and was slung back as well. He was headed back for the portal again. My eyes stung and my chest hurt with the crushing reality that I might not be able to save him no matter what I did. I ran for him anyway. "Ryan!" I wanted to protect him more than anything. My fear turned to fury, I couldn't let this happen. I wouldn't.

Save him.

And that was all the voice had to tell me. She finally offered me the power and my entire body lit up with a golden glow. I was quicker and my steps lighter.

Just don't kill yourself before you're free of Fear.

I didn't pay attention to her words at that time. Grim took down a few of the werewolves in order to get to the charred demon. Once he was there, I hollered, "Hold him!"

He took one look at me and did as I asked. The charred demon didn't make it easy and there was a struggle before Grim finally held him to where I could do something. The power was tingling and burning my fingertips at this point, and I knew it was time to release it into him.

I grabbed the charred demon's wrists and let it all go. My power wrapped around his wrists and formed a golden band on each arm. His burnt skin began to fall off his body and his hair grew back. Ryan stood in his place. He looked at me confused, and Grim released him.

"What the hell?" Penny looked at me surprised.

"What's going on?" Ryan asked, and I looked at the werewolves still entering through the portal.

But, dizziness hit me and I felt wobbly on my feet. Grim was there to scoop me up in his arms. "She can't keep using this power." I could hear the panic in his voice as he spoke to Ryan. I supposed it was scary for him to see it chip away at my time alive, especially when he was the only one that could see how it affected me. When I thought about it, his time would never stop but our time together would be limited to mine.

"Take her somewhere safe, I have to figure out a way to shut this portal or they'll never stop coming through." Grim placed me into Ryan's arms and walked away. My weight shifted in his arms as he walked with me. He looked down at me with a worried expression.

"I can probably walk," I told him and rubbed my head. I could hear the ruckus going on around us and wondered how we were walking away without anyone attacking us.

"I got you, besides Grim's making sure no one can get close to us." That made me smile. "You saved me, didn't you?" He smiled down at me.

"It's the least I could do," I replied.

"I can't believe that you actually have powers... how is that even possible?" he asked.

I tried to shrug my shoulders and sighed. "I honestly don't know, but Killian and I... I think we were meant to meet each other as crazy as it sounds... Fate, destiny, whatever you wanna call it, I think that's how we are," I gave him the truth. His smiled faded, yet his eyes softened in understanding.

"So, fate never gave me a chance to begin with?" he tried to speak lightly about the subject, but I knew we were past that.

"No one can replace you in my life and in my heart. You will always hold a special place there. Ryan, you've kept me sane all these years." He looked up, but I had already seen the tears glisten his eyes. "I will always love you but not the way you want me to and not the way I once thought I did."

He finally looked back down at me. "You didn't have to tell me. I'm going to love you regardless of what you've decided." For a moment my heart fluttered at his words and maybe in another life, one without ghosts and demons... I might have been Ryan's.

"I didn't tell you that to make you feel better. It's the truth," I told him.

"Just as well, Melanie, I spoke my truth right back."

CHAPTER EIGHT
Melanie

"I still don't understand how you saved me?" Ryan asked for the thousandth time as we sat on the couch together. My eyes were closed and I was beginning to feel a bit better. Grim and the other Reapers had managed to close the portal by tossing every dead werewolf back into it. Something about what came through the portal had to go back in it in order for it to close—it had been spelled that way.

"I don't know." I raised up and sighed. "It comes and goes and the voice speaks and suddenly I know what to do," I answered him.

He gave me a funny look. "Voice?"

"Yeah, the *me* inside my head," I replied and then placed my head in my hands. "That made me sound super crazy, didn't it?"

He grinned at me. "I wasn't going to say anything, but since you said it…"

I pushed him away from me and he laughed. "You never told me about a voice." Killian stepped into the room followed by Lincoln and Penny and a couple more Reapers I didn't know.

"Really?" I said.

Ryan looked at Lincoln limping and went pale. "If I did that—"

Lincoln swiped his hand in the air. "It wasn't you that threw me into a wall but the demon that you become. No worries, I'm a healer." Ryan didn't seem to feel better after his words.

"He wasn't the only one that you managed to get a swing at." Penny pointed to the bruise on her face and glared at Ryan.

"I hit a girl, too?" His voice was full of regret.

"It wasn't him," Killian told Penny.

She shrugged her shoulders and turned her focus on me. "I've never seen any sort of power like that before—the color…" Her eyes were on the gold bands on Ryan's wrist before she looked back at me. "So, Lincoln wasn't lying when he told me she healed Rixen?" she asked.

Killian sat down next to me and placed his hand on my thigh. He let his head fall back and sighed wearily. "She didn't heal the dragon, Penny," Lincoln spoke up. "The dragon was already at Death's doors. Neither mine or Grim's healing would have saved him."

"You're saying she brought him back to life?" she asked skeptically.

"I didn't say that. I don't know what she did." Lincoln was healing himself as he spoke. When he was finished with himself, he healed Penny's bruised face.

"I just don't understand." She crossed her arms. "I don't sense any sort of demonic presence coming from her…in fact, I don't sense anything at all. She's nothing more than a human." When Lincoln was finished healing her, he stepped back.

"Not exactly. Whatever power Melanie wields rivals my own." All eyes fell on Killian but his were on me. "She has a scythe," Killian said it like it should mean something.

Silence. *Tick-tock, tick tock,* the grandfather clocked filled the empty echo. Then they finally went berserk and the room filled with gasps. "She has a scythe?" Lincoln repeated.

Killian nodded and smiled at me. "I told you she was the reason I was able to merge, yet you didn't seem to believe me," he huffed at Lincoln. "She pulled it from her chest. It's golden." He glanced down at Ryan's wrist. "Her power seems to emit that color. Even her skin and hair change when she's using it."

"Yeah, I saw her earlier," Penny acknowledged.

"If she has a scythe like you…" Lincoln's words died out, and for the first time since meeting the centaur, he seemed to acknowledge me as a person—a hint of admiration touched his cheeks.

"She's something else," Penny mumbled, "if she really pulled a scythe from that human body of hers." She didn't sound bitter about me—just confused, maybe curious as well.

"Do you think you can try calling it out?" Killian asked me. Call it out? What the—I didn't even know how to use the power properly, how was I going to make the scythe appear?

My mouth tilted upward as I bunched my shoulders up. "I can try, but I don't think I will be able to." I blinked innocently at him. "Truthfully, I've been trying."

"I know," he told me. Huh? He wasn't going to chew me out? "Try again."

I sighed and stood up. There were too many people in the room, it was making me nervous. I decided to close my eyes instead and focus on bringing it out. *Scythe, scythe, where are you?* I was rambling with my thoughts and shook my head. *Be serious, Melanie.* I didn't want to look like an idiot in front of all these Reapers. In my head, I visualized my scythe. Golden, just as big as Grim's, yet more feminine, and it had a hook-like blade that went inward like his as well. I moved my hand to my chest and it went no further than the valley between my breasts. I tried a few more times before I gave it up.

"I can't. I don't know how I did it before," I admitted.

"I thought so." Killian nodded like he finally understood something. "She can only wield the power when she's in extreme danger or if she has an intense desire leading her to use it. Like earlier, it was her desperation to save Ryan that allowed her to use it. I think it's protecting her that way."

"What do you mean?" Lincoln asked.

111

"She's human, her body can't handle using it."

"It's a shame, really," Lincoln shook his head at me. "A power like Grim's and it can't even be used properly." His eyes lit up. "I've heard that angels carry a light on their skin…"

"She's not an angel, Lincoln," Killian was quick to tell him.

"I didn't say she was—"

"Neither is the power. Although, it is similar," he added. "She's my counterpart."

"She's human!" Penny hissed. "It's not even allowed. It's against our way of things unless she were to have your mark and she most certainly does not have a mark from you." I brought my hand over the X out of habit as she spoke. Killian noticed and wasn't happy.

"Am I missing something here? Did I ask for an opinion from any of you about who I choose to be with?" Killian looked around the room at his Reapers and none of them said a word. "Yes, I know that it doesn't make sense that she's human, and I have no idea why God made her one."

"Wait," I spoke up. "What do you mean? You're making it sound like you already knew about me."

Killian ran his hands through his hair before he looked at me. "An angel came to me a thousand years ago or longer and told me that I had a lover—only she hadn't been born yet. It wasn't until you were on the rooftop wearing my cloak and wielding a scythe and piecing me back together again—even calling yourself

112

my light," he laughed softly, "that I remembered the angel's words from that night and realized who you are to me."

I felt happy and worried all at the same time. "But you said you had no idea what I was," I told him.

He grabbed my hand and smiled. "I know you are meant to be with me, Love, but that doesn't mean I know what your power is supposed to be or why you were born a human."

"I'm so confused. And I thought you were complicated before all this," Ryan mumbled beside me and I shot him a look.

"We'll find out more about you as soon as Fear's out of the picture. Right now, he's a top priority." He picked up one of the papers Fear had sent across his land up and glared. "I want every wolf den found and searched. One of the packs in the Underworld is helping him."

"Yes," Lincoln answered for us all. "Then we might get some peace around here again."

———————————————

It was becoming a habit of Killian's to take me home when all I wanted to do was stay with him. I sighed loudly, making it obvious I wasn't happy about it as he pulled into my driveway. Once the car was in park, he looked over at me. "You wanted to stay that badly?" he asked with a smug look.

"I don't see why I have to be home. I could stay days with you before I'd have to come back home each night. How do you manage all that time without me when half a day kills me," I admitted, testing my girlfriend privileges out.

"I don't," he replied. "But I still have my duties as Grim as well as using every chance we can to track down Fear. I want nothing more than to give you all my time."

"I could stay in the bedroom you set up for me while you're busy…" I mumbled.

Butterflies swam in my stomach when he laughed. "The next time you stay at my house won't be spent in that hidden bedroom but with me. In my bed." I felt my face turn red. "Do you understand?"

"You say those things on purpose." I made a disapproving sound in my throat.

"Only because I love to see those cheeks turn crimson for me," he added and my insides turned to mush. I tried not to look too happy as I opened my door and stepped out.

"I guess I'll see you tomorrow after school?" I asked.

He nodded. "Just say my name and I'm there." He winked and I rolled my eyes and shut the door.

What a day, I thought as I made my way inside. Mom and Alex greeted me as I came in. I fixed myself a BLT sandwich before heading upstairs to my room.

I saved Ryan. I smiled as I ate my sandwich on my bed. I felt closer to Killian. Fear was still a problem, but it didn't go as planned for him today. I stopped him from taking Ryan. That was enough for me to feel satisfied. I placed my plate on my nightstand and slipped underneath my covers. I was exhausted and showering would have to wait until the morning.

I studied my shade lamp on the nightstand. I've conquered so much in the past few weeks… maybe it was time to finally overcome my fear of the dark. Now that I knew my real fear, the dark should no longer be scary, right?

I leaned over and shut it off. It was a lot darker than I realized without any light. It took several seconds for my eyes to adjust enough to make out the furniture in my room. Even my ears were straining—I could hear my heartbeat.

That shape looked odd next to my bookshelf. And I had no idea where that shadow was coming from—it was unrecognizable. Wait, did it move? I turned back on the light and scanned the room.

Nothing.

Okay, maybe I wasn't that ready to conquer the dark.

———————

Another day at school spent evading ghosts. The Reapers were doing their job, but they had their hands full. Penny was back with Tess, and I didn't forget to ask her how she managed to be everywhere all the time. She replied with, "We take shifts watching you, Tess, and your family." Surprisingly, she hadn't been snarky about it, but her attitude was still the same regarding me in everything else. She enjoyed gossiping about me to the ghosts before she sent them to their afterlife.

"I finally talked to Mike," Tess surprised me at lunch by saying.

"Really?"

"Yeah. We decided to end things," she said while taking a drink of water.

I looked at her for several seconds trying to figure out how she was taking it all. "I hadn't expected that outcome," I told her honestly.

She smiled at me. "He didn't cheat. You were right about that. He did get with Haley before we were together but I had already known that. We just decided to see how we do apart." She shrugged her shoulders casually.

"So, it's more like taking a break from each other?"

"No, I think we really are over. I don't know, I guess it was just nice to hear from one another that maybe we can get back what we lost. It felt good to leave him on good terms."

I looked at her like she was an alien. "Who are you, and what are you done to my irresponsible, carefree Tess?"

She laughed. "I finally realized I had no right to be upset if Mike had really cheated on me… not when the whole time we were together I had regarded him as someone I'd eventually leave. I wasn't happy with myself and I didn't want to stay in a relationship where I was that way, so we ended it." She looked down at her plate with a smile before she looked over at the football players. Mike was in the group laughing. "Who knows, maybe in the future we will find something between us again, that is if we don't fall in love with other people. I don't plan to hold myself back when I'm with someone anymore, and I'll probably get hurt because of it, but losing Ryan made me understand that nothing's guaranteed. I hope Ryan knew how much I loved him and I plan on loving the hell out of the poor soul that catches my interest next."

Tess had the tendency to say something real then turn around and say something silly to try to take away from the seriousness. I smiled at her. "He does," I replied then corrected myself, *"Did."*

"Yeah… let's never grow apart, Melanie, no matter where life takes us." Her words caught me off guard.

"Yeah…" I tried to smile back.

Only I didn't know if staying alive was in my future, despite Fear's upcoming death.

CHAPTER NINE
Melanie

It was another evening of Killian coming to pick me up in his car so that we could leave at his place in the human world and fade to his actual home outside the borders of the Underworld.

Only when we arrived things were in a slight uproar. Ryan was yelling at Lincoln for something and when we appeared, his anger turned on Killian. "You can't expect me to sit here and do nothing!" he yelled.

"What can you do?" Killian placed his hands on his shoulders and glared at Ryan.

"What is going on?" I asked them both.

Ryan pulled a crumbled piece of paper from his pocket that I recognized and shot another piercing stare at Killian. "He figured out where Fear plans to open the portal."

"So, you managed to find Fear?" I asked Kilian.

"No, we haven't been able to find him," Killian answered.

Ryan sighed in frustration. "He plans to open the portal in Denver." His words caught my attention and I turned his way. "He's going to unleash a hoard of demons that's out for human blood in our town, Melanie! Where our families are!"

My eyes widened. "And we are going to be prepared," Killian tried to calm Ryan.

"You're not leaving me here while my sister's in trouble." For the first time since everything had happened to Ryan, I saw real panic stir in his eyes. I thought that seeing him crack in front of me would bring out my own fear… it didn't. Instead, I wanted to be what kept him from breaking any further… the person he had always been for me.

Honestly, I was afraid. If Denver was Fear's destination with the portal he planned to open, then Ryan was right… we couldn't do anything, but unlike Ryan, I had enough faith in Killian to know that he was already planning.

"Ryan, everything's going to work out," I started out.

He squinted his eyes at me and shook his head. "You can't say that. You don't even know what might happen." His hands were in his hair and he was pacing frantically.

I went to him and gripped his shoulders. "Ryan." I forced him to look at me.

His face broke and I knew he was falling apart. "Oh God, Melanie. Our families are going to be placed in danger. OUR FAMILIES!"

"I know," I told him. "I'm scared too, but we have to keep them safe."

"She's right. He plans to open the portal on Halloween, that's still months away down here. We have time to stop him before he even gets a chance to open it."

I didn't know which of us calmed him down but he visibly relaxed. "Killian's been keeping Reapers at our houses to keep our families safe already. He was already prepared if Fear tried to use someone I cared about against me again. This time is no different."

"His death is on Halloween," Killian finally revealed the day Fear would die.

"It's weird that you know that." Ryan gave him a strange look. "So, you knew I would die that day as well?" I looked back at Killian.

"Yours was different, one minute it was clear and you were meant to live a long life, then it would change again—it was constantly back and forth. I could never get an accurate feeling with you. I tried to tell you to stay away from Melanie because I figured she was the reason." Killian raked his hand through his hair. "I think the day you touched Melanie's mark, it altered your death so that it could go two different ways and because of that, it was always shadowed for me… I see every death perfectly and what I encountered with yours has *never* happened."

"I won't regret my choice. Whether it was when I was nine and saw her on the floor of the classroom or my recent choices now that led to my death… if you are trying to imply that I should have stayed away from her."

"It was for your own good," Killian tone was dark. "But I do understand what you mean. I would have never

120

stayed away either." They were glaring at each other like morons.

"If you think hearing you two talk like this will make me happy, think again. It doesn't make me happy that you died Ryan." I looked to Killian. "And it doesn't make me happy to know that if put in the same situation, you would have done the same thing." I sighed. "Idiots," I muttered before walking off.

———

"Are you safe to approach?" Killian walked a step behind me as I toured his castle.

"If you keep saying things like that, you're going to make it very unsafe for you," I answered with a smile as I turned around.

"Come on, let's go to the key room," he said as he grabbed my hand.

"Do I get to use the key?" I asked.

"This time I'm in charge of the key. I'd like to show you something other than food." I grunted in response.

"Maybe I should have stayed with Ryan. He wasn't taking it well and honestly, neither am I. We can't let Fear open that portal in our small town."

"No words are going to make either of you feel at ease, not until Marcus and Fear are out of the picture." He grabbed my hand as we walked. "I'll do everything I can to protect that town and everyone in it."

"I know you will." I squeezed his hand and smiled.

121

It took us a couple of minutes to get to the "key room" as he called it. I would have added the word magical in there somewhere to the name, but that was me…

He stood in front of the door with a goofy grin on his face. "Don't get me wrong, Love. You can use the key whenever you want, just not right now. It's my turn to show you something." I arched my eyebrow at him.

When he opened the door, I couldn't hide my disappointment. "I can't even see anything in there. It's completely dark." I tiptoed beside him trying to get a better look at what was in the dark.

He had to know I disliked the dark…

He shoved me forward with a grin. "Stop stalling and go inside. You'll never be able to see what I'm trying to show you unless you go in."

I had an uneasy feeling right before I stepped through the door. I gasped and staggered forward, but Killian was there to hold me steady. I had no momentum or sense of gravity in this room, considering it didn't look like a room at all, that wasn't surprising. It looked like I was standing right in the night sky. Stars surrounded us. Bright, beautiful, and right at my fingertips.

If I reached out my hand… it looked like I could touch one. Only the stars were huge despite how they looked in the sky, so I knew this little one that I could reach out and touch wasn't real. "Okay, I'll admit. This is beautiful," I told him.

He let go of my shoulder and I didn't dare move. I still felt a little off. It felt like I was standing in a galaxy. "You gonna get down here with me?" I turned my head very slowly and saw that he was lying down on a blanket with his hands behind his head. He looked like he was floating on a blanket in the stars.

I smiled and joined him. It was easier to look around when I wasn't standing. "What made you want to show me the stars?"

The stars were moving all around us and new stars were taking their place. I gasped. Was that the Milky Way? "What? I thought humans enjoyed this type of thing… like it gave you all the chance to wonder if there was something more out there."

I shrugged my shoulders. "Yeah, it does, but in my case wondering if something more was out there was terrifying. I mean, I saw ghosts… looking at the stars," I tried to think of what I thought of them. "I actually don't think I ever looked at the stars. I was too busy being afraid and too concentrated on the fact I saw things others didn't. I probably did as a kid." I sighed. "I didn't mean to get all gloomy," I told him quickly. He was watching me from the corner of his eye. "Thanks for giving me a chance to appreciate something that I should have already."

"You're welcome." A screen formed above us. Mom and Alex were sitting on our couch. They weren't moving, though. "What is that?" I asked.

"It's what those two are doing right now," he answered.

I squinted my eyes at the screen. "But they aren't even moving."

"Because time is that different between our worlds. Time in the Underworld moves so much faster that it looks like they aren't moving when really they are."

I was quiet for a long time then I moved my head to look at him. "Why are you showing me this?" My stomach knotted with anticipation. He was making me hope for things that might not ever happen. Would I get to stay here with him until I died? For some reason, the thought was both sad and happy.

When he didn't answer my question, I asked another one, "Doesn't it bother you?"

"Does what bother me?"

"That I'm going to age. You even know the exact date that I will die… doesn't that bother you?" I asked. I found it cruel.

He moved one of his hands out from underneath his head and brought it into my hair. He said nothing until he raised up. Now he was looking down at me, running his hand across my stomach with a sad smile. "It looks like I shouldn't have said anything to you," he told me before sighing and raking his hand through his hair. "I don't plan on losing you, and I won't. There are plenty of ways to keep you by my side. I just have to choose the right one. The one that makes sense." His words warmed my stomach but at the same time, the unknown reality of it all seemed terrifying.

"What do you mean?"

His fingers trailed up my ribs and along my chest. Goosebumps broke out over my skin. He stopped above my breast. "I'm not sure if I'm willing to cross that line yet," was his answer and I decided not to pry him for any more. I figured I would know soon enough when he had made his own decision.

———————

Another day at school was another day of Reapers keeping ghosts away from me and the ones that got close enough were dissolved into the light that bounced off the necklace Killian had given me.

But one thing I noticed was Tess. She seemed a little less sad and a lot more like the girl I grew up with. Penny wasn't the Reaper that was watching over her today and Tess had asked me if I wanted to visit Ryan's grave with her after school. His tombstone had been delivered.

I called and made sure Mom was picking up Alex before we left after school. She followed me in her Mustang and it took us about twenty minutes to get to their family's cemetery. It was on their grandparents' property and wasn't very big, but was well taken care of over the years. I knew their grandma was buried up here, but I wasn't familiar with any of the others.

Tess was stepping out of the car when she said, "It's weird that we were here last week burying him."

I nodded and we walked up the hill together. The male Reaper that was with her was silent as he followed behind us. I kind of felt bad for the Reapers that had to

125

constantly watch over us. Protecting us wasn't their actual job, yet none of them complained. Except Penny.

We were panting by the time we reached the top of the hill and it was easy to spot the new tombstone that wasn't there before. It was black, different than the normal ones and I found that it suited him.

Ryan Jones

Beloved Son and Brother

Followed by his birthdate and death.

Surprisingly, no ghost had followed me here, but they were still a huge problem at school and home. The grass still hadn't grown, it wouldn't until next year. Looking at his tombstone, knowing his body was six feet below me…. it made me sad all over again. Ryan's body was here, but his soul was stuck in a new one created by Fear. The gold bands were keeping him safe right now and I wanted to believe it would continue doing so.

When I spotted Tess in the corner of my eye, I saw her tears. "I bet you're doing great wherever you are," she whispered to the grave and I swallowed my feelings. "I bet you're causing trouble, too." She wiped her eyes and looked over at me. "Do you think he can hear me?" she asked.

No. Only I couldn't tell her that, so I prayed my silence would be enough for her.

"I also talked to Mike and we ended things on good terms and I feel good about it," she continued like that for several minutes. Rambling on to his tombstone, telling him everything she would have if he was here. I would tell him everything she couldn't.

I placed my arm over her shoulder and we stood there silently until we could no longer handle the cold. I wrapped my jacket around me as we walked back down the hill. "Are you going to bring Killian to the Halloween party?" she asked.

I shrugged my shoulders. "I wasn't aware I was going," I told her. Now that I knew Fear planned to open the portal on that day… unless Killian stopped him beforehand, there was no way I was going.

"Come on, you have to. I'm going as Batgirl." I could see Tess's version of Batgirl already.

"I might have plans already," I told her so maybe she would stop asking, but this was Tess I was talking about…

Tess and I went separate ways after leaving the cemetery. When I got home, Mom and Alex were watching TV together. "You're back?" Mom called to me while I was still in the hallway.

"Yeah, it's freezing," I replied, rubbing my arms.

"Killian stopped by but left before you got here," she mentioned, and I felt my forehead wrinkle up with wonder. He always knew exactly where I was, so I wasn't sure why he stopped by.

"Oh?" When I entered the living room, Miles was sharpening his knife leaning next to the doorway. He greeted me with a nod and walked into the hallway with the Reaper that came in with me.

A couple of ghosts already arrived since I got here. They only seemed to find me at the places I was most likely to be at.

"Yeah, he stayed and chatted for a few minutes with us," Mom added softly, almost like she was pleased with him for doing so.

"Did he?" I asked. "I'm going to head on upstairs."

"Foods on the stove," she yelled as I was going on the stairs.

I wasn't surprised to find Killian waiting for me in my room. I smiled and shut the door behind me. "You ready?"

I nodded. "Of course." He took my hand and we faded to his castle.

I could only stare as Ryan sat at a table with Penny. He looked pale as she laughed about something. "Don't worry, it'll grow back," she told him. He stood up quickly when he saw me. Cards were laid out on the table and the butler, Ralph, was bringing out drinks, but what I was most curious about was what Penny was talking about… something told me I probably didn't want to know.

Ryan looked guilty about something as he looked at me. He was even messing with his shirt, looking down at it as he did so. It was very odd. Ryan was never an awkward person. That was my job. "Oh hey, Penny was just telling me the rules of poker in the Underworld and I believe I'll stick to the human way," he said too quickly.

Even Penny was watching him strangely. Killian was silent next to me. I arched my eyebrow at him. "Are you okay?" I asked him.

"Yeah," Penny added, "I haven't even cut anything off yet."

My eyes widened. "What kind of poker do you sickos play?" I looked to Killian for an answer and he shrugged his shoulder.

"I'm not." He fidgeted with his shirt again.

"He's hiding something," Killian said.

Ryan was tense. "I'm not," he denied again.

"You didn't want her to see you hanging out with me?" Penny teased and he looked at her like she was crazy. I couldn't blame him. I had seen Ryan date countless girls over the years and it never bothered him. It was something else. "Well, you weren't acting weird until she showed up," Penny went on.

"What's that on your neck?" Killian pointed at his own neck to make his point. Ryan looked away and hid his neck from our view.

"It's nothing." Now I was afraid. The clues were there and yet, I didn't want to acknowledge them.

"Stop putting up a front, your odd behavior the moment we got here is enough to prove that something is wrong," Killian practically ripped the words out of his chest.

"Piss off." Ryan headed for the front door.

I looked at Killian hopelessly and he tilted his head forward for me to follow Ryan. I took off after him. He was already out the castle doors before I caught up. The doors shut behind us and he stopped but didn't turn around to face me.

"How long?" I whispered. My palms were sweaty and I squeezed them shut.

"How long what?" he mumbled, still not turning around.

"Ryan!" Tears were in my eyes and I grabbed him by the shoulder and jerked him around.

"Don't cry, Melanie…" his voice was pleading, desperate.

I saw the blackness on his neck, disappearing into his shirt and lost my breath. I cupped my mouth and brought my hand out to his shirt and pulled it up. I gasped at what I saw. Starting at his chest, the charred blackness was vining out in every direction. Three jagged marks were trailing up his neck. Most of his chest was already covered and the vines were spreading over his ribs.

He pulled his shirt down and brought his hands out to wipe my tears which only made it worse, but when I looked up I could see the tears forming in his own. "Don't cry," he said, even though he was on the verge of doing so himself. "I knew this was going to happen. You were the only one that couldn't accept it."

I thought I had saved him. I looked down at the gold bands on his wrist and it was the first time I noticed that they weren't as bright now… they were fading…losing the battle against his demon.

I couldn't breathe. I couldn't think. I only realized the reality of the truth I refused to accept. I breathed in so hard my voice was terrifying coming out of my throat as I said to him, "I can't save you… can I?"

His arms were around me before my crying got worse. I hugged him back and it didn't take me long to feel the tremor in his own back and I knew that he was crying too. "It's okay, your tears are enough for me… it was enough that you tried to save me," his voice was muffled as he spoke into my shoulder.

"There's a lot I have to tell you, your sister spoke to you at your grave today." His shirt was soaked with my tears.

"Tell me everything," he said.

And I did.

———

Lincoln inspected Ryan's chest and sighed. "I've never dealt with anything like this before, so it's hard to say how fast it'll spread."

Killian and I stood next to the couch where Ryan sat. I talked him into letting Lincoln look at it. "Will I still be me on Halloween?" he asked.

Lincoln tilted his head and shook his head. "I don't know."

"That's all I'm asking… I just need to know that Fear is taken care of and Melanie and everyone are gonna be safe before I… I can't lose who I am before I see him destroyed." He clenched his fists and shook his head.

Lincoln nodded. "I'll see if there's anything to slow down the spreading, but don't get your hopes up."

Ryan grabbed his shirt and put it back on. "Fine." He looked at me. "I'm okay, Melanie, so stop looking at me like that."

"I wasn't—" Was I?

"We can't kill Fear, you keep forgetting," Killian said to Ryan.

"Which is bullshit." Ryan clenched his teeth together and glared at him.

"Even so, Marcus has always been the one pulling all the strings and he *will* die. If you can keep yourself alive until then… who knows, maybe we can figure out a way to do something about Fear."

Ryan stood up and walked past us. "We both know I won't have that much time, so stop trying so hard when really you could care less."

"That's where you're wrong." Ryan turned around and looked at Killian. "Your soul matters to me because it matters to Melanie. I don't want her crying over you any more than she already has."

"What?" Ryan was angry. Killian was no better next to me as he arched an eyebrow at Ryan.

"If something happens to you, there'll be no getting over it for her, you know that."

Ryan was in Killian's face before I had time to grasp the situation. He grabbed ahold of his shirt and glared. "Do you think I want to leave her knowing she will be with you? I'd much rather be alive and making her mine!"

"Oh?" That one word from Killian sounded terrifying.

"Stop it, you two!" Neither of them was listening to me.

Lincoln intervened and pushed them apart. "Grim," his voice was full of lecture and disappointment as he scolded him. He turned on Ryan. "When he says he wants to save you, it's true, but he doesn't know how to handle his jealousy when it comes to your relationship with Melanie, either."

"Jealous?" Killian scoffed. His reaction even to me was a dead giveaway that he was, in fact, jealous.

"Yes, jealous." Lincoln felt like the one in control at the moment because Killian went quiet. "Good Devil, I mean look at you. You baited the human into arguing just to release your frustration." Caught red-handed, Killian scratched his chin innocently and looked away.

"Well, well," Ryan said. "I've always known you were." He placed his hands behind his head and grinned cockily.

Killian's hand turned into a bone and the scythe materialized in his hand. Lincoln and I both moved at once. "I should put him out of his misery right now," Killian growled.

"Now you're the one baiting him," Lincoln stated to Ryan and he shrugged his shoulders. "I think you should probably go," he added, and Ryan walked out of the room.

Lincoln looked at me and we both sighed together.

———————

Killian and I hadn't spoken much after his argument with Ryan. He took me back to my room and left. He was probably feeling guilty about how he acted earlier. Or maybe, I wanted him to feel guilt instead of just hoping he was.

I ended up watching a movie with Mom and Alex, although she fell asleep thirty minutes in. I showered and went to bed only to toss and turn. I knew why. Killian and I hadn't got the chance to spend time alone with each other today. The more time I spent with him, the more I wanted it.

I was curled up underneath my cover when I called out, "Killian." He came immediately and took one look at me and smiled.

"You called?"

"Will you stay with me until I fall asleep?" I asked lamely. I couldn't think of a better reason for why I called him here.

Without another word, he took off his leather jacket and tossed it on the floor. He didn't take off his boots, though. When he got in bed with me, he moved his hand underneath me so I placed my head on his chest.

"Talk about something," I ordered him and he chuckled softly.

"About what?"

"I don't know," I whispered. "How about your real age for one thing? You're a lot older than three thousand years, aren't you?"

"As Grim, yeah," he admitted. "But I didn't start counting my age until the merge. Melanie, I never lived until then, I only longed to be more than what I was. Then once I discovered what it meant to live, the rest of my years would be waiting to find love—waiting for you." He was rubbing his fingers up and down my arm. It was relaxing and his words topped the cake and I couldn't help but smile.

"Gag," I mumbled, and his laughter made his chest vibrate and I felt it against my cheek. "If I hadn't been the one you were destined to be with—"

"It would have still been you. The moment I laid eyes on you, I knew that you were going to turn my world upside down."

"Gee, thanks," I told him.

"You continue to make me feel things no one has ever done before." He placed a kiss on my forehead. "This madness they call love—what I've always wanted, you pull it from me so easily. The one thing I've discovered, the one thing I've desired and craved to have with someone, you gave to me just by crossing my path. How many ways do you want me to word it for you?"

Smiling, while I listened to the rhythm of his heartbeat against my cheek, I fell asleep.

CHAPTER TEN
Molly

Two more witches dropped dead, the other ten was chanting together. Blood seeped from their eyes and nose—they were all slowly dying and yet, none of them stopped. Either way, they knew they were dead if they didn't listen to Fear.

He forced them here in order to keep himself hidden from Grim and it was working. When they started to die off, he made the werewolves find more. My stomach was coiled up with a mixture of irritation and fear these past few weeks.

My boss had always been a sick demon, but now, he had clearly gone mad. He was desperate to escape his own death. I kept clinging to the body I wanted, but I was beginning to understand Fear had never planned to give it to me. He kept me baited all these years just so I would do what he wanted.

I had been young when he found me and naïve. He got me to believe him so easily. I didn't know what Grim would do to me once Fear died. Sometimes I didn't want him to die because of that very reason, but then, I wanted him gone—out of my life more than the rest of my troubles. I wanted to get away from him.

But Fear couldn't be killed. It was Marcus that was meant to die… was there no escaping regardless?

Fear looked up and smiled at me. He looked like he expected good news. It made me nervous to continue to tell him the same results. "The ghosts can't enter her body. Even when Grim's not around, the necklace she's wearing dissolves them before they can even get close." Not to mention, the Reapers he was keeping around her house.

"So, he plans to keep both my marks from me?" Fear laughed. "I don't think so. I don't know how they are keeping the boy away from me, but it won't last forever. As for Melanie, there's a way to get the ghosts inside her. And once the spell activates inside her, things are going to get interesting." The look in his eyes twisted my stomach. I didn't even know what kind of spell he placed over the ghosts.

"I think it's time I come out of hiding to pay her a visit," he told me.

I nodded and he ported. I assumed he expected me to join him. I took a deep breath and followed, only something interrupted my portal and I ended up somewhere other than Melanie's.

Something sinister lurked in the darkness before me. "What the hell? Who brought me here?" I asked. I was still trying to use my portal chip to get me the hell outta' there, but it wasn't working.

"Molly." Recognition of the voice turned me to stone. "I've come to make you a deal. One you won't want to refuse."

CHAPTER ELEVEN
Killian

It was in the crook of my arm where her body lay close to mine. Her breathing became softer and more even, letting me know she had fallen asleep while mine, on the other hand, continued to quicken.

My eyes lingered to the X on her chest and the dark thoughts I was having these days were growing on me more and more. I knew Melanie had noticed as well, but she didn't pry me with questions. Instead, she was waiting for me to come out and tell her what was on my mind.

If it was one thing I learned about her, it was that she hated when I kept her in the dark about things. Which was why she was constantly asking questions... and that was why I found it funny that she wasn't trying to get this answer from me. I grinned and stopped as quick as I started. I probably looked foolish... looking down at her while she slept with a lovesick expression.

I wanted nothing more than to spend all my time with her and to steal all of hers, but I was still Death. I would always have a balance to deal with and looking for Fear was making my impatience grow. I couldn't relax until Marcus was dead and Melanie was free of Fear's mark.

I slowly slid my arm out from underneath her head and placed it on her pillow. She didn't even flinch and that alone made my heart swell. The girl that once could hardly sleep when I first met her… so easily succumbed to sleep around me. The fact that I could give her that bit of peace despite everything going on… it had me feeling like I was on top of the fucking world and that only proved how caught up I was in her completely. I put my jacket on and took another look at her lying on her bed before I faded to the Underworld.

At this rate, I knew the chances of me finding Fear before Halloween were slim… if I was going to find him, I would have been able to do so already. His death clawed through my veins and knocked against my bones everyday it grew closer. Whatever he was using to keep himself hidden was working, but it wouldn't work on the day he was supposed to die. Nothing would keep me from him on that day, but I couldn't stop his plans if I didn't find him before then.

I found myself at another wolf den. There was no sign of Fear or Molly. I faded to a new place. My thoughts drifted back to Melanie—much like they always did when I was away from her. It was agony waiting to see her again, and sometimes I wanted to wake her up through the night just to satisfy my need to be around her. A night of her sleeping and going to school was no time at all for her, but for me, that was days turned into weeks.

Love wasn't what I expected it to be. It was more. So many other emotions came with loving someone. I cared for a lot of demons over my lifetime, and I knew what it felt like to lose friends and allies—I outlived everyone, so it came naturally for me to expect that, but with Melanie… everything was amplified to the point that the thought of losing her drove me insane. I was terrified.

Loving Melanie meant constantly worrying about her when she wasn't around. It meant fearing for her life. Worst of all, I was always untouchable by any demon that wanted me dead and now that I loved her, she became that weakness everyone wanted me to have. A weakness I would never let go of.

I was helpless—completely taken by her and she didn't even know the extent of my love for her.

Every time I sent her back home, I fought myself to keep her with me. I didn't want her to leave. I wanted to treasure her, but then I also wanted to ruin her. I wanted to feel her crumble beneath me as I showed her what it meant to be born *mine.*

The thoughts both worried and excited me. Just because we were meant to be didn't mean I could claim her—I wasn't an animal… then again, the more I let myself think about all the things I get to show her—all the things she had never seen before and the desire I saw blazing in her eyes as she looked at me even when she was nervous… I couldn't keep myself away from having the dark thoughts.

I wanted Fear out of the picture. For good. Then I'd take my time in showing her my world. And I'd do whatever she'd let me do to her. I smiled at my own inner dialogue. When the danger was gone, I'd show her what it meant to be loved by me.

To be loved by a guy that carried the weight of death on his shoulders.

To be loved by Grim Reaper.

Then it might make her realize how long I've been waiting for her to love.

Like a plague—when I least expected to feel his presence, it popped up clearer than ever before. My heart died out. I knew exactly where he was. *Melanie.* I faded to get to her as quickly as I could.

CHAPTER TWELVE
Melanie

I woke to the sound of Alex screaming. I jumped up and touched the part of the bed where Killian had been. I didn't have time to wonder when he had left. Alex was still screaming. "Alex!"

I was already opening the door and immediately stopped at the doorway. Molly walked on the bannisters on the second floor. Her tiny arms were out as she balanced herself and when she saw me, she flashed a smile. "It's been awhile."

I ignored her and ran for Alex's room. "Alex!" I yelled again. I was pulled back by the hair and panic was already gripping me—I had to get to Alex. My arms swung out as I fell on my butt. The power came out like static at my fingertips, but Molly dodged my attempt to hit her with it and punched me in the face. It knocked me back and for several seconds I was too stunned to do anything.

When I opened my eyes, Miles was thrown out of Alex's room. He smacked against the wall and didn't move once he landed on the floor.

"Too bad your mom's at work to join in on the fun," Fear's sinister voice drifted out of Alex's room.

"Sis!" he was crying out for me, and I quickly stood up.

"Alex!" I screamed. "I'm right here." I clenched my teeth and felt all this hatred and fear fester to the point that it was suffocating. "Leave him alone! He has nothing to do with this."

He stepped through the doorway gripping Alex by the shoulder. His claws dug into Alex's skin and he looked close to passing out. Fear was going all out; his horns and tail were there for Alex to see—to make him terrified.

"I don't know." Fear looked down at Alex with a smile. "I'm perfectly okay with marking him as well." The very thought made my blood boil.

"That's a nice necklace," Molly added next to me.

Grim appeared out of nowhere and slammed Fear against the wall. Alex stumbled a few steps back but was quickly able to get away from them when Fear lost his grip on his shoulder. He ran my way but when I brought my hands out to scoop him up in my arms, Molly kicked me in the stomach. A sound escaped my lips right as I doubled over in pain.

"Sis!" Alex cried out my name again. He squatted down in front of me. "What's wrong?" He couldn't see Molly because she was a ghost, but he had no problem with seeing Fear.

"Stay back," I told him.

Molly grabbed him up by the shirt and shoved him away. He was freaking out and looking around frantically. It hurt to see him look so afraid of something he couldn't even see.

"I thought this necklace was supposed to be protecting you?" Molly studied the necklace with a smirk. "I think I'll get rid of this, what do y'all say?" I looked behind her to see who she was talking to. Ghosts were in the hallway, floating behind the bannisters and in the stairway… all of them were waiting for something.

I couldn't even make out Grim. He was surrounded in his dark colored essence. Fear laughed. "Why are you so angry? And here I thought you'd be happy to see me since you've been trying so hard to find me." A guttural sound ripped from Grim's throat. One minute they were in front of Alex's bedroom door, and then the next, they weren't. I could hear them in another part of the house.

"Stop looking for Grim, he can't save you right now," Molly said to regain my attention.

Alex was covering his ears and there was a wild look in his eyes. "Sis, what is going on? What were those things fight—" Grim and Fear appeared on the stairs. Fear's tail shot out toward Grim and he caught it and slung him against the wall. The wall caved in with his weight and Alex started screaming.

"Alex, it's going to be okay!" I tried to tell him, but I wasn't sure that it was.

"Geez, you don't even care that I'm right here in front of you," Molly huffed. "Guess I'll get straight to the point then." She reached for the necklace and it reacted, sending her flying back through the hallway. She went through all the other ghosts and instead of landing on the floor—she fell straight through like the ghost she was.

I stood up and went to Alex. I scooped him up in my arms and placed his legs around my waist. "Come on," I said. He was crying and hiccupping against my shirt.

"I'm scared," he whispered, and my heart broke. I took us to my bedroom and slammed the door shut. I glanced at the door and quietly waited.

"Alex, I need you to go hide in my closet until this is all over." I placed him on his feet and gently wiped his eyes.

Next thing I knew, I was being yanked backward by the hair. I grabbed my bedpost and took ahold of my hair and looked back. There was nothing, but I knew why when I looked back to Alex. Molly held him by the shirt with a knife against his neck. "Lose the necklace." She tapped Alex's neck with the blade and he squealed almost silently—his bottom lip trembled as he looked for what was holding him back.

"Stop!" I cried. "Let him go and I will," I promised. I was already reaching behind my back to take it off. She grinned in triumph, and I sneered at her. "You're no different than Fear," I spat the words out without thinking, but she was the one that looked surprised by it. Her expression faltered and gave way to what I could have sworn looked like shame.

She recovered quickly, though. "We all can't be perfect. Someone has to be the villain."

"No, no one's forcing you to do these things. That's all you." There it was again, that expression on her face.

She glared. "You're right. Not all of us make the right choices to begin with, and we are stuck paying for them until it's all over and we're done for." I got the feeling the 'we' she was talking about was actually her, but I didn't care—I didn't want to try to understand the one that was holding a knife against my brother's neck.

"You're stupid if you expect me to believe someone has to continue to make bad choices like they have no choice. That only makes them selfish—*weak*."

I was making her angry. "Take. Off. The. Necklace." She moved the knife against his skin and he started panicking worse. "You're only valuable to Fear because Grim cares for you. Now that he knows you're Grim's Light or whatever, instead of the Vessel, let's just say things only got worse for you. I've never seen him loathe someone as much as he does Grim Reaper."

I knew that if I took off this necklace, I was screwed. But Alex's life came above mine. I promised myself no one would end up like Ryan—especially not my little brother. My fingers were on the necklace when Grim faded behind Molly. "You're a ghost, it matters not where I'd send a soul such of yours," He was talking down at her and she looked up—wide-eyed and fearful. "Fear's death has a set date, you, on the other hand, are already dead."

He lifted the scythe out and she and I both knew he planned to open a passage that sent her straight into flames. She tossed Alex down and disappeared. Fear appeared where she once was and Grim grabbed him by the neck. "Go ahead, I'd like to see you try," Fear goaded him.

I bent down and Alex scrambled away from them and closer to me. I noticed ghosts were filling up the space around us in my room. Everything about this made me uneasy. Why did Fear come out of hiding when he knew Grim was looking for him and the missing portal chips?

He had a trick up his sleeve and whatever it was started and ended with me and the ghosts. "Don't be afraid, go ahead and jump inside. The power inside her can bring you all back to life," he was lying. The devious smirk on his face was so plain to see. Only the ghosts were desperate enough to believe anything he said.

"I can't bring any of you back." I forced Alex to his feet and tucked him behind me.

"What's going on?" Alex asked behind me.

"If you honestly think going inside her body will bring you back to life—you're all pathetic," Grim said to them, and Fear only grinned wider.

"Only one way to find out," Fear mumbled. Grim tightened his hold around Fear's neck, but he made no move to try and get away.

"If anyone even tries to go near her, you'll never get to your afterlife. I'll make you suffer a terrible fate," his teeth were clenched together as he spoke.

The ghosts were all around us. Their eyes were going back and forth between me and Grim and Fear. They were contemplating their chances of making it near me before Grim got to them. They made their decision—five came at me at once and Grim let go of Fear and swung his scythe toward them—they screamed and evaporated to nothing as the blade touched them. Two were already near me and the necklace reacted.

"What an irritating sight. No wonder I had to come out of hiding," Fear studied my necklace as he spoke. Grim refocused on Fear instead of the ghosts when he saw that my necklace was still doing its job. "I wonder, though…" He pointed a finger over his chest, in the very spot his mark rested on the skin of mine. "Can she be protected from the one that practically owns her?" He pretended to draw an X on his chest and laughed.

The X was burning to the point that it burnt through my shirt. The knowledge of what he came here to do only seemed to hit us when it was already too late. "Melanie," my name fell from Grim's lips like a cry for help. Every ghost in the room ran for me at once. His scythe morphed into a sword and a scream that sounded more like a roar escaped his throat as he swung out and obliterated some of them.

But they were coming at me from every corner of the room. And when the first one reached me, the necklace didn't react and the X continued to set my skin on fire.

The ghost went inside me and I fell to the ground like a brick—I was a deadweight. I couldn't move. I didn't know how many managed to get inside me. I could hear Alex crying next to me and Grim went ballistic.

Heavy… my eyes were so heavy, but I was terrified of giving in to the sleepiness that suddenly filled my entire body.

No wonder Grim fought so hard to keep me away from Fear. Because even he couldn't protect me against his mark.

I didn't want to close my eyes. I didn't want to think that Fear finally succeeded in killing me.

But the darkness came whether I wanted it to or not, and with it, who knew what followed.

CHAPTER THIRTEEN
Killian

I could hardly grasp what was happening—how fast things fell to ruin. A murderous sound came from my throat as Melanie fell to the floor the second the first ghost went inside her. Behind me, Fear was laughing like a maniac and he knew there was nothing I could do to kill him today. I focused on destroying every ghost in the room, but I wasn't quick enough—I didn't know how many had already slipped inside her.

Panic held me like a vise and it didn't help that Melanie's brother kept asking her to wake up as he shook her body. His eyes kept going back to me and Fear as he cried out for his sister.

My essence was as dark as my anger and continued to hide me within it. Once there were no ghosts left, I turned to Fear and slammed him into the wall. I held him by the chin and I squeezed so hard that if he had been a normal human or demon, his jaw would have shattered. "What did you do?" I screamed in his face.

His eyes leveled with mine. "She's somewhere not even you can reach her." His words were meant to set me off and it worked.

I was furious—ready to push my boundaries. I didn't know what he did to her. "I'm going to kill you," I said through clenched teeth as I dropped him on his feet. He ran his hands down his shirt with a smile and mocked me with it. He didn't expect me to bury my hand into his chest. For a moment, I reveled in the look on his face as I held his heart in my hand. It beat wildly and with fear— he should be fearful… I was pushing every limit that existed as Grim.

"You can't," he hissed, yet his eyes were unsteady… I had him afraid. "I'm immortal, it doesn't matter what you do to me," he spat in my face, and I growled—pressing my skull into his forehead.

"Fear is the only one immortal, remember that," the words echoed with my rage and power. "Marcus, you are a dead demon. You won't be able to hide inside of Fear much longer. Death has a way of getting its way."

I squeezed his heart harder and even now, I felt my anger going past its limits. My fingers were clawing and I felt my energy trying to pull out Marcus even now—I was reaching as far as my power would let me go, and inside of me, my own warning came knocking—my own power wouldn't let me go any further. It wouldn't let me get Marcus, no matter how easily I could pull him out right now… I could feel his sick, pathetic presence burying himself deeper inside of Fear.

I finally stopped trying to fight myself as Grim—I knew I couldn't take Marcus's life right now and so did he, because he laughed. "That's what I thought. How incredibly pathetic, to be stopped by your own fate." My hand was still in his chest as he leaned in next to my ear. "Don't worry, I'll take my time in ruining her before she finally gives in and accepts death as a means of escaping the hell I put her in." My essence pooled around us.

"Even if she's not the Vessel—I'll have my fun in snuffing the light out of what was meant to be yours."

I clamped my hand over his heart until it burst. His eyes went wide before shutting. He wasn't dead, he would be back. I flung him across the room and turned to Melanie and Alex. He looked petrified as I moved toward them.

"Stop. Don't hurt us—" My hands were over his forehead—wiping his memories clean before he could finish his sentence. I caught him before he fell and gently placed him on the floor. Through the house, my power was already sweeping over everything and fixing the damage.

Skin took form on my bones and I was Killian again as I picked Melanie off the floor. Her pulse was strong but when I placed her in my arms, she dangled like she wasn't okay at all—my fear was coming at me full force, and I was reminded of how fragile her life was compared to mine. I tried to come up with a logical reason as to why she was born human… but I couldn't.

I never experienced any type of fear until Melanie came into my life. Now it came to me all the time— naturally and so fast that it was crippling.

"Melanie," I could hear the quiver in my own voice. She was shaking then I saw that it wasn't her shaking but me. I pulled her limp body closer and when I looked back to where Fear had been laying—he was gone like I expected him to be. "What did he do to you?" I whispered to her.

I faded to Tess's house and Penny greeted me outside when she sensed my presence. She took one look at Melanie and her jaw tightened. "What happened?" she asked.

"Fear. I have to get her to the castle, but I need you to call another Reaper to come stay with her brother. Miles is unconscious at her house and the boy is alone." She nodded and her eyes lingered on my hands… they were still shaking and I couldn't stop. It took everything I could to hold myself together. She'd never forgive me if I left her brother alone…

"Get a grip… you're no good to her if you fall apart before helping her," When I opened my mouth to say something, she held up her hand. "Go, I got everything handled here."

I didn't waste another second and faded into the castle.

When I saw Lincoln, I started to unravel. I lifted her further up against my chest and held back what might be tears. The Grim Reaper didn't cry, but Melanie was giving me all sorts of firsts. "Fear got to her," I told him in a rush.

"What happened? Bring her to the couch!" I followed Lincoln into the room and sat her down on the couch.

"What's going on?" Ryan stepped into the door and took one look at Melanie and rushed over. "What happened to her?"

"Fear was there and because of him, the necklace couldn't protect her from the ghosts entering her body," I panicked. "I don't know what he did to her. Can you do something?" I asked Lincoln.

"Have you tried using your healing on her?" Right, I could heal as well. I couldn't focus on what I might be able to do for her myself.

I brought my hand above her chest and my healing sparked to life. Only there was nothing to heal... absolutely nothing. "I can't!"

"Calm down," Lincoln told me and shoved me out of the way. His healing came to life under his fingertips as he hovered his hand up and down her body. After a minute, he sighed in frustration. "There's nothing wrong, physically," he said.

"Something's wrong, look at her!" I yelled. "She won't wake up." I gripped her shoulders and gently shook. "Melanie, Love, wake up." Nothing. I placed my hand over her heartbeat—it was steady.

"I think he might have trapped her in a dream state," Lincoln told me.

I didn't like the sound of that. I've been around since the beginning, so I had seen plenty of death within the realms of dreams. "What do you mean? How could he with ghosts?"

"Easy. He just needed a witch or any demon that deals with spells and there you have it." Lincoln studied me. "Grim, you should know more than I, nothing is impossible when it comes to the resources in our realm."

"Then all I need to do is force the ghosts out." I fisted my hand as it became bone and right when Lincoln yelled for me to stop, I reached into Melanie's chest. It was easy to feel what wasn't supposed to be there, but when I tried to pull it out her entire body jerked forward.

'Stop! Are you mad? You could do more harm than anything!"

I sunk to my knees beside the couch as I watched her. She looked like she was sleeping peacefully. "I can't do anything! Who knows what he's putting her through right now."

The tremors were running through my body again. I was powerless. I didn't want to fall into despair—no matter what. I couldn't do anything when he could kill her in her sleep.

Lincoln moved behind me and placed his hand on my shoulder. "You have no choice," Lincoln didn't even hesitate to say the words. "The only one that can save her is herself. It's all up to her."

"Melanie," Ryan was behind the couch. He grabbed her hand as he smiled down at her. "You didn't come this far to lose in your sleep. Your entire life has been a nightmare because of Fear. I say give him hell." I was stunned by the boy's words… how could he take it with ease? Then I saw his hand that held hers was shaking. That was how I knew the extent of his feelings for her right now were no different than mine. And right now, I couldn't hate him for it.

I looked at Melanie. I focused in on the sound of her heartbeat—the only thing that gave me comfort. I decided to hand it over to her. The only thing I could do was have faith in her.

I grabbed the hand closest to hers while Ryan still held the other one tight. My resolve was clearer than ever before. There would be no more hesitating on what was right or wrong…

Looked like, in the end, I would have to use a page out of Fear's handbook.

When she woke, I was never going to leave her side.

Then, her heart rate spiked and water started shooting out of her mouth—she was choking.

CHAPTER FOURTEEN
Melanie

Water.

Something had a hold of my foot and I was being dragged down… further and further. I was finally able to open my eyes but when I did, I couldn't breathe. I made the mistake of sucking in water when it should have been air. I looked up and saw the light growing distant—the surface was so far away and the water was so dark.

My lungs were on fire, and I thought that I should be dead. I didn't know what was happening… it was hard to focus on anything besides the pain of drowning. It hurt so much, I almost wished for it to end sooner.

"Already want to die so soon?" I looked down in the direction of the voice—it belonged to Fear. He was the one pulling me down. I couldn't see him, but I knew he was there. His voice was muffled from the water, but I couldn't be mistaken. I struggled and tried kicking him away. "I want to make sure your death is slow and painful," he laughed afterward. "Just because you aren't the Vessel doesn't mean I won't make use of you once you die and belong to me."

Then I remembered. Fear had used Alex as leverage, and Molly was there as well. The ghosts managed to jump inside me, then what? What happened? Where was *this*?

He released my foot and the next thing I knew, I was falling onto my bedroom floor. Water came down over me. I spluttered and coughed up water, only when I lifted myself to my feet, I wasn't wet. Which was odd...

Nothing was right about all of this.

My bedroom was dark—I never left my shade lamp off at night. I was confused and disgruntled—what had Fear done? If not for the small bit of light peeking in from the window, I wouldn't have been able to make out the objects in the room. But the first thing I made myself do was run over to the light switch, it wouldn't come on. I tried the lamp on my nightstand—no luck either. There was a creak outside my door—possibly somewhere in the hallway or... Alex's bedroom. I never worked well with my own fear—my irrational dread of the dark amplified everything and made it worse.

Where was Killian? I couldn't wait on him, not if Fear or Molly was somewhere in the house. I had to find Alex. There was another creak on the other side of the door and I lost some of my nerve. I took a deep breath and walked to my door and opened it. I heard Alex scream and all that mattered to me was getting to him—I ran through the hallway, forgetting that I was scared myself.

"Alex!" He stopped crying by the time I got to his door. It was slightly open but not enough for me to look inside. I pushed it open. Only it wasn't Alex that awaited me. A faded silhouette stood a few feet in front of me. I scanned the room for the person it belonged to but there was no one. It wasn't a silhouette—it started to expand and where it once stood in the form of a human was now disfiguring into something unrecognizable. Only I did recognize it from a recent encounter and it chilled me to the bone.

The black fog fell to the ground and started moving after me. I took a few steps backwards before I turned around and ran. There was no light in the house— nothing about the house felt normal. Something kept bothering me about what was happening.

"Killian!" I yelled as I ran down the stairs. I looked back and the fog was already dropping down through the bannisters.

I figured it was best to get outside… I didn't want to be trapped in a corner of the house with that thing but when I tried to open the front door, it wouldn't open. Of course, it wouldn't. I slammed my hand against the door in frustration.

When I started to run in a different direction, something caught my eye outside the window. I stopped and pulled the blinds back. There was nothing. Everything was gone.

Someone was raking a knife against a metal counter. It was coming from the kitchen—the screeching hurt my ears. Wait, maybe it wasn't a knife… but claws? Fear.

This wasn't real. It couldn't be. Killian would never let Fear take me.

Those words were what kept me from falling apart. I wasted too much time and the fog was closing in. I couldn't run in any direction. The living room and kitchen were both blocked.

Hands expanded out from the fog—coming closer. "Melanie," those voices slithered my name.

I backed into the door. This wasn't real. This wasn't real. Fear was messing with my head somehow. The ghosts! I tried to think. I passed out and... this was a dream? Yes, it had to be. I was in water before I landed in my room, that alone didn't make sense!

One of the hands latched onto my arm and I couldn't even jerk away—instead, it felt like I was being sucked in. I was breathing hard, trying not to scream.

This realm is real. You die in this place; you die for real.

With the voice, my power sparked from my hand and vaporized the fog. I gulped in a lungful of air. I didn't get all of the fog, but the blast from my hand was enough to make a path through it. I ran for the living room because I feared I knew what awaited me in the kitchen. Only I chose wrong.

Fear's red eyes met mine and that was all I saw before he was slinging me across the room. I didn't know how hard I smacked into the wall but it was enough to make me feel like I was paralyzed. I rolled over on my back and gritted my teeth. I was scared to move—this pain was real. Which meant the voice wasn't kidding around—my dreams made the perfect place to kill me—it completely isolated me from the one person that could stop him from hurting me.

"Are you beginning to understand what's going on?" Fear walked toward me. "It's just you and me here," he chuckled before he went on, "and anything I decide to use against you. Tell me... what are you most afraid of? You were always the scaredy-cat." He brought his finger to his bottom lip and smiled. "But that's right, I'm to blame for that."

I was slow to get off my back, but just when I did, he used his tail to wrap around my waist and bring me to my feet. I grabbed his tail and tried to loosen it—he made it tighter. "Hmm, what to do?" Red eyes roamed over my body. "What would mess with Grim in the worst way?" Bile rose in my chest at the way he was looking at me. He was using me to get back at Killian.

"He's going to kill you," I said through gritted teeth.

"Not if I can stop it—or at least not before I kill you," he answered. "Death is only the beginning of the pain you'll see once your soul belongs to me."

I was afraid of him. I couldn't even get untangled from his tail—how was I supposed to survive this nightmare? He smiled at me knowingly—he could sense how I felt. He grabbed my hand and forced me to touch one of the horns on his head. "How am I, Melanie, do I look like the perfect nightmare?"

I had to have lost my sanity for a moment because I smiled. "You look like a pathetic demon who crossed the line a long time ago. You're desperate to escape what's coming for you, so you hide from Death." This time I was the one to laugh in his face. "But he's coming for you whether you like it or not."

His hands wrapped around my neck as veins traced his face, showing his anger—he was pissed and I may have just cost me my life.

You know his weakness just as he knows yours. Look for it.

Look for it? I hated how the voice—the *me* inside my head who I believed was the very power I possessed—never gave me enough information. Only enough to get me searching…

 I couldn't breathe… I scratched and pulled at his face… my vision blurred.

I startled myself awake and jumped into a sitting position. I must have passed out again and I wasn't dead. Which was good, but who knew when Fear would grow tired of playing with me. I had to figure out a way to wake up—not like I've been doing, I needed to *actually* wake up.

I looked around and saw all the desks around me. I recognized this room. It was the very room he attacked me in as a child—this was Alex's current school now. Only this was all an illusion, I knew that, but it didn't stop my heart from racing faster. He chose this place on purpose.

The lights were on. I stood up and like déjà vu, the sky outside the windows turned dark. In my mind, the logical thing to do was try to open the door, but as I turned around in that direction, I knew that he was wanting me to reenact our first encounter.

"I won't play your games," I called out into the room. "I'm not afraid."

The lights flickered and when I squeezed my hands into fists, they were already clammy. I took one step back and bumped into the teacher's desk. It squeaked and that alone caused me to panic. I pulled myself together quickly and focused on the back of the room.

Just like I expected, the back row of lights went out. Everything was the same. Only I wasn't a helpless nine-year-old girl who didn't know what was happening to her... I've been through so much more and I was alive, and I sure as heck didn't plan on dying in this place with him.

Another row went out and I looked around. I spotted the windows and started pushing the teacher's desk across the floor until it hit the wall. I went back and grabbed a chair. I took it with me as I climbed on top of the desk. The windows weren't very big and they were high off the ground. I jerked the alphabet curtain off one of the windows—the one that I was going to climb through. I lifted the chair up and used the two back legs to break the glass.

Another row went out and I hurried up. I threw the chair down before placing my hands in the window. I still felt a few pieces of glass against my palms, but I had no time left. I pulled myself up and hesitated the moment my head was out the other side of the window. I couldn't see anything. It was pitch black.

My heart pounded in my ears and throat. I took a deep, brave breath and pulled myself through the window. Glass grazed my stomach and I hissed, trying to ignore the little sharp jabs of pain. I fell into the darkness.

Only to land right back in the classroom. He controlled everything in this dream. I screamed in frustration and got back on my feet. The room was way darker now, and I saw that there was only one row of lights left before it would be complete darkness.

This was the worst kind of fear. The kind you waited for—the kind you couldn't see. I'd rather deal with him face-to-face then be forced to wait like I was now. I didn't know why I looked, but I pulled my shirt down and the mark was gone.

"I found you." My skin crawled. I knew why it wasn't there. He planned to put me through it all over again.

Last of the lights went out.

My breathing was quick and heavy, and my hands were out in front of me as I waited for what I couldn't see. What could I do? The voice told me to look for his weakness, but how—

My feet were knocked out from underneath me. I screamed and my hands were searching for Fear— waiting to feel his presence crawl above me. And he did. I brought my feet out between us and kicked him. He was completely silent, and I knew he fed on my fear. My hands found his horns and I pushed at them—keeping him away from me. I could feel his breaths and something in me cracked.

I was losing. I was terrified. And that pissed me off more than anything.

"Get off me!" I screamed.

His claws tore through my shirt as he began to draw the X onto my chest. I screamed out in pain and frustration, then I saw them.

Despite the dark, I saw two chains running out from something—oddly they were just there floating. Fear was still above me and when I brought my hand out to feel where they were coming from—it was his chest. Now I was confused. What was I seeing?

My chest was on fire as he continued to slowly carve the X onto my skin, but I ignored the pain and tried to focus. One of the chains seemed never-ending and floated all over the room in a ghostly glow—it looked solid and strong. The other one was totally different. It was shortened to the point that it was only a few feet long running out of his chest—it looked brittle and old… no that wasn't the right word for it… dying.

The chain looked to be dying. I knew what I was seeing. I understood perfectly. I was seeing Fear's lifeline as well as Marcus's. I found it: his weakness.

"I see it," I grunted through the burning I felt on my chest.

I reached out and grabbed Marcus's chain—I couldn't see anything in the dark except the chains, but I felt him stiffen above me. "You really are dying, Marcus." I jerked the chain and he made a sound in his throat—like he was sucker-punched in the stomach.

He disappeared above me—the chains faded away as did the darkness. We were back in my room.

Now it was my turn to frighten him. There was a certain calmness I felt. I wasn't dying here, yet… someone might.

"Marcus," I whispered with a smile as I walked out of my room. The house was still dark—silent. Fear's chain floated all over the house, I just needed to follow it.

Then I heard them downstairs. I leaned over the bannister and saw the wolf demons. There were three of them, but they didn't have any chains running out of their chests which meant that they probably weren't real, but that didn't mean they couldn't kill me. One jumped up over the bannister in front of me while the other two took the stairs. I needed to find Fear, and if I was right, maybe I could end Marcus right here and now before he did me.

I climbed onto the bannister next to the wolf demon and before I lost my balance—I jumped and grabbed a part of Fear's chain floating in the air. My legs gave a little with the fall and I fell to my knees in the hallway—ouch! I didn't look up to see what the wolf demons were doing; I didn't want to think about how easily they could kill me if they got ahold of me—which would be easy trapped in a house with no escape.

I tugged at Fear's chain—it was everywhere, so it was hard to pinpoint exactly which direction he was in. Only I think he found me first when I was yanked backward by the shirt. "What is it that you see?" He turned me around to face him only to kick me in the chest.

Oh, God. Did he break something? I didn't want to stand back up and face the pain I felt. I placed my hand over my chest and stood—I bent over and focused on breathing. There was a catch in my ribs—not a good sign.

"Don't act like you don't know." I smiled, but I couldn't hold back the groan as I held my chest.

"I'll admit, I am very intrigued. Just what are you, Melanie?" he asked. "As much as I would love to find out—I think it's better if I kill you right here and now, no more games, but do you blame me? Who knows when you'll decide to do a Grim on me and bring that scythe out."

I grabbed Fear's chain again right as the wolf demons came up behind me. They held my arms down, and I tried to wiggle out of their grasp, but it was a futile effort—compared to my strength and theirs as well as the pain shooting through my chest, I could do nothing.

But I did still have a hold of Fear's chain, and Marcus's floated close between us but not close enough that I could reach it. "I feel bad… honestly. I wanted to play with you more—drag the pain out, but I'm a smart guy and I know when to quit." He rubbed his chest as he spoke, "For a second there, it almost felt like you were pulling me—" He laughed and shook his head. "Nah, even with the powers you possess, you're still human."

I grinned at his casual attempt to be at ease—I knew I spooked him earlier. "Do you want to know what I saw—what I'm seeing now?" I asked. His eyebrows raised as he stepped closer. The wolf demons still held me, but I relaxed in their hold so that it would hopefully loosen their grip. One kept growling into my ear and it took everything in me not to gag from the stench of them. Fear was a dangerous demon, but his own games would be his downfall. He could have killed me in the water— the very moment I woke up in this place, but he didn't.

Stu-pid. But I wasn't complaining.

Lucky for me was more like it. His need for games, torture, and drawn out pain was the reason I knew I was getting out of this alive and for once, I was glad that he was the way he was. His game of cat and mouse—his need to hurt Grim by making me suffer—all of them were mistakes he couldn't help but make.

"Two different chains are coming out of your chest. One's solid and strong—unbreakable... the other, though, it's short and brittle and right there at the end..." I pointed to the tip of Marcus's chain. I knew he saw nothing there from the look on his face. "It's like a wick and it keeps on getting shorter and shorter, I wonder, *Marcus*, why that is?"

He looked confused as well as angry. He clamped his teeth together as he growled at me. "I'm going to enjoy taking your life. Just know that it's only the beginning once I own your soul." His eyes grew redder as he stalked closer.

"I don't think so." I jerked at Fear's chain so hard that he was thrown forward on his knees. The wolf demons were no longer holding me as tightly as they should, and I slipped out of their grasp without any real effort. Fear was holding his chest as I came at him. He looked up at me with a shocked expression. I let go of Fear's chain and grabbed ahold of Marcus's.

I planted my shoes on both of his thighs as I leaned my face down over his. I felt no fear as I looked down at the monster who used to be the thing I was most afraid of. I flashed my teeth. "I'm going to end your life right here and now, Marcus," I yelled and brought his chain between us. "By breaking this chain!"

His eyes were wide and he gasped—I took pleasure in his horror.

When I started pulling at his chain, he threw some sort of light at me and suddenly he grew distant—far away. I lost my grip on the chain.

"Don't think that this is the only thing I planned when I placed those ghosts inside you," his voice echoed in the darkness that closed in around me. "You'll see soon enough."

Then, I was waking up. I raised up into a sitting position on the bed I found myself in. I felt sick and feverish—I knew something had to be let out. Something awful seemed to be lodged in my throat and I couldn't stop myself from opening my mouth. Blackness flew out—talk about gross and terrifying. The dark cloud floated above my head.

Killian sprung from his chair and gave the cloud a hostile look. It expanded right before exploding. The pressure from the explosion was violent—I felt it go straight through me and from the look on Kilian's face, he did too. The castle even seemed to shift and move, and

I realized whatever came out of me was still expanding further through the castle.

As soon as the castle stopped shaking, Killian bent down on the bed. He looked worried—anxious. He had a five o'clock shadow outlining his jaw. He touched my cheek and said nothing for the longest time—I don't think he knew what he wanted to say, but his eyes looked like they held a whirlwind of emotion.

"No," I said out of frustration. I pulled away from him and placed my hands through my hair that felt all sweaty and icky. "I could have killed him!"

"Melanie, what are you talking about? Kill who?" I looked back to my left where he sat next to me and recognized his worry.

"Marcus," I told him. "He forced me out of that place—wherever he had me—right before I got the chance to."

"He's not supposed to die until the 31st."

"Your rules, not mine," I stated quickly.

His eyebrows bunched together. "How could you have killed Marcus? He's still Fear as of right now."

"Not exactly. Now this is gonna be hard to explain, but I saw their life—" I motioned with my hands dramatically and brought them up to my chest. "Two chains hung out of Fear's chest. One is his and you're right, Fear's definitely not dying. *Ever.* Marcus's, on the other hand, is short and it was lit like a fuse. Don't you get it? It's because he's about to die like you said, and all I had to do was break his chain and I just knew he was a goner," I said through pants and all of my dramatic flair because I had *almost* killed Marcus. I took a deep breath and looked at Killian who was dead silent. He ran his hand across his unshaved chin. I squinted my eyes at him. "You don't believe me!" I tossed my hands up in the air because I was all about being dramatic right now—I *almost* died and I *almost* took care of Marcus once and for all—I deserved to be, even though it was nothing but almosts.

"Think back, Killian," I told him, "wasn't there a moment right before I woke that you felt his death right in the moment like he was dying?" I pleaded with him.

He looked at me for the longest time before he took my hand and smiled. "How could I have been focused on that when you were lying here stuck in another realm that Fear put you in? And how can you be angry that you got pulled out of the dream realm when I was right here worried," he cut himself off and straightened his voice. "I believe in what you saw and thankfully it scared Fear enough that he woke you, but you don't know for sure if breaking the chain would have killed him, right?"

I wanted to nod my head, but I couldn't. "I wasn't positive; it was just a feeling. A very strong one."

Lincoln stormed into the room, followed by Ryan. He took one look at me sitting up and smiled. "What the hell just happened?" Lincoln looked to us both. "The entire castle shook."

"The spell Fear used on the ghosts left her body and whatever it was… caused that huge tremor," Killian told him.

"Something didn't feel right about it." Lincoln shook his head.

"I know," Killian agreed. "I think we should sweep the woods and everything just to be on the safe side… it almost felt like a new spell instead of the one he used to keep her in the dream realm."

"I'll check it out." Lincoln left the room, and Ryan stepped on in.

I took a deep breath and noticed my chest no longer hurt. I grabbed it and tilted my head. "My injuries must not have been permanent while I was in that realm."

"No, your injuries were real," Ryan told me and I looked up to him. "He kept healing you every few seconds and he got so crazy, that we had no choice but to leave him alone with you so that maybe he could relax." He nodded toward Killian. "That guy was a nervous wreck."

Killian sighed. "You scared the living dead out of me." I grinned and he added, "And that was supposed to make you smile." I shook my head at him. "But, I wasn't the only one worried about you." He looked to Ryan. These two were being weird… since when did they try to acknowledge one another?

"That's a given," Ryan said.

"Somehow, I made it," I told them both with a shrug of my shoulders.

Killian had that sort of intensity about him that came out of nowhere. One minute he was worried and relieved I was okay and then, he was watching me with a pair of steely eyes—a look of determination and a hint of something much darker lurked beneath the surface. I shifted my weight on the bed—unable to handle the heat of his gaze. Even Ryan must have sensed the change in Killian because he said, "You probably want some time to relax. Come find me later if you want." He walked out of the room and left me to face the imposing man sitting next to me who had suddenly turned all predator.

"You're not leaving my side until this with Fear is taken care of," he said out of nowhere. "No, even then, you won't leave my side."

My heart skyrocketed. "What?" I mumbled.

"I'm saying I want you to stay here with me," he answered, and I hadn't expected him to be so straightforward. I felt the heat in my cheeks rising.

"You said you didn't want me to stay here unless I was going to be sleeping in your bed," I spoke too quickly. My emotions were all over this place. Happy. Excited. Scared. Loved.

"That's where I want you." His dark eyes held me captive. "But that's not all I've thought about while you were lying here." Something about the way he was behaving—his actions and words had my stomach in knots—the kind that was sure to go up in flames. His hand was on my shoulder, tugging down my shirt until the X was in view. "Actually, that's not the truth. I've been thinking about the mark for a while now, but it wasn't until I could do nothing while you were facing Fear on your own, that I stopped hesitating and gave into the idea." I waited for him to go on. "I wonder… what would Heaven think if I were to place my own mark on your skin? I wonder if it will be enough to keep you away from Fear even after you die."

My face must have mirrored my emotion—conflicted. The first thing I thought about every time the mark was mentioned was pain—agonizing, brutal, and wrong on so many levels. Fear gave me his mark when I was only a child and with it came the trauma and years of seeing ghosts and wondering if I was crazy or different than everyone else. It meant ownership in the Underworld of my very soul.

Then there was Killian—my protective, gentle, dark, loving Grim Reaper who wanted to turn something horrible into a way of saving me. I also hadn't overlooked the storm in his eyes or his voice when he brought it up. It stirred something in him more than protectiveness. Something primal—dark and it made me wonder if it stemmed from his incubi traits or me alone. And if I was right about it, then I didn't know how I should feel. The idea was tempting and heating my body right now, that I wouldn't deny, yet the idea of going through what Fear already put me through again…

"I haven't seen you look at me that way since we first met," he told me. "Cautious and afraid," he murmured as he pulled my shirt back up and leaned away. I could see him backpedaling with his actions as he tried to give me some distance. "I would never do something you wouldn't want me to do, but I can't lie to you and say that I'm not willing to do anything to keep you from him—and to keep you with me." Butterflies weren't just in my stomach but my heart.

I scooted over to him and I saw the flicker in his eyes. "So, this is what's been on your mind lately? Every time you were gazing at Fear's mark, you were wanting to add your own to my skin?"

"Yeah," I hoped he wouldn't avoid the question and smiled when he didn't. "I never thought that I'd want to put a mark on someone... until now." I didn't say anything. "The choice will always be yours to make, I won't ever stop looking for a way to protect you from Fear's mark if killing Marcus doesn't work... but you will stay here until this is over."

Anticipation rolled over my skin more than nerves. I looked around the room—it was the one I stayed in during my last stay here. The hidden room behind the piano that sat in the ballroom. "So... will I be sleeping here?" I asked because I wanted to know what he really felt, whether he wanted me here or with him.

"You know exactly where I want you, but that is entirely up to you as well." The intensity of his gaze felt smothering, but it wasn't just his gaze, my body was feverish and suddenly all this built-up desire between us was close to igniting—there was no incubus voodoo, no doubts, no unspoken words left—we were heading for the inevitable.

How could he not know my answer? I've wanted him long before I wanted to accept my feelings for him. Since the night I took his hand behind Deb's Diner—in every way, physically, mentally. My feelings were so strong that sometimes it scared me—the need to just *exist* with him.

I must have been lost in thought and before I could give him my answer, he said, "I'm going to go check the woods out with Lincoln. I won't ask you to come to my room, though you know that's where I want you. You can stay here." He brought his hand to my cheek. "Later, if you decide to come to me, all you have to do is say my name." He had to make everything sound sensual and sexy, which caused an ache to spread between my thighs and I squeezed them together. "Or get Ralph to take you to my room."

Did he know what his words were doing to me? With his incubus traits coursing through him, how could he not? He stood from the bed and leaned over me—all dark and mesmerizing and lifted my chin up. I met his eyes—that smirk, he knew there was no resisting him. "Just know that if you come to my room, we won't only be sleeping."

He left me there without me being able to get one word out. He was giving me time, but I didn't need it. With him, I was always sure.

As I walked past the full-length mirror, I had to do a double-take. I looked horrible. Not horrible, horrible, I supposed just… rough, and a shower would do me good right now. I made a mental note to do that before I made my way to Killian's room—heat spiraled through my stomach again at the thought of being with him. I was in a permanent state of arousal, thanks to him.

I left the room and went to find Ryan. My stomach growled in protest and I placed my hand over it. Okay, I hoped he would be agreeable with eating and talking. Luckily, Ralph was present in the hallway, and he told me Ryan went outside a few minutes ago. It didn't take me long to find him with Sky and that alone made me smile. I arched my brows at her, the dragon who didn't trust him at first was now rolled over on her back across the steps as he rubbed her stomach like she was some sort of dog.

"She came around a lot more than I figured she would with you," I said, interrupting them both.

Sky rolled her head around to look at me before she got up and came to me. Ryan sat on the steps as he grinned at her then me. "How are you feeling?" he asked.

I rubbed my hand across Sky's scales as I sat down next to him. "I'm okay, I just need a good soak."

He looked me over and nodded. "That you do," he agreed.

I snorted. "You weren't supposed to say that." We both laughed and I watched Sky make her way back over to him. "Seriously, I'm kind of jealous, you've already got to spend a lot more time with Sky than I have. I mean, look at her." I squinted my eyes at her. "I feel betrayed, somehow." She tipped her snout up at me and looked away.

"Are you really okay?" he asked again.

"Yes, why?"

He sighed. "Because Melanie you were stuck in that dream—or whatever— for a day with Fear. You didn't see the way we saw you lying there, it was messed up."

"Ryan, I'm perfectly fine. Maybe I'm just used to almost dying all the time." There was that word again. *Almost.* My world revolved around it.

"You shouldn't have to be."

"Maybe once Marcus is gone, Fear will let us both go," I said it like it was an actual possibility when I really couldn't imagine Fear doing that. He was Marcus and I doubted his thoughts were any different—or would be any different once he was separated from him.

"Yeah," he said like he had the same thoughts as me.

The charred skin was spreading up his neck and slowly running onto his face. "It's spread even more," I told him.

"Don't worry about it. I'm okay with whatever happens to me." I could tell that he genuinely meant it. "Just more than anything, I want to see for myself that our family and town is gonna be okay."

"You've given up on you, but I'm still holding out for a miracle."

He looked at me and shook his head with a smile. "I think we're too far down in Hell to get one of those miracles you're hoping for."

I shoved him, and he wrapped his arms around me. I leaned into him and sighed. "I think I'm okay with you being with him now," he said out of nowhere.

"Huh?" I tilted my head to the side.

"He really cares for you, I don't know how deep that goes, but it was strong enough for him to fall to his knees and lose himself when you weren't waking up. Because of that, it's easier to accept why you can't love me like I want you to."

"Thank you for finding me that day in the classroom. Thank you for being my best friend ever since." I felt like I should tell him that.

"I really wish Tess could have heard you say that." And we both laughed.

My stomach growled. "Want to go with me to raid the fridge?" I asked.

Fifteen minutes later, we were propped up on the kitchen counter as I devoured two ham and cheese sandwiches and a bag of Doritos I found in the cabinet. Killian had the kitchen stocked with food. Ryan only took a water.

"Do you not have to eat anymore?" I asked him.

"I didn't when I was a ghost but now I do. I feel alive, only I'm not—I'm just part monster." Me and my stupid mouth.

"I'd rather you be part demon than nothing at all," I blurted out, and his eyes went wide. "Don't look at me like that. I accepted the fact that I can't save you myself,

181

but you're still here right now." I grabbed his hand. "And until there's no sign of you left, I won't stop holding out for that miracle." I made him smile.

"I saw that he found out your love for ice cream cake," Ryan brought up.

"Huh?"

He motioned with his head to the fridge. "One's in the freezer."

My mouth did a giant O as I nodded. I glanced at the door. "Who are you waiting for?"

"What?" I said nervously.

"You've been eyeballing the door every few seconds." So, he noticed, did he?

I sighed. "Have I?" I feigned not knowing.

He looked me in the eyes. "Go. It's written all over your face that you're waiting on him."

His words made my heart speed up because I *was* waiting. I was getting anxious and the longer I sat here thinking about it, the more nervous it made me. Ralph still hadn't come for me but then he told me all I had to do was say his name and he'd be there. Only wouldn't it better if I bathed before I saw him again?

I didn't know. My mind was back and forth with all the things I wanted Killian to do to me and all the insecure little things that came with having my first time with him. Would it hurt? What if it was bad for him or me? What if I did something weird? Then I'd go right back to the pain, I hated pain and I was pretty sure the first time for anyone was a disaster, right?

Why did I start thinking?

I knew what my heart wanted—it screamed for Killian in every way, with each beat, and with every conversation, every touch we shared, it only reached for him more. I knew what my body wanted. The sweet, torturous ache between my legs was a constant reminder of how bad I wanted him.

"Is everything all right? You're shaking," Ryan couldn't help but ask me. I could only nod in reply. My body had a will of its own, and my mind was slowly cracking under the pressure. It was insane, how much I felt with just thought alone.

"Melanie," Ralph's voice drifted from the doorway and the relief I felt when he finally came for me made me weak in the knees.

I slid off the counter and looked to Ryan. "I'm going—"

"You're nervous about something, relax." Embarrassment crept against my cheek and I wondered if Ryan sensed what I was nervous about. I didn't know what to say and thankfully if he knew, he pretended not to. "I'll see you later." He walked out the door and left me with Ralph.

"Do you wish for me to show you to Grim's room?" he asked.

"Yes," I said within a heartbeat.

CHAPTER FIFTEEN
Melanie

Killian's room was on the first floor and in the same hallway as the kitchen. When Ralph stopped in front of the door, it looked no different than most of the doors in the castle, yet it was the place Killian slept when he *did* sleep. A few weeks ago, he invaded my privacy by barging in my bedroom unannounced all the time and now… I was finally invading his. Not invading, he wanted me here.

"Go ahead," Ralph told me as his feline tail swayed behind him. It took me a few seconds before I nodded and he smirked. "You can use his bathroom to bathe," he added, and I felt the scarlet wash over my cheeks. Oh, God. Of course, he knew and it wasn't that I was ashamed. I just preferred privacy.

He left, and I opened the door to Kilian's room and shut myself in. One look around his room and I could tell it was his. It was simple and not at all grand. I've never seen him wear colors that weren't dark—he was plain in that way. He never tried to impress anyone because he didn't have to, he was impressive as is.

The light in the room was coming from a few floor lamps. The colors in his room consisted of multiple shades of gray. The walls were stone as well as the floor—like most of the castle itself. The floor was almost a black color, though. His bed was huge with black and gray covers. A dark blue, circular mat poked out around the bed, it looked soft to touch.

The wall in front of me was nothing but shelves covered with all kinds of trinkets and things that looked valuable. I walked over to look at them. There was some sort of white globe that rested in a hand, a few necklaces in closed displays, a set of knives, a pair of claws (I had no clue), and even more that I couldn't put a name to. The curiosity of it all was killing me. Did he have a certain taste for weird things or did each of these tell a story from his past? I clutched my necklace with a smile. He had this necklace made from the pearl he took from the demon in the lake, so maybe these were all no different.

I spotted the second door in the room and figured it had to be his bathroom. Before he decided to show up, I hurried inside to bathe. I slid my hand across the wall until I found the light switch. The room was bright and clean. The tub sat in the middle of the floor. It was huge, and I was going to enjoy cleaning off. My hair felt icky and my body needed a good scrub down after today.

I let the water run while I took off my clothes and sighed in contentment when my body sunk into the water. I took my time dipping my head in the water and washing my hair. Killian must have been anticipating this because I found a new razor, so I shaved next and with each stroke I slid up my leg, I was reminded of what I was about to do. I was already warm from the water, but now I was scorching.

Once I got out of the bath, I dripped water across the floor as I grabbed a towel. It wasn't until I dried off that I realized I had nothing to wear. The black robe materialized in front of me as soon as the thought came to mind. I looked around the room expecting to see Killian, but I was alone. I smiled and took the robe knowing that he must be on the other side of the door.

And holy crap, my own thoughts were killing me. I was going to exhaust myself before anything even happened between us.

I placed my wet, tangled hair against the robe and didn't care that it needed to be brushed. With no second thoughts, I opened the door. The room was empty and I couldn't help but feel disappointed as I stepped into the room. Once I was halfway in, two muscular arms enveloped me from behind. It was unexpected and my body lit up for him just like that. He dropped his chin over my shoulder and his nose pressed against my hair as he breathed me in. I closed my eyes and tilted my head to the side.

"I should treasure you," he whispered. "But first I must ruin you." He trailed a finger down my cheek. "Ruin me."

"Why is that?"

Then before I knew it, I was facing him, being pulled in by his eyes. They were warped with desire or maybe it was the reflection of my own. "Because there'll be no escaping each other after that." Somehow, I knew his words were the truth. "I told myself I'd wait, but lately, I'm only desperate to get you beneath me."

I was overcome with emotion. My chest was close to bursting and I couldn't keep the words to myself. "I love you." I kissed him and he kissed me.

"I love you," he replied.

With our pleasantries out of the way, his eyes shifted from desire to longing, from want to need. I knew it was finally time for us to collide—our emotions, our bodies—our souls.

I stepped back. He came forth. I took another step back, he took a step forward again… and again. We waited several breathless seconds before he snatched me by the wrist and pulled my arm over my head. His lips smashed into mine. A throaty moan fell from my lips onto his—tongues collided and my desire became a throb to the point that it hurt.

My free hand sought out his skin and I raked my nails across his shirt, I was so desperate to feel him. Only he took hold of it and placed it with my other hand above my head. He gripped them both with one hand as he continued to kiss me. His other hand was already at the opening of my robe and soon it was covering one of my breasts. That small amount of contact was enough to make me fall into him.

"Killian," I cried out.

He released me and I was so bent out of shape, I stumbled backward. He didn't smirk, he relished in what he did to me. I started walking backward quickly in the direction of the bed. I wanted him there and he knew it. I stopped once I felt the presence of the bed against the back of my legs. This time he did smirk and with the wave of his hand, my robe fell off my body as black feathers. They floated to the floor until they made a puddle around my feet.

I was butt-naked and instinctively my hands flew up to cover myself and his jaw tightened. "Don't," he warned me. "No shying away from me, not when I've already seen everything," he told me as he came for me. "By the time we're finished, your cheeks will be stained crimson and you'll no longer have a reason to hide yourself from me."

It was a natural habit to cover oneself when naked in front of a guy like Killian. I was a tad nervous was all, but more excited than anything. I dropped my hands and waited for him. "Fuck," he muttered, sending ripples of pleasure where I was already throbbing. "You're beautiful. No wonder I'm a lost cause when it comes to you."

"Take off your clothes," I told him just as he stopped inches in front of me. He grabbed his shirt from the back and pulled it up over his head. I practically drooled as I admired his abs. He was a big guy and right now, I loved feeling small next to him.

"Want me to keep going?" He met my eyes with a smoldering look and I nodded silently, mouth still hung open. He tore at his zipper and my heart soared, I was about to see what I wouldn't dare look at when we were in the pond together. He kept his eyes on my face as he tugged his jeans down—nothing underneath and his erection stood for attention like it was begging for me to look, touch. I felt myself get hot and a little bit of fear crept up my spine at the size of him. Nothing about him was average, and I suddenly wondered if maybe we weren't compatible down below. What did I expect with Killian? He was big in general and especially down there. I swallowed hard.

"Come on." He jarred me out of my thoughts. "Up ya go," he said right before his hands grabbed each of my butt cheeks and hauled me against him. His hard-on lay on my stomach as he got up on the bed and tossed me down. My wet hair stuck to my back as I watched him above me.

God, he was handsome, manly, rugged perfection in every way.

In this position, with him hovering over me, I saw how massive and imposing he truly was. He dropped down over me. His hands found my hair. "Blonde strands," he muttered as he slipped his fingers over my face. "Blue eyes." He found my lips. "Lips that are normally pale pink are now red and swollen from my lips," he whispered.

"What are you saying?" I asked softly.

"I'm branding every part of you—this moment—into my memory so that when I take you again, over and over each time, I'm going to feed them back into your memory."

My stomach fluttered. "You can do that?"

He nodded and trailed down further until his hands were covering my breasts. He pinched each nipple and I arched my back. "Perfect tits," he mumbled to himself and when I glanced down, his mouth was already taking in one of my nipples. I cried out, his mouth delivered pleasure and sweet agony. "You're very sensitive." He rolled my nipples between his fingers as he went further down. My stomach was tight with anticipation and the throbbing of my sex wasn't going away, it was only getting worse. "Sexy stomach." He planted kisses between my breasts all the way down until he reached the most important part. He raised up once he got there and I felt like I was going to combust if he didn't give me some sort of relief. "And the part you've been waiting for," his voice was throaty, and I was positive he was affecting himself just as bad as he was me.

He lifted one of my legs straight up in the air as he slid his hand up and down once before he positioned himself between my legs. I held my breath and he met my eyes with a heated look—I couldn't look away as his face lowered toward me down there. "I'm pretty sure you'd cause a flood if this keeps up down here," he groaned and his breath only increased everything I was feeling.

I groaned in frustration. "Stop detailing my body and do something with it already," my words came out as a throaty command.

His tongue swiped over me and the new sensation was too much at first. I jumped, but he pinned my hips down and his tongue went over me again. "Oh, my God." His hand made its way down and he worked magic with his tongue, the pleasure was building like a tsunami inside me. My stomach muscles were tight, waiting for what I desperately needed. His tongue invaded me for several torturous seconds before being replaced with one of his fingers. He built me up so that I could fall apart. He didn't let up, even when my whole body quivered.

When he finally released me from the orgasm, my legs were already made of Jell-O. He raised up until he towered over me. I felt drunk off the orgasm, my body was lax. I ran my hands over his chest and loved the feel of him at my fingertips.

He held himself up by one hand as his other moved between us. When I looked down and saw him palming himself, it was the most erotic thing I'd witnessed. The pleasure was already wanting to build again and I squeezed my thighs against him, trying to relieve the oncoming pressure.

"There's no way I'm not going to hurt you," he told me, voice raw. "The pain won't last forever, but I'll make sure our pleasure will."

Nervousness and excitement clashed inside me. I nodded and slid my hands up his neck onto his face. His gaze was fixated on me as he lowered himself on me— just enough so that I wouldn't feel uncomfortable with his weight. I felt his hand between us, and I knew what he was doing. The anticipation was killing me, and I gave him a desperate look so he kissed me.

I went still as the length of him pressed at my opening, I could already feel the reluctance of my own body to let him in. "Killian?" I called his name nervously, giving away my worry.

He lowered his head onto the bed next to mine and took a deep breath. "I'm going to hurt you," he said again, almost painfully like it was the worst thing in the world. "You feel so fragile... soft, and perfect against me." I could hear it in his voice, he was afraid of something, possibly the idea of ruining what we have by doing this so soon.

"I want this," I whispered to him. "Put me out of my misery already and give me what I want. Stop blurring the lines of right and wrong in your head—we're right. We'll always be right."

"Yes, we are," he agreed.

He lifted his head and kissed me hard. I moaned into his mouth as he took hold of both of my wrists and pinned them above my head with one of his hands, while his other was already guiding his length toward my opening, and using a lot more force this time. Pain overtook the pleasure and my whole body jerked as I tried to pull away. I wasn't trying to fight him; I just couldn't help it—the pain was awful. But he held me firm and now I knew why he held my hands down to begin with. He stopped pushing at my entrance, but he wasn't letting me go. My stomach still caved with pleasure for him and all the things he could do to me despite it all.

"It really hurts," I admitted.

"This barrier between us isn't going anywhere until I take it." He was all in now—dark words and throaty voice, and all *mine*, like I was soon to be all his. "You're ready for me, Love. You're dampening the bed, you're so ready."

His mouth crashed onto mine and with a single, painful thrust, he took my virginity. He swallowed my cry and held me down as my body tried to fight it—the brutal pop of my virtue being lost seemed deafening to my ears. He didn't move once he was completely buried inside me. Then he released my arms, touched my face, kissed me softly, ran his hands over my breasts. My hands found his hair and he feathered kisses across my face. He was loving me, steadying me as he built me back up with pleasure.

Killian's whole body shook as he traced his hands over me and my pain slowly turned into a dull ache. I didn't have to voice that I was ready—he knew—and he slowly began to pull out. The pain was there, but so was the pleasure. He eased back in and repeated the process until my fingernails were raking over his back and the heat overcame everything else.

"Killian," I whimpered his name.

"Wrap your legs around me."

I did and he sunk in even deeper. It felt amazing. Perfect. I already felt myself getting thrown into another orgasm. I tossed my head back and he bit my chin lightly, forcing it out completely. Killian was more frantic now as the aftershocks of my orgasm pulsed around him.

When it subsided, I could feel that I was sore. "One more, come on," he was ordering me to get off again. "With me."

I wanted to, but I didn't think I could, I was afraid of falling apart in his arms. "I can't," I groaned, fighting what I desperately wanted.

But he was relentless and wasn't going to stop until he gave me another. Each thrust became more ruthless and demanding. He cupped my breasts and grabbed my butt off the bed and rammed into me. I couldn't stop the noises that fell from my mouth and the buildup that refused to take me completely over the edge. His lips found mine, kissing me just as roughly as he made love to me.

"Let it go, Melanie." His gaze held mine. "And take me with you."

Like my body had any choice but to obey him. We teetered off the edge together, and I shattered beneath him. He swelled, succumbing to the pleasure, heightening and extending mine.

I was gazing at him and he was already lifting his head off my shoulder to look at me. I couldn't explain what I felt. I just saw him like I knew he saw me.

A slow grin spread across my face. I felt exhausted but satisfied. He kissed me on the forehead before slowly pulling himself out. I winced from the soreness that I felt now that the heat was gone. My blood stained him and the bed. Instead of feeling ashamed or shy about it, it gave me a thrill.

But then I realized something disastrous. "Killian, you didn't use a condom." My pulse thudded in my ears I was thinking about it so hard.

"You won't get pregnant." He smiled. "I can control that, too." Relief hit me and I fell back against the pillows. "We have no need for one. No diseases here. No chances of getting pregnant. And no other lovers. Just

195

you and me." I gave him a smile and tried to get underneath the covers. "I don't think so, Love. We're not finished."

I dropped my mouth. "What?" I was feeling every bit of the ache and tenderness from what we just did.

"You heard me." He walked over and scooped me up in his arms. I let out a surprised squeal.

"I'm sore," I protested. "Ladies can't just do it again right after giving away their virtue."

He grinned wickedly. "Says who?" His mouth opened in an O. "Ah, those erotic stories you read." Darn it, I still managed to blush after what we just did. "Is one time really enough for you?" He went on, "Not for me. Besides I got a cure for that too." Tingles heightened the ache I was feeling, and I clamped my legs together as he held me to his chest. I looked at him. I hoped he wasn't going to say something corny like his penis was the cure for my pain when it was really the reason for the ache.

Both of us completely nude, he faded us outside the door to the key room. That meant we were right in the hallway—naked! "Why are we in the hallway?" I yelled in a whispery voice, which only made him smile. I scanned the hallway both ways praying nobody was around.

"You've got to give me a minute. It's not easy to use the key with you in my arms," he said completely at ease, and I huffed. A door opened and Lincoln walked out. I hid my face in his shoulder and he laughed. Lincoln took one look at us and shook his head, proceeding in the other direction.

"Just open it already before I die of embarrassment." I covered my eyes with my hands and groaned.

A delightful, deep laugh spilled from his lips as he unlocked the door and opened it. Steam rolled out of the room as we stepped in. A gorgeous watering hole awaited us. Clouds of steam rolled off the top of the water. That was the only thing in the room despite the rocks around it. Killian might have noticed my love for ice cream cake and food, but I was beginning to see his love for water. "It's healing water," he told me.

I took a deep breath. "It feels like a sauna in here. How are we supposed to breathe?" I asked.

He didn't answer as he carried me to the water and lowered us in. As soon as my butt and stomach hit the water, it soothed me, taking care of what was aching. I sighed happily. Mm, it was some sort of healing water like he said. "Feel better?" he murmured as he started to shift me around to face him. I gave him a lazy smile and nodded. He placed my legs around him so that I straddled him. The hazy effect from the water lifted when I felt the length of him pressing against me. He threaded his fingers into my hair and pushed me into kissing him. My hands were everywhere, his too. Slow, yet demanding.

He gripped each butt cheek, hauling me up as he moved across the water with me again—that wasn't very deep. He ended our make-out session and forced my legs to drop into the water. I unwrapped myself from him with a protest, and he twisted me around. The length of him grazed my butt and a ripple of pleasure shot through me. "What are you doing?" I asked as he forced me to my knees, lowering my stomach over the giant rock in front of me. My nipples rubbed across the rocky surface as he positioned me the way he wanted me sending jolts of pleasure through my stomach.

I twisted my head back to look at him. The way the rock was made, my butt was lifted perfectly. By perfectly, I meant, perfectly exposed. Behind me, he stood on his knees as his length bobbed. I didn't care that my thoughts were all cave-girl. I loved how dangerous he looked behind me, all big and dangerous, with a lusty look in his eyes.

Then he was placing his giant hands on my butt cheeks and spreading me apart. I dropped my face back onto the rock, I couldn't handle what I felt with seeing him so blatantly exposing me. "Killian." I couldn't suppress the moan that came with saying his name.

"I haven't even done anything to you yet and you're already coming undone." His words only made me want him more. "Just like I knew you'd be. The moment I saw all those lusty romance novels on your shelves, I was already picturing you something like this," he admitted, and I writhed against the rock.

"You okay?" he asked, and he knew I was way above okay—I was delirious. I lifted my head up and met his heated gaze again. My face must have shown my need because he was at my opening, sliding in the very next second. We both moaned. There was no pain this time, only exquisite pleasure.

He was slamming into me. My nipples and stomach all raked across the rock with a pleasant sting.

His hands were on my butt, gripping, rough handling me as I cried out. I felt myself on the verge of an orgasm but every time it got right there, Killian would change his thrusts into a torturous slow one that kept me on the edge without sending me over. He was doing it on purpose, keeping it from me and not letting me move. I could only take what he gave me.

"I'm close, stop torturing me," I whimpered.

"You're at my mercy right now, try doing something about it," he challenged me in between his easy, slow strokes. His body was glistening from the steam and sweat in the room. He stole my freaking breath he was so handsome.

But right now, he was a jerk—one that withheld me from my orgasm. Fueled by his words, I was desperate to move beneath him. My legs were of no use in this position and he had complete control over my hips, but not for long. I applied pressure to my palms and waited until he was pulling out and coming back in before I pressed everything I could into him.

Oh, and it had been worth it. He moaned and I followed after him. "Bloody hell," he murmured. When I met his eyes, there was no challenge, only love. "That felt good." I took that as an invitation to keep moving into him every time he thrust. Soon his movements were more erratic and coming faster, harder. And I was back to getting what I wanted.

He pulled out completely and flipped me on my back. My stomach and breasts were blotched in red spots from the rocks sliding against my pale skin. He spread my legs and slipped right back in. My eyes rolled back it felt so good. "These look sensitive now after rubbing against the rocks." He pinched a nipple and I arched my back for him. Oh, God, I could feel everything through my nipples now. He pumped into me as he continued to torture my sensitive flesh. He took one into his mouth, and I tugged at his hair.

I was so close—he lifted my legs back and went in deeper. His eyes locked on the mark and I sensed what he must be thinking. "Do it," I whispered.

He lifted his gaze. "Melanie…"

"Please, I want to be with you. Always." I didn't care what method we had to use to stay together. The thought of ever being apart was more than I could stomach.

He planted a bruising kiss on my lips before his hand covered the mark. Light shot beneath his palm and my skin felt blistering hot. I hissed and Killian stopped. When he moved his hand, Fear's mark was still there. A little bit of my hope was crushed, but Killian yanked me up by the arms as he positioned himself to where I would be on his lap. He thickened inside me and some of that fire returned.

Killian looked determined. One look in his eyes and I knew he was studying my eyes to see if I wanted him to stop—I didn't, even if it might not work, I wanted to try.

He stretched his hand out to the side and that part of him turned skeletal—his scythe materialized in his hand. His essence circled and rolled around his boned fingers as he moved the tip of the blade to my skin. I watched as he placed a new mark over the one I had. He cut my skin, and blood slid down my breast. Unlike Fear's mark that was full of pain and discomfort, Killian's gave me a whole new feeling—warm and tingly. I felt staticky and hot like I was a coming alive like a livewire. I brought my mouth to his neck kissing and sucking on his skin. He groaned in pleasure.

Then the mark was on fire. I looked down to see two different marks. Fear's red X and Killian's blue slash across it. Only Fear's mark was trying to burn through it. I bit Killian's shoulder while I rode the pain. But it dulled and when we looked at it again, the blue shined brighter. I didn't know how it would work now that I had two different marks but it gave me hope. I smiled at Killian. His scythe left and he said, "Now, where were we?"

He picked me up by the hips, sliding out of me almost completely before bringing my hips back down. If not for his hand against my back, I would have fallen completely as I let the passion consume me. He controlled me by the hips, slamming in and out.

Oh, my God.

I gripped his shoulders, my hands were slipping from the sweat. My breasts bounced with every jerk. His eyes were all over me. The room was suffocating and overbearingly hot—it felt like I would pass out if not for the passion driving my willpower. He squeezed my butt and stopped altogether.

He let me take control. I wrapped my arms around him and rocked into him. Back and forth, circular rotations, up and down until I found the right rhythm. He held me by the waist and it was getting close, but my legs were protesting and I was getting desperate now that I was on the verge of one. I panted and he finally put me out of my misery. He thrust once, twice... third was the one.

I moaned into his neck, toes curled. My feet and legs gave out completely and it slipped him into me even deeper. Killian groaned and the pleasure consumed me. Owned me.

I went slack in his arms. I felt completely exhausted and something felt light about me. When I opened my eyes, I saw why. I was glowing like I did when I used my power. Killian looked mesmerized as he slid his hands over my glowing skin. I started to pull away from him—not pull, I was floating and I couldn't prevent it. It reminded me of how the power first awakened inside me. I had been dreaming of Killian. He held me close to keep me from going anywhere and smiled.

He switched us again, pinning me beneath him. "What's happening now?" I brought my arms around his neck, studying it.

"We're bringing it to the surface," he said in admiration as he began to make love to me. He gave me everything and more. My power seemed to influence his, shifting different parts of his body over into Grim's as we stayed tangled together on the rocks until we came apart in each other's arms.

It was beautiful. Intense. The most surreal moment of my life.

In his room, I collapsed on the bed. I felt wobbly, weak, and satisfied and just when I thought I'd fall asleep his hand would slide across my hip. I shivered and he woke me back up with the help of his power. He'd slide up against me from the back and he would kiss my neck before taking my body once again. He would be soft and gentle this time but just as passionate.

It continued for so long, I didn't know what existed beyond it. I stayed in a permanent state of fever. We fit so well... so right. Now I honestly thought we were two halves of something whole.

Maybe even then, the reason we were so desperate for one another was because we could already sense what would become of us.

———————

"Melanie," he whispered, voice tender and full of affection as he hugged me from behind. I had no idea how long we've been trapped in his room together, but no matter how much I slept, I was positive I couldn't keep up with him.

"Hmm," I mumbled as he lazily guided his fingers across my arm.

"Melanie," he said again. I couldn't help but smile with my eyes still closed.

"Hmm?"

"Thank you."

"For what?" I somehow managed to ask through my sleep deprived mind.

"For existing and for being here with me. For letting me love you."

I searched for his arm until I found it and wrapped it around me. I fell asleep with the biggest smile on my face.

CHAPTER SIXTEEN
Melanie

I was awake the second Killian jerked next to me. I raised up as he moved his arm off me and climbed out of the bed. His jaw was set, and his whole body radiated trouble. I scooted off the bed, still nude. He was already putting on his jeans.

"What's wrong?" I asked him.

"His death... it's already here." I assumed he was talking about Marcus.

I bunched up my eyebrows. "What? How did that happen?" Not that I was complaining, but Killian didn't act happy about it. "Isn't that a good thing that we don't have to wait until Halloween?" I asked him.

He sighed. "If my hunch is right, Melanie, it's already Halloween."

That was crazy! "Killian, Halloween is still two weeks away in my world."

He nodded as he put on a shirt. "I don't think killing you was his only objective when he placed the ghosts in you. Whatever left your body must have been a time spell."

"Time spell?" I muttered.

"Meaning, his goal was to slow time here. Slow enough that time in the human world slipped right by while we were here…" *Screwing each other's brains out!*

Bile rose in my chest. "What are we gonna do?"

His expression relaxed when it saw my distress. "Don't worry, we're prepared," he assured me. "The other Reapers are always prepared for anything at any given notice, and we made sure to get our hands on every portal chip we could find."

"Then why are you so tense?"

"I don't like being caught off guard." His face darkened again. "When I felt his death crawling all over me, it set me in motion. I don't understand what good this would have done him; I'll sense his death, no matter what. Maybe he wanted to throw me off… unless." He didn't move for several seconds. "Bloody hell," he muttered.

There was a knock on the door. "Grim…" Lincoln sounded worried. I looked down at myself and quickly grabbed one of the sheets.

Killian walked to the door and opened it enough so that Lincoln couldn't see in the room. "Have you tried leaving to the Underworld?" Killian asked.

"That's what I came to tell you, none of the portal chips are working. I didn't think much of it but normally we'll have a Reaper checking in—"

"No one's checked it?" Lincoln nodded and Killian cursed. "I can't leave, either. I couldn't fade."

"Then the tremors last night were a spell?" I could hear the alarm in Lincoln's voice.

"Wait for us in the main room." Killian shut the door and turned to me.

Their conversation set me into panic mode. "Killian… we have to get there before Fear opens that portal." I couldn't even imagine what would happen if we couldn't get there to stop him.

He went to his closet and grabbed a black t-shirt. He pulled the sheet from my body and lifted me to my feet. I couldn't help but notice my body was sore in all the right places as he did so, even though it was hardly the time. "Here, put this on. You can find you something to change into in your room—remind me to make a place for your clothes when we get back." I let him put the shirt on me. It fit me like a nightgown. My heart did a little flip when I thought about what he just said.

"What?" I whispered, taken aback.

He smiled. "Round two when we get back?"

I blushed. "I'm pretty sure that was several rounds last night." He arched an eyebrow at me and I gasped. "That was one round for you?"

He laughed and started walking to the door. "Come on, Love. Let's end this once and for all."

Oh, did I love the sound of that.

I changed into a pair of tight black pants and shirt with some lace-up boots. When I stepped back into the ballroom, Killian, Ryan, and Lincoln were immersed in a conversation. "There's no way to get in touch with any of the Reapers until we can port out of here," I caught what Lincoln said as I moved next to Killian.

"Then I guess I'll have no choice but to destroy the spell," Killian told him. His eyes drifted to me and brightened before turning back to business.

"How do you plan to deactivate a spell—you may have a few tricks you can do with your powers, but a spell is a spell," Lincoln said as we followed Killian out the castle doors. Ryan sent an uneasy glance my way—the charred blackness covered half his face now. It spread a lot through the night. Panic gripped me, but I swallowed it back down.

Killian turned around with an arrogant smile. "The way I take care of everything else," he replied cockily and my stomach fluttered. His eyes caught mine again as if he knew.

"How's that?" Lincoln asked, crossing his arms across his chest.

Killian shimmered—fading in and out as he turned into Grim. His scythe materialized in his hand, he placed both hands on the rod and brought it above his head. No one had time to question what he was doing; his blade was in motion, breaking through the pavement. He lifted the scythe back up almost like he expected something to happen.

Lincoln sighed. "Brute strength isn't going to work this time."

"Yes, it will. It always works." Grim was already lifting the scythe back over his head. Only this time, his blue essence traveled away from his bones and wrapped around his scythe. He swung down—the ground trembled beneath our feet and a violent wind came from the ground where he hit. Ryan and I hunkered down until it was over.

"Show off," Lincoln grumbled.

"Did it work?" Ryan asked.

He got his answer when several Reapers started appearing around us. "Grim!" I could hear the alarm in his voice. "We haven't been able to get in this place, we didn't know what happened," one of them said.

Another added, "We thought something happened to you…"

Penny appeared with a scowl. "What—" She stopped and closed her eyes. "We were all guessing it was Fear, but that's not the problem." Dread pooled in my stomach at her words. "Fear's already in that town these two are wanting to protect so bad." I assumed she meant Ryan and me.

"He already opened the portal?" Ryan asked, fists clenched together as if he were keeping himself from going berserk that way.

"Not yet," Penny told him.

"Make sure the Reapers are prepared," Killian told one of the males. He nodded and left.

"What about my mom and brother?" I asked Penny.

"They're fine, but you've been missing for two weeks…" Penny trailed off and looked to Ryan. "As for your sister, she's no different."

I hated to think what they've been through the past two weeks. Ryan took my hand and held it. "It's going to be okay," he told me. Only it wasn't. He might not last another night before the demon overtook him completely.

Lincoln handed a bag to Killian—who must have switched back from Grim while I was talking to Ryan. Killian opened the bag and flipped it over. Hundreds of portal chips fell out. He moved his hand above them and they all started lifting from the ground, flying in the air— they connected and formed a circle, forming a massive portal in front of us. An eerie, dark mass twirled around inside it.

"What's the portal for?" I asked. "We don't need one." Because he could fade us anywhere we wanted.

Killian looked at me and smiled. "Who said we were using it?" Devilish smile, cocky attitude—what was he planning? I knew the moment Rixen and Sky dropped down in front of us. My mouth hung open.

"They are coming, too?"

"Not just those two; *all* of them."

"Dragons in the human world?" I shook my head. "In Denver?" I asked.

"Man, this is going to be interesting," Ryan muttered next to me. Not interesting, more like chaos.

"We need all the help we can get," Killian said to me. I liked the idea of Sky being by my side but people seeing her? Some idiot with a gun would try to shoot them! "Don't come through the portal until you get my signal," Killian told Lincoln, and he nodded.

"They aren't coming right now?" I asked as my gaze fell on Sky. She tilted her head at me.

"No, they're our leverage. I'm hoping to close the portal before bringing them in." Something black formed in his hand and once it was completely visible I saw that it was a cloak. He placed it over me. "When I'm Grim, I want you to draw power from me instead of yourself when you use your power." I smiled. He said 'when' instead of 'if' almost like he accepted the fact that he couldn't keep me from using it.

"Is that even possible, and how do I even do that?" I asked.

"That's what the cloak's for, steal from my power that way," he answered. "Truthfully, I don't know if it'll work, but I'm counting on the fact that we're linked by our fates that you can take from me in a way that no one should be able to." He didn't give me a chance to respond. He tossed a portal chip to Ryan and he caught it. "If you plan on coming, that's your only way," Killian told him.

211

Ryan looked at it. "How the hell do I use it?"

"Just press the damn button and think of where you want to go," was Killian's answer. Ryan muttered something under his breath that I couldn't hear.

Killian's eyes were on me again. "Are you ready?"

"To get rid of Marcus and hopefully sever our link to Fear once and for all? I arched an eyebrow at him. "What do you think?"

"It won't be easy to stay next to you once we start dealing with all the demons." He tucked my hair behind my ear.

"Let's hope this power of mine decides to help me out," I said to ease his mind.

He sighed. "Your safety will always come first no matter how many demons I'm dealing with." He grabbed me by the waist and pulled me into him.

The darkness came.

He took us to my bedroom. Ryan wasn't with us; I had no idea where he took himself. My room was a mess like someone had torn it apart looking for something. We hurried out of my room and I could hear Mom's panicky voice talking to someone. "She's been missing for two weeks!" She was on the phone. "You guys haven't even been looking enough!"

"Mom!" I ran down the stairs. All I wanted to do was ease the worry I knew she must have been feeling this whole time.

"Melanie?" Her voice was barely even a whisper… I wondered if maybe she was second guessing if she heard me. I heard her set the phone on something and a second later she was standing in the hall. She saw me and broke completely. She was ugly crying as she ran to me. "Oh, Melanie, my baby," she sobbed as she spoke. "Where have you been? Do you know how scared I've been? How much everyone's been searching for you?"

I let her hug me and I hated that I couldn't give her more comfort right now. I pulled away from her. "I didn't mean for this to happen, I'm sorry. I don't have time to explain. The town's in danger!"

Her tears stopped and she just looked at me… maybe I shouldn't have said anything right now… maybe we should have dealt with Mom after we saved the town. "What are you talking about?"

"Sis?" I looked to the top of the stairs and saw Alex—so much emotion filled that one word and the look on his face. He came running down the stairs, pushing Killian aside and threw his arms around me.

"Hey." I had no clue what to say to him or Mom. "I'm sorry."

"We'll explain everything as soon as we get back," Killian informed my mom. He looked to me with urgency. "We have to go."

I nodded. "Just what is going on?" Mom no longer looked happy—she was furious as she glared at Killian. "You're not going anywhere young lady." She turned on me.

"You guys go, I'll stay with her family," Miles told us as he appeared next to Mom.

Killian nodded a silent 'thank you' and then he was taking my hand, and we were running past Mom as she screamed bloody murder. "Melanie Rose!"

Killian opened the front door and I turned around to look at her. "Sorry, Mom!" I said hurriedly as we ran out the door.

She was not far behind us, but by the time she would get to the door, we'd already be gone.

We stood in front of the town library. The portal was even bigger than the one opened at his place. It was right above the library—across the street was Deb's Diner where so many were eating right now. And Fear had to choose Halloween of all days, the town was crawling with people. The line at Wendy's was backed up.

The worst part of it all, everyone could see the portal. People were already gathered around the library taking pictures, pointing, gasping, and whispering with bewilderment—some were smart enough to look afraid while others took it as a joke.

Everyone was in costumes—families stopped with their kids and studied the portal. People were even stopping and getting out of their vehicles. My nerves were tingling against my skin, crawling with unease. The children's laughter only made me worse.

I took a deep breath. We must end this.

Killian was holding my hand. "I'm going to protect these people," he told me, whether to ease my troubled mind or his, I didn't know.

I noticed something against the Library window— a picture. "Is that…"

"Yeah, it's a missing person's photo of you," he told me. I would make it up to Mom, Alex, and—

"Melanie?" I heard Tess scream my name. I turned around to see her running across the two-lane road— through the traffic. How could she tell it was me from that distance? Only I didn't get to think much about it, I took one look at her face and released Killian's hand so I could brace myself for the hug she attacked me with.

Her shoulders shook violently. She was… crying. "Melanie… I thought we agreed that we'd always have each other… you asshole, how could you leave like that?" she said through violent sobs. She squeezed me tighter. Her words made me understand how devastated everyone would be if something were to happen to me… or if I'd leave. For good. I bit my bottom lip to keep from crying with her.

"I didn't leave." I didn't know what to say to her.

She pulled away from me. "Do you have any idea how much we've been searching for you? We gave them Killian's description," her eyes went to Killian next to me, "and they couldn't find anything on him… it was like he didn't exist. We were thinking the worst."

"I'm sorry. I'll explain everything later, but right now I need you to go home. It's not safe here."

She looked at the portal. "Does it have something to do with that?" she asked. When I didn't say anything she added, "Just what is going on? You're scaring me, Melanie."

A deep, menacing laugh—that was engraved into my memory from my childhood—came from the top of the library. Everyone went silent. People were turning their heads in the direction of the library, if not looking already. The look on Tess's face as she saw Fear on the rooftop was what I imagined mine looked like all the times I had encountered him before. He was in his ugly form—his truest—with his horns, jet-black hair slicked back, glowing red eyes, pale skin, and giant tail that matched the color of his hair.

People were screaming and a few generics laughs were in the mix as well. "Nice costume," someone yelled, having no idea that they were baiting an immortal entity—the monster that preyed on my childhood.

"It looks so real," a girl said as she giggled with her friends.

This was bad. There was a giant hole above the library with a horned demon about to unleash Hell upon the town and everyone was taking it as a joke. "Get the hell off the roof, man," the same guy as before said to Fear. Several laughed.

Fear ported and Killian faded the same time he did. Fear reappeared in front of the guy that had been laughing—claws going for his chest—who had no idea how close he had been from dying just now, but Killian faded in between Fear and the guy. The guy staggered back. "Killian." Fear sneered. "Or should I say, Grim? How do you plan to keep all these humans safe when you can barely keep one girl alive?" I saw Killian's jaw tighten even from this distance.

"Is this some kind of act?" someone asked in the crowd. I looked around at everyone, I didn't even know this many people lived in Denver until now.

"How did he do that?" Tess whispered to me. "What's going on?" There was a helplessness in her voice that I hated to hear. Where was Ryan? I figured he would have gone searching for Tess, but she was right here.

"Are you so desperate that you want to resort to this?" Killian asked Fear. Fear's eyes looked a darker shade of red as he glared at Killian. "Even demons have rules about showing themselves to humans—which is why the mark even exists so that demons can't wreak havoc on the human world. It's over, Marcus, your death is here."

Fear laughed. "Which is why I searched for the Vessel—why I was meant to be Grim!" he screamed. "Satan is a terrible ruler of the Underworld, if I were to takeover, I would've let demons do as they wished. Humans have always been beneath us, we shouldn't have to hide in the ground for their sake."

Killian shook his head. "I can't believe I chose to ignore the kind of monster you were before, Marcus, but I won't anymore." Fear's tail shot out toward Killian and he caught it with his hand. They glared at each other. "Besides, do you honestly think Heaven would sit back and do nothing if that were to ever happen?"

Fear's eyes lit with madness. "I don't see them doing anything right now." He ported again and Killian faded right after him. People were freaking out and looking around for them, as was I.

Swords clashed—everyone looked to the library. Killian was Grim now as their swords met on the slanted roof. Everyone was screaming, some were smart enough to run away. But not enough.

"I'm going to enjoy taking your life, Marcus, and when you're gone, Fear will go back into the darkness where he belongs," Grim said to Fear.

Fear looked crazy. "Never!" he roared. "There's no way I'm dying—at least not without destroying the thing you love."

A thunderous echo came with the opening of the portal. Demons were pouring out—a blackness, some sort of fog glided through the night air. I saw wolf demons jumping out. So many... it was overwhelming to see so many different demons coming out. People scattered, screaming, and trying to put distance between the things that were coming out of the portal.

Tess had my shoulder trying to pull me away with her. "Melanie, let's get out here!" she screamed at me.

I pulled away from her. "I can't. I have to help Killian."

She looked frustrated—she also looked terrified. "Melanie… what are you talking about? Don't you see what's happening?" She looked to the rooftop. "Is that Killian?"

I pushed her. "Go home or something. Get far away."

But she wouldn't. "Melanie!" Tears pricked her eyes. "Tell me!"

"Demons, Tess, it's demons! You claimed you believed me when I saw ghosts, well you already know that the skeleton on the roof is Killian. He's Grim Reaper and he's been keeping me safe from demons since my birthday last month. The reason I've been acting weird lately," I motioned with my hands to look around us, "is because of all this!" I took a deep breath after letting it all out.

She looked at me wide-eyed and completely stunned. Out of all the things she could have said or asked, she yelled, "What the hell, Melanie? Those two on the roof are scary as hell!"

"Really?" I looked at her in disbelief. "Our town is being attacked by demons and you tell me my boyfriend is scary looking?"

Tess grabbed her head and muttered, "I've been friends with you for too long, now even I'm going crazy."

"Tess-uh," I dragged out her name with my frustration.

"Can you guys save this conversation for after we deal with the demons?" Penny ported next to us. Tess saw her—Penny must have made herself visible to humans.

"Who the hell are you?" Tess asked, giving Penny the evil eye.

Penny tipped her head back and rolled her shoulders. "The one that's been keeping your ass safe the last few weeks," Penny hissed.

"Melanie!" I turned to Ryan's voice and saw him running toward us. Tess looked the same time I did and her eyes lit up—she saw him.

"Ryan?" she said his name in disbelief.

"Tess?" He looked at her carefully. "You can see me?"

Tears pooled in her eyes, she was about to lose it. "Ryan," she said again as she ran to hug him.

He wrapped his arms around her. "It's okay," he told her. "I went home, but you weren't there. Mom and Dad were, though."

"Yeah, they've been doing that," she spoke through tears.

"Doing what?" he asked.

"Staying home." He looked surprised and met my eyes with a sad smile. He realized it, too, what his parents were trying to make up for.

She looked up at him. "What's all over your face?" she asked and he pulled away from her quickly.

Penny was shoving Tess to the ground as a demon attacked. She sliced its throat open with a sword and it fell to her feet. "Behind you!" she yelled at me.

I turned just as Ryan stepped in front of me. He locked hands with the demon and his strength was that of a demon—he must be stronger because of his demon trying to get out. Once he tackled him to the ground, Penny took her sword through the demon's head.

I looked around. Reapers were fighting off the demons easily. They clearly had no problem taking care of demons, but the problem was the portal. They kept coming.

It was loud—people were panicking, kids were crying. My eyes darted around to see if anyone needed help—I didn't know where to start or look. The demons were running all over the place.

"Stay close, I don't want to be responsible for any of you dying," Penny told us.

A group of males walked toward us. Pale skin—I saw the fangs in their mouth as they smiled at us. Vampires. Penny swore under her breath. "Ohmigod, ohmigod, ohmigod," Tess chanted next to me. Her fear was completely out in the open. I gripped Grim's cloak. I was scared, but I wasn't weak. I wanted to stop Fear just as much as Killian—if not more.

I felt my power beneath my skin—vibrating with urgency. Good, it was willing to fight tonight. Penny twirled her swords in her hands and took off after the vampires. They were quick. One was already behind her and kicked her. She grunted and swung her sword out. He moved again with a laugh. Ryan ran—he moved almost as quickly as they did. He grabbed one by the shoulders before hauling off and punching him in the face. He grabbed him again before he took off. Penny killed the vampire he held right before another bit into her neck from behind. She screamed, and it put me in motion.

My skin was lit—golden, and when I got behind the vampire, I placed my hands on the sides of his face and let go of the power. His head exploded and he dropped to the ground before dissolving to nothing. Penny grabbed her neck and Ryan was atop of one of them. The arm that was completely covered in black, dug into the vampire's chest—he turned to dust. The last vampire was fuming and lunged in our direction. Penny scooped down and picked up her swords she dropped and rammed one into his chest. He turned to dust.

A gunshot went off as Ryan was getting off his knees. We looked in the direction it came from, several men stood together with guns. They shot another demon as it came toward them. Two of them high-fived each other and laughed. They wasted no time in finding a new demon target.

"Isn't that Big Bill from the liquor store?" Ryan squinted his eyes at the guy with the gun.

Tess rolled her eyes. "Yeah, I think so. Stupid ass," she hissed. "Which reminds me, we are idiots, too, for not making a run for it. This placing is crawling with monsters." She looked back at me. "No offense Melanie." I suppressed an eye-roll because I got the feeling she was talking about Killian. "What's up with your skin? You're freaking glowing!" Tess looked at me bewildered.

"Hello, Gorgeous," a demon said behind Tess. She went stiff as a board as she looked to me rather hopelessly. She turned slowly to see what was behind her. The male demon was covered head to toe in nasty, yellow boils. When he smiled, you could see his rotted teeth. Bile rose in my throat as I grabbed a hold of her wrist and jerked her away from him.

He laughed before lunging for us. "Not so fast," he yelled. I didn't want to touch his skin—who knew what might happen. I managed to kick him in the knee, he grunted and came at us, but I was already running, dragging Tess with me.

Only while running away from him, we ran into something worse. Dread turned in my stomach as I watched the shadows move around us. "What the—what are those things?" Tess asked, clutching my hand tighter.

"Shadows," I whispered.

It kept getting worse. People were running away from them, but shadows were slipping inside of them easily. They stopped running and turned in our directions—grins broke out on their face. My panic grew—I never wanted to lose that kind of control again and be stuck seeing from the inside as your body did as the shadow commanded.

I moved in front of Tess as the shadows closed in—my necklace blocked any of them from getting inside me and I sighed in relief. A hand clamped down on my shoulder, I turned to see an unnatural grin on Tess's face. She gripped me harder to the point that it hurt. Goosebumps covered my skin and it was obvious one managed to jump in Tess. She attacked me. I fell to the ground with her on top of me. "Tess!" I yelled her name even though I knew she couldn't do anything to help her or me.

The others that were being controlled by shadows were getting closer. I gritted my teeth together and focused on Tess. She was strong. I placed my knee against her stomach, giving me enough room to get my boot between us. I managed to get my boot at her crotch and I put all my force into slinging her off me. She gripped my shoulders to try and stop me, but I still managed to throw her off. I scrambled to my feet. "Shadows are jumping inside humans," I yelled to any Reaper that was close by, but they were already ahead of me.

A couple of them were already plucking the shadows out and destroying them much like Killian did the one that jumped inside me.

"If I kill you, Fear will be happy," the shadow said through Tess. She was already up and charging for me again. I dodged her and tried to figure out how I was supposed to get the shadow out of her.

"Tessa," Ryan called out to her, but she never turned. She went for me again and this time, Ryan was there to stop her. He tried to hold her arms, but he was being too gentle. She pulled away from him easily, and her tiny fist was connecting with his nose before either of us could stop her. I grabbed my own nose and flinched at the sickening crack that came from his nose. He hollered from the pain, but still tried to get a grip on her.

She got away from him and went after me. "Tessa." I went at her with my own tackle, managing to knock her on the ground. She was thrashing and yelling and trying to bite me, but there was no way I was letting her go after seeing what she did to Ryan's nose.

Someone picked me up effortlessly. "Hey," I hissed, ready to start kicking and putting up a fight until I saw that it was Grim.

"Easy there," he told me in a hurry. Tess was about to take off running when she saw Grim, but his hand was in her chest before she got the chance. He ripped the shadow out and she fell to the ground with a deep breath. He crushed the shadow in his hand.

"Are you okay?" I dropped to my knees next to Tess.

She met my eyes. "Melanie, I'm so sorry," she started, "that wasn't me—"

I cut her off, "I know." I looked up to Grim. "Where's Fear?"

He sighed, gripping his scythe. "Playing hide and seek, he's messing with me—"

Fear appeared and rammed into Grim, sending him flying. Grim faded in the process and reappeared next to him. Fear's tail was in motion—at first, I thought it was Grim he was aiming for, but it was me. Grim yanked his tail away from me and slung him with it.

"Getting tired of protecting her yet?" Fear laughed. "How about all these pathetic humans? The demons will keep coming."

"Too bad you won't be around to see me close the portal," Grim told Marcus. Fear ported again and Grim rolled his shoulders before looking down at me. "I need you to use your power, Love, or get out of harm's way, or I'll never be able to concentrate." He reached his skeletal hand out to me and I took it. Ryan was next to Tess as she continued to apologize for his nose. Her eyes went to Grim and she fell silent, unable to do anything but hang her mouth open.

He was right. He needed to end this. "Go, I'll be fin—"

My feet were jerked out from underneath me—it happened so quickly that Grim lost his grip on my hand. My chin smacked the blacktop and a metallic taste filled my mouth—blood. My shirt rode up as I was dragged over the blacktop, my stomach was on fire. I was close to getting trampled on by demons, humans, and Reapers. I turned on my back and could finally see what had me— Fear's tail—and he came into view with a nasty smile on his face. "I'll make sure he suffers," he sneered down at

me. "I'll make you both suffer. I only wanted power—
who are you to stop me when I almost had Grim!
Worthless human! You're nothing, not even the Vessel—
I was tricked by whatever I sensed in you!" He was
delirious.

All I felt was hatred. I smiled even when I knew
my mouth was filled with blood. "We both know that I
am not, nothing." I glowered at him. "I think you've
already experienced a taste of what I'm capable of." It
registered on his face and for a second, I thought I saw a
hint of uncertainty—fear. "This is the end for you."

I radiated energy—close to bursting and power
came to me as simply as breathing. I was the beacon of
light. My scythe materialized in my hand, and I lifted
myself to my butt and swung the blade down over his
tail. It severed and he cried out. I was on my feet in no
time, waiting, surging with power. Grim faded next to
me, but Fear was gone again. He looked to me and I
smiled. "You're hypnotic and so fucking beautiful," he
told me and in my head, I pictured Killian whispering
those words in my ear as I lay beneath him. He grabbed a
piece of my hair that was glowing. "I wish you could see
yourself in my eyes." His essence brightened around him,
and his presence had my power tingling all over my skin.

Grim faded seconds before a child screamed—he
must have sensed it. I scanned the crowd and for a
second, I was too stunned to do anything but study what I
was seeing.

Chains.

Chains everywhere.

I was seeing every person and demon's lifeline. My head spun. They were all different colors. They floated out of people's chest and every time a Reaper killed a demon in front of me, I watched the chain light like a fuse and in a matter of seconds, they were gone.

One chain stood out to me—it pulsed and I knew why as soon as my eyes locked on Tess. It was her chain and a demon stood above her—female, four arms and four legs with a giant mouth stretched open; big enough to fit Tess's head in there. I was there within a second and my scythe ripped into her back. Tess sagged in relief when the demon dropped to the ground. She looked up at me. "You're glowing," she stated.

"Where's Ryan?" I asked her.

Her eyes lit up with worry. "He led a bunch of demons away from me."

"I think he'll be okay," I told her. He was already dead. They couldn't do any more damage to what Fear had already done to him.

I took a good look around—most humans were gone; dead demons lay all over the place. The Reapers were doing good, but the problem was the portal, demons kept coming through it.

"The portal's a problem," I said to myself and when I looked to Tess again, I studied her chain. It was long and full of life, yet if I hadn't saved her life just now, her life would have been cut short… exactly like her brother's. I couldn't let that happen.

Tess's face filled with horror. "Another one?"

I followed the direction she was looking and smiled. A second portal formed. "This one is for us," I told her.

Dragons spilled out of the portal and if demons weren't enough for people to scream about; the dragons gave the rest of them a reason to panic.

"Is that…" Tess lost her words as she watched them.

I saw Rixen in the front, he dropped down and took one of the demons in his mouth before flying back up. Then I saw Sky, the one, and only white dragon. She was bright across the night sky and just like I found her, her blue eyes found me. My glowing skin was probably like a beacon to her.

She landed gracefully in front of me, tucking her wings against her so that I could climb on. Tess was scrambling away. I took one look at Sky and said, "Get her."

"Melanie!" Tess screamed right before Sky scooped her up. I pointed to where I wanted Sky to take her. We dropped her off on the rooftop of Deb's Diner.

"It's better for you to be up here than down there," I told her as we took off back in the direction of the chaos.

"Melanie!" she screamed.

CHAPTER SEVENTEEN
Melanie

Sky dived into the demons and plucked one up by the mouth. Blood spewed all over her from the wind as she bit his head off. The body fell to the ground, and I could hear her crunching on the head. "Spit that out!" She tilted her head enough that her eyes looked back to me questioningly. "Who knows what diseases these demons might carry." She looked amused as she cocked her head to the side as if to say, "I don't pick and choose my food like you." Still, she opened her mouth for me to see and the head fell out.

I wrinkled my nose up. "Gross." I looked up just in time. "Watch out!" I said right before a feline looking female jumped for us. Her body landed on Sky's head and she bucked and jerked her neck around to get her off. The demon smiled—revealing pointed teeth and just as her claws came at me, I brought my scythe to her neck and with my swing and the added pressure of her jumping at me—it was a perfect cut. Her body and head fell from Sky in different directions. "Who knew we specialized in head-hunting," I said lamely. I hoped she understood my crack at a joke— since we both just killed a demon by taking off its head. A weird cackling sound came from her throat, and I smiled.

Okay, my gaze traveled through the masses until I spotted Ryan fighting with a demon twice his size. I was about to tell Sky to fly to him, but she was already doing so on her own. The demon threw a punch—his fist was twice the size of Ryan's head—and he went sailing through the air, knocking into two others. He got up slowly and shook his head. "Ryan!" He looked up, and I extended my hand out to him, using my other to hold onto my scythe and Sky both. The two demons were looking at him like he was a target. His hand grabbed mine—one of the demons reached for him and I had to let go of Sky and swing my scythe out. I sliced into his chest. Ryan jumped on behind me and we were back in the air.

"I had everything under control," he clarified, and I looked back at him—my eyes moved to his chest where I saw no chain. My heart plummeted. I kept holding on to a way to save him, but my own power reminded me that he'd already lost to life and death—everything. "There's too many of them," he added, and my eyes roamed over the chaos below us.

"All we can do is keep killing them until Grim kills Marcus," I said.

"Will that really be enough?" His words sent a chill up my spine.

Another chain started pulsing to me—exactly the way Tess's had and I followed it until I saw the woman it was connected to—human. I thought that everyone had managed to get away, I guessed wrong. What was the pulsing? Was I supposed to save her... I gripped my scythe. She wasn't supposed to die today. Her chain was trying to turn into a fuse when it wasn't supposed to.

She screamed, scrambling to her feet until she was backed up against the bricks of the library. Demons with horns and red skin surrounded her. They were average size men and women, but there were a lot. "What is it?" Ryan must have noticed I had gone tense. His eyes followed to where I was looking. I looked down at my scythe and wondered... I was starting to realize how similar my power was to Grim's, yet it was different, but...

I visualized what I've seen Grim do before and closed my eyes. When I looked at my scythe again, it was a chain in my hand. It moved like a snake and before I knew it, it was slithering out of my hand and racing toward the demons. One by one, it wrapped around them until it rounded them up in a circle. I gripped what part of the chain that was left in my hand and yanked. The chain ripped through them—it was disgusting and satisfying all at once for me.

"Really." Ryan took a deep breath. "What are you?" he was genuinely asking me, and I couldn't give him an answer that I still didn't know myself.

Something rammed into Sky while we were distracted—she let out a furious cry. I looked around to see a shadowy figure slipping around us, it looked like a shadow in the form of a dragon. Ryan was yanked off Sky and I was too late to reach for him, then I was knocked off right after.

Sky shrieked in fury as she whipped her tail out to smack the dragon—her tail went straight through it. I looked up to the one that held me in its talons as it took me higher. In my head, I imagined what I wanted my scythe to be and soon after, it became a golden sword in my hand. I stuck it into the shadow and unlike Sky's attempt, my sword destroyed it.

Only I didn't think it through, and now I was falling from the sky. Grim was there to catch me in the air—he was always there to save me. I smiled at him, but it quickly turned into an 'oh crap' look when I saw Fear coming at us with a sword. It was out of nowhere and somehow, I instinctively moved my sword up to block his attack.

Then, Grim was placing my feet on the ground as Fear attacked again. He turned on me, and Grim faded in front of me to block him. Fear hissed—he was desperate to end me just to get back at me for not being what he wanted and for piecing Grim and Killian back together. But most of all, he wanted to make Grim suffer.

Rixen jumped Fear from behind and was lifting him into the air. He didn't get far, though. Fear ported on him. I searched the sky for Sky and saw red when I caught sight of a shadowy dragon biting at her while she landed close by. She couldn't fight something she couldn't touch. I ran to her and my sword was inside the shadow before it even knew it was a goner.

My heart caved when I took another look around us. Dragons were fighting alongside Reapers, yet the demons kept coming through the portal. Denver was being overrun with demons.

MICHELLE GROSS

CHAPTER EIGHTEEN
Killian

I watched Melanie go to help Sky and in my head, I chanted, *"I see her, I can feel her, she's safe."* That was the only way I could concentrate on what I needed to. I always sensed her, no matter what I was doing.

I grew tired of this game of cat-and-mouse with Fear. Marcus's death was crawling all over me—humming, burning, ready to ignite. Even though he was meant to die, it didn't make it easy since he was merged with Fear. He kept porting on me every time I was close, and he would keep doing so because he knew the moment I get my hands on him… First, I needed to take his portal chip away from him, but he was always popping up when I focused on another demon or Melanie. What made it worse, he had a witch spell him with some sort of invisibility spell.

I relaxed and concentrated on finding him through Marcus's death. When I was meant to kill something, I could always find them by that link, but I couldn't keep them in one place like I needed Fear to be. My essence brightened when I found him in my mind and I faded to a rooftop. The only person I saw was Melanie's friend, Tess, but I knew he was up here.

Her eyes widened when she saw me, and she started backing up as I hurried to her. "No more running," I told Fear just as he became visible behind her.

She screamed, and I pushed her to the side right before his tail moved after her—it still hadn't healed from Melanie chopping a good chunk of it off. I stepped on it and reached for him, but he pulled back.

"Still not tired of protecting them?" It always came back to that with him. He couldn't understand my willingness to protect lives that weren't meant to die. "If not, then do you really have time to worry about killing me?" My essence flooded with darkness, giving away my anger. So, he thought by distracting me with all these lives that it could protect him from his own death? I was a damned good multitasker.

Melanie was right, I was vain.

There was a tug in my chest, a pulling, a wrongness—someone was close to dying and they weren't supposed to, but even so, they could still die under unexpected glitches in fate. Like this situation right now, it wasn't supposed to happen, yet it was. There was a major shift in lives right now, and I couldn't sit back and do nothing.

Not when it was my job to keep it right—balanced, restore it to how it should be.

Fear smiled, knowing the demons were sparing his life with every second they pulled me away from him. I willingly turned away from him and stepped toward Tess. She scrambled back and squealed. It made Fear laugh.

"It's funny, really, you spend an eternity looking after mankind, guiding the dead, and ridding us—the evil ones—from the world and all you get in return is screams and terrified looks." He made an example out of Tess, and her eyes moved over him in realization.

I scooped her up and faded. I took her to her bedroom and placed her on her feet. Her eyes were full of uncertainty as she looked at me and it didn't bother me— I knew the way I looked as Grim would be frightening for any human and that had never once bothered me, until the day I met Melanie.

Melanie's fear of me had been the only one. She unraveled me and filled me with dread at the thought of showing her a part of me. That was why I held it off for so long until I couldn't anymore and became Grim in front of her for the first time… and when she had left me and drove off that night out of fear…

She ripped my heart out.

But she was the only one with that kind of control over the way I felt and now when she looked at me, I knew there was nothing but love, admiration, and even desire… I've noticed the look on her face when I used power around her… she even loved me this way and what I could do.

Her thoughts were the only thing that mattered.

The heaviness in my chest was getting stronger and I faded again. Demons were all around the car I faded next to. A family of four was stuck in the car in the middle of the road. When I looked around again, I saw that they weren't the only one. The traffic was starting to back up and before any of them had a chance to turn around, demons surrounded them.

I changed my scythe into a chain and whipped it around to hit the demons. It got them away from the car and a second later, I faded and sliced through every one of them until not one was left standing. I moved through the vehicles, killing demons and trying to make a way for them to turn around. They were just as afraid of me, though, as they were of the demons.

Ron, a Reaper, joined in to help me out. Around us, the souls of the demons we've killed were piling up—they were like clouds of darkness moving around, but none of us had any time to send them to Satan's Flames when we were too busy killing more of them.

Another Reaper moved in beside me. "Go, we'll protect them. You take care of Fear so we can end this for all of us."

I nodded. In moments like this, I was reminded all over again that I wasn't the lonesome Reaper that I once was. I had Reapers—a family I created, in a way. I had a home. I had demons around me that lived for the same thing I did.

And now, I had Melanie.

She was the very reason why I needed to end this.

CHAPTER NINETEEN
Melanie

Sky was in the air, biting off heads and limbs while I stuck to the ground. I alternated between my scythe and turning it into a sword. I was getting quicker at it and my body was showing no signs of fatigue. My power must be feeding off Grim's through the cloak—he had been right about it.

Something jumped me from behind, and two ogre-looking demons stepped in front of me. I switched my scythe into a sword and impaled one in the stomach. I couldn't get the sword back out, and the ogre didn't even look affected by it. Whatever was on my back laughed—it was a she—and covered my eyes with her hands. Then one of the ogres must have punched me because it had enough force to throw me onto the ground with the she-demon still on my back.

She swiveled around until she was the one on top, and I was too stunned by the punch to do anything. I looked up to the demon and the pain in my jaw suddenly became less important as her mouth opened to the size of my head. I panicked, grabbing her shoulders and neck careful not to get close to her razor-sharp teeth—her face was all mouth now, it was messed up.

I looked to my right where my sword was and couldn't even risk taking my hands off her to get it. Saliva dripped onto my face and I gagged. Now, I was good and worked up, the queasy feeling in my stomach

239

was all I could take. I gritted my teeth and sent power through my hands. She screamed as my power lit up her skin. She tried to get away, but I wouldn't let her—her face went back to normal, her eyes rolled back, and her entire weight sagged over me. She was dead.

I pushed her off me and grabbed my sword. The ogres were waiting their turn, and I was plenty pumped up to do it with all this adrenaline coursing through my veins. One was behind me and I swiveled around to face him before he could do me any harm. This ogre's chain was a dark orange and the length of it told me he had a lot of years left—if only he hadn't decided to come here. I decided to take a chance and do what I wanted to with Marcus before he kicked me out of the dream.

His arms were coming out to grab me but I dodged him easily and grabbed his chain in the process. I brought it to the ground and held it there with my feet. I gripped my sword with both hands just as the ogre went at me again. I slammed the tip of my blade down over the chain, breaking it in two. The chain lit a fuse where I broke it and not even a second ticked by before it was at the ogre's chest. His eyes widened as he gasped, falling over dead.

I smiled, knowing the truth now. I could kill Marcus myself.

I was yanked back by the hair and dropped my sword in the process. I scrambled to gain my footing, but the second ogre lifted me up to my feet, bringing his hand to my neck. He moved me around to face him as he held me up and laughed—his belly jiggled in the process. I kicked at him but he wasn't affected. I tried reaching for his chain but I wasn't close enough to where it floated from his chest so I went back to holding his hand over my neck in an attempt to ease the pressure there.

"Hey, ugly as fuck!" Ryan yelled, and the ogre turned his head to face him the same time I did. Ryan was running at us and I knew he was going for a football tackle. My body tensed up because I could already tell how it was going to go. The ogre was easily seven feet tall or more and when Ryan hit into him; he bounced off his belly. The ogre laughed again as Ryan got back up ready to go at him again.

"Ryan, stop!" I coughed, starting to feel the pain in my neck. "Hand me my sword!"

But the ogre took one look at my sword and went after Ryan with me still in one hand. Ryan's jaw tightened as his eyes leveled on the ogre's grip on my neck and went at him again, but he didn't get anywhere because the ogre's free hand went straight for his neck.

He lifted Ryan up next to him and now we were side by side in the same awful situation. We exchanged a look that spoke volumes, something like "we are so screwed". "Melanie, your power," Ryan told me, and my eyes widened. Oh, yeah, I still had it! I felt my hands heating up over his that held me by the neck, but before I got the chance to use it, a sword burst through the ogre's chest. His eyes rolled back and blood splattered us in the face. The blade continued to move up his chest and into his face, splitting him. We fell to the ground and Fear ported on top of the ogre's shoulders right as the body was beginning to fall. He was jumping at someone—I realized it was Grim when the ogre's body finally fell to reveal him on the other side.

Grim took hold of Fear's leg as he was trying to port and slammed him to the ground. His boot was on his neck before Fear got the chance to move. Fear grunted and hissed trying to move.

Grim's eyes darted to Fear's hand and I saw the portal chip he was holding—Fear was about to use it. Grim's sword went through his hand and Fear hollered from the pain. The portal chip shattered as Fear's blood coated its remains. "Demons!" Grim's yelled—his voice was like thunder, intimidating and frightening. Most of them stopped fighting with the Reapers and dragons and saw Fear beneath his boot—a lot of them suddenly looked wary. "Go back through the portal and live another disgusting day of what you call life or," he brought up his sword—it changed back to a scythe, "become a part of my scythe and know what it means to be killed by me."

I saw Fear's chain floating around but couldn't see Marcus's—it must have been underneath him. There was a dark expression in Fear's eyes as he gazed up at Grim, almost like he was still expecting to get out of this. I wanted to snuff that last shred of hope—he more than deserved what was coming and where he was going once he died. Grim's eyeless sockets were peering down at him—I couldn't tell what he was thinking, but his thoughts couldn't be much different than the dark ones filtering through mine.

One minute Fear was on the ground, under Grim's boot, and then the next he was up on his feet—eyes murderous as he charged at me. But Grim was toying with him, letting him have a bit of hope, thinking he'd get his way. A black chain with Grim's blue essence snaked around Fear's torso and arms, and he screamed in fury. His tail started to move, but Grim was in complete control of everything.

My hands were twitching, begging me to do something—the feeling was so fierce that I was moving before I even knew it. I spotted Marcus's chain—it was so small now that it was almost completely at his chest—and smiled. This was it, it was the end for him. I felt Grim's eyeless gaze on me, he was probably wondering what I was doing—why I stopped right in front of Fear. He wasn't the only one that wanted to hurt Fear in some way.

Fear jerked in the chains. "You can't do this to me!" he was practically screaming in my face, I was so close. I took it all in with a smile, like his end was my euphoria, but I wanted Marcus in despair. The way he was now wasn't good enough for me, not after everything he'd done.

"Finally," I blew the word out. "You reap what you sow." He didn't look afraid, it still looked like he wanted to murder me and everyone in his path. I didn't like it. "Do you even realize where you went wrong?" I asked him.

He laughed in my face, making me breathe in the smell of him—his filth. My anger was at a new high. "You took nine years of my life!" I screamed in his face. "You took a life that wasn't meant to die—you killed him just to spite me when you couldn't kill me and all this—everything you've done and the reason you're about to die, Marcus… do you realize it was all for something that I never was… Do you realize you were wrong?"

He smiled and my tears were starting to form—I wasn't going to cry, I couldn't, not in front of this smug demon that didn't understand he was a monster. "And…?" was all he said.

"Melanie…" Grim was behind Fear as he called to me. I met his eyes. "He doesn't have a shred of humanity; he won't ever see the error in his ways which is why he's a dead man."

As Fear tried to turn around and face Grim, I gripped Marcus's chain in my hand. His eyes widened as he looked back at me—good, he could feel it. "He's only strong because he's Fear, let's see how he feels without him." Grim's eyes were on my hand, but I didn't think he could see what I could and he cocked his head to the side.

I pulled the chain and Marcus screamed. We all saw why when I forced him out of Fear. He fell to his knees in front of Fear, his blond hair falling into his face as he lunged for me, but I jerked the chain and he fell to his knees again. "How'd you…" Grim muttered, then he changed his focus to Fear—he looked different without Marcus now, more monstrous without any hints of a man or Marcus's traits on his face. He wasn't trying to fight the chains that bound him, either.

For some reason, it made me wary. "You're not going to try and save him?" Grim asked Fear but he stood emotionless. Marcus whipped his head around and glared.

"Do something," he yelled at Fear. "You can't live without me!" He never responded. Grim even let the chain drop from Fear's body and he just stood there, watching, waiting.

Grim moved next to me. "The entity that once chose you, refuses to help. He doesn't care that you're about to die." Marcus glared, and I gripped what was left of his chain tighter in my hand, wishing to see some of that fear I've seen before flood his face. "There's no end to the suffering where you're going," Grim added.

Marcus never flinched, instead, he laughed like a lunatic. "You were always a goody—" He never got to finish. His head tumbled off his shoulder, followed by his body smacking the blacktop. It happened so quickly that I could barely process what happened. The chain disappeared in my hand—there was no life left. Grim's scythe dripped with blood in front of me. I finally blinked.

"He was never going to show any regret but believe me, he was afraid," Grim said and maybe it was because he knew how much I wanted to see him suffer. His dark soul rose from his body. Grim opened the passage and the soul started screaming and panicking.

I staggered backward, the passage was filled with every horrid emotion and pain. Like the time with Vengeance, I was overcome with all of them at once. Marcus's soul put up a fight and even I jumped when a giant hand snaked out and grabbed it, pulling his soul in before disappearing.

"Looks like we weren't the only ones wanting Marcus dead," Grim said.

I took a deep breath as Grim looked at me. I instinctively touched the marks on my chest—Fear and now Grim's as well. It wasn't over. Grim and I turned where Fear was—he was gone. Grim's essence darkened and unease crept up my spine.

"Where'd he go?" I asked him, my eyes scanning through the quiet demons—some resumed their battle with the Reapers.

"He's still here, I can sense him," Grim told me and I immediately started looking for his chain—I found it. I ran for it, but it moved as if Fear knew I was going for it. Grim faded and I spotted him again on the library as his chain came back into view—brilliant blue and vibrant with life. Fear was there as well.

"Take the mark off Melanie and the boy and leave with every demon you brought here." Grim stepped toward him, gripping his scythe. Fear seemed to be searching for something or someone… his eyes fell over everyone until they stopped. I looked in the direction and for a moment, my heart stopped.

It was Ryan. He had a hazy look in his eyes as he gazed up to Fear—almost like he was in some sort of trance. "Ryan…" I called to him in a whisper almost.

I turned to Grim with urgency and hopeless feeling. His stance told me enough, something bad was about to happen. "You're going back!" Grim sounded desperate as he jumped at Fear. He cut him wide open with his scythe and sent him flying in the direction of the portal, but Fear made sure he missed the portal and regained a spot on the roof. His focus was on Ryan again.

"Ryan!" I ran. I ran to get to him in time. I ran to save him. I ran because it was all I could do and when I got to him, I shook him with fury. He wasn't budging, he didn't even respond. It was almost like he wasn't in there anymore.

The walls were caving inside my chest.

Then horrid cries were torn from Ryan as the blackness started to spread. Grim was there next to us. "It's time." My eyes widened. No. I started shaking my head, gripping him tighter. I didn't even get to say goodbye. I wasn't ready. I was never going to be ready.

Grim tore my hands from Ryan—I could feel his scythe pulsing as he brought it up. Fear attacked Grim, pinning him to the ground. His tail moved rapidly behind him. Grim threw him off and they were back on their feet.

"Melanie," Ryan said my name. I turned around and gasped at what I saw peering out of his chest. He had a chain again.

MICHELLE GROSS

CHAPTER TWENTY
Ryan

It was a dark, twisted feeling losing yourself to something on the inside—a demon, a monster, whatever you'd want to call something that shouldn't exist. It made me sick and the rage I felt was more than on the surface, it was skin deep. It was crushing my entire being.

My memories were changing—they were fading, in and out, every few seconds. I was terrified because I kept forgetting that I was Ryan Jones.

And then I was even more terrified of what would become of me when I no longer remembered that I was *me*.

But that fear always helped in the end. It would kick-start my heart and I'd gain back a part of me that I had lost to the demon. Her face would take over my mind and as for my heart—she had been a part of since the day I met her. Blonde hair, perfect blue eyes, pale kissable skin. I'd always thought she was meant to be with me—be mine. And a part of me would never be able to let it go that she wasn't. I was bitter and happy for her all at once.

Melanie Rose had gone and found herself without me.

I was okay with that, though. Loving her was something I would never be able to change. I would not know how—it was as natural as breathing.

Then the other woman in my life, the one that was the female replica of me was the only other person that'd bring me back from the darkness. Tess. My throat got all tight and it hurt to even breathe, or think that I left her alone. We grew up in a home that lacked love and affection, but now I hoped more than anything that my death did something to our cold parents, and they figured out how to be there for her when I no longer could.

Lastly, I prayed that the only two women in my life that ever mattered remained a part of each other's life.

Yes, these were the last few things I was telling myself in case it was my last chance to think of either of them.

I studied Melanie in front of me—it was clear she was scared, scared for me and shocked that I even called her name. She must think this was my end, the place where she had to let me go. In a way, it was but it most certainly wasn't my end. I moved my eyes over to Fear as he fought with Grim.

No, it was far from over for me. I feared something far worse than ceasing to exist awaited me because I sensed exactly what he wanted from me. The tug and pull, the need to go to him, that link that waited between us as I met his red eyes.

I closed my eyes and tried to fight it, ignore it—just enough so that I could get a goodbye in, in case it was my last chance.

"Melanie," I said her name again.

She didn't move, she didn't even blink. She was too terrified of what I was about to say. "Ryan," she managed to say my name. She was glowing, like really glowing, and it was so weird for me to see her like this—strong and powerful—when I knew her as the scaredy-cat, the introverted girl that saw ghost so she didn't mesh well with anybody except Tess and me. And secretly, that was the way I preferred it. I didn't want anyone to get to know the girl I knew, but someone did… and he helped her more than I ever could. I glanced to Grim before looking back to her.

"You and Tess look after each other," I told her first because suddenly I didn't know what my last words should be to her. "And be happy…" I brought my hand to her cheek—it didn't even look like my hand anymore and cupped it. My eyes fell on her lips and more than anything, I wanted to kiss her there, but instead, I chose her forehead. She would always be the treasure I couldn't have.

"Don't hate me for what happens next," I whispered as I stepped away from her.

"Ryan!" I could no longer fight it and Melanie's voice was nothing but a distant sound in the back of my head.

The pulsing was back full force, clawing at me from the inside. My eyes were heavy and the darkness began to filter back in… yes.

Fear would leave, I knew he would. He was waiting for me. I just had to do what he wanted. This would all be over if he left and never came back, right? I would do this to save her.

And I ignored the feeling in my chest that told me I craved what I was about to do more than I wanted to admit.

That fear came back, though. What will become of me?

Demons were starting to aid Fear as he fought with Grim… his attention turned to me. The darkness was closing in, I had to hurry before I lost myself completely to the demon. Fear was the only one that could stop it all… he was in front of me before I know it. Red eyes drifting over me. Grim saw and he looked desperate to get away from the demons that ganged up on him… Reapers were joining in.

The pull toward Fear was irresistible, and I didn't even want to run. His eyes burned into mine. *I'm Ryan Jones, I'm Ryan Jones,* I chanted over and over to myself, *don't forget—*

His clawed hand latched out and grabbed mine. I stiffened as all this pain hit my body at once. A door inside my brain was thrown open and between us, every dark and wicked deed entered in its wake.

CHAPTER TWENTY-ONE
Angel Sanctuary

"Should we have really let that happen to the boy?" Michael whispered next to Faye as they stood around the seeing glass.

"Yes," Gabrielle answered beside them. "The boy's human life was already lost and this is his new fate. One you're to blame for, Faye." His eyes fell over her in disappointment again.

She took a deep breath and closed her eyes. Faye had watched Melanie and Ryan the last nine years, she knew just what kind of man Ryan was… if anyone could survive that kind of fate, it was him… she prayed she was right.

"Are you ready?" Gabrielle asked her.

Never in a million years, but she'd never admit that to him. Instead, she reopened her eyes and stared down at the seeing glass, determination filling her eyes. She would correct her mistake, no matter the pain it would cause. "Yes," she told them.

The angels were ready and gathered to go. "Now let's fix what we can and set fate back in the right direction," Gabrielle said. "Let's enjoy this night, we get to destroy some demons. And Faye…," he called to her, and she turned to meet his eyes. "You'll be the one to rip two people apart."

His words sent panic through her soul. She never felt as sad or horrible as she did now.

CHAPTER TWENTY-TWO
Melanie

"Ryan." I was always too late when it came to Ryan. Too late to save him. Too late in figuring out what was happening. Too late with my words. Always, too late.

I ran toward him—Grim was, too. No, please, no. I stared at Ryan and Fear in panic, but it was what I expected. I stopped running when I saw the two of them step into each other. My heart sunk—twisted. Oh God, what had I done to him? Only one stood where two used to be.

I thought destroying his soul was the worst thing that I could have let happen to him—I was wrong. Now, he was the very thing that caused all this pain.

I was in a state of confusion and panic, but I was thrown off, even more, when I saw Grim shift back into Killian. He was running for me—panic and fear laced his beautiful features. This moment between us was only a few seconds, but in my head, it felt infinite and slow; the time it took for him to get to me.

And when I saw what caused the panic in his eyes, I fully expected him to reach me in time. Molly stood by me, her hands coming at me. His hand was extended out, he was reaching for me so I did the same even though he was still too far away for me to reach him. In my head, I kept imagining that he'd get to me before she did. But he didn't, and she pushed me into the portal that she opened behind us.

"Melanie!" he screamed and I lost sight of him as we entered the portal.

———

"What are you planning?" I hissed at Molly as I took in our surroundings. A dungeon? It was dark and dingy and smelled like rotten flesh in here. I covered my mouth as I stared at the empty cells on both sides of us— we stood in the middle of some sort of prison? I heard screaming all around me, but the cells were empty. I followed Molly as she walked quietly in front of me. Something told me we were moving in the direction of the noise.

My skin was crawling… something was off about this place, more like, I shouldn't be here. "Where are we?" I asked.

"This is the Pits of the Underworld," she answered but never turned around as she kept walking. She didn't seem worried that I would escape. I instinctively gripped my hand and frowned when I realized I no longer had my scythe. My skin wasn't glowing, either.

Then I stopped abruptly, finally letting her words sink in. She stopped in front of me, turning her face around to look at me. "Yes, this is where the bad guys go that Grim descends, and these empty cells you see are *nothing* compared to what really happens to them. He'll often leave them here waiting, starving, filling their head with the vilest things he can come up with for months before he finally sends them to the next cruelest punishment. It goes on forever until he finally sends them to the flames and that's when they'll be begging to go back to these cells, but they never can. The pain and suffering are everlasting once you're down here." She turned back around and resumed walking. Her words engraved themselves onto my skin; a chill I knew I wouldn't be able to shake.

In front of her, I could make out the end of the cells and a brick wall with a dark opening that looked like a stairway leading down.

"Why are we here then? It hardly seems like a place a living person should be," I told her, masking the fear I felt.

"You're here for me," she didn't turn around as she replied.

"What?'

"To get what I want… I need you," she answered, and the unease I felt only got worse. When we came upon the last two cells, one had someone in it. My eyes roamed over the man… or I thought that might have been what he was, now he looked more like a skeleton. He didn't even see us as we walked by, his mouth and eyes were opened as if he were looking at something in horror and it was frozen like that… wait, I studied what I could make out of his sunken in face. Vengeance.

"Don't stare at him for too long, you might get sucked into whatever hell he's going through." At

Molly's words, I snapped my gaze away from him. She started moving again, I took a deep breath and followed.

I studied the long circular stairway leading down to who knew what… I didn't expect Hell to look like this… I meant, I had already been in the Underworld, but this place was the real deal… wasn't it? I expected it to be hot since Grim called it Satan Flames, yet as I followed her down the steps, it was so cold my breath created fog. As we reached the last step, the screams quietened and I scanned the room. It was completely empty. Freezing and eerie, but empty, quiet… gray and dull.

Lonely was what I felt here, to the point that it was suffocating. Molly stopped without me noticing, and I almost bumped into her tiny frame. She peered into the distance. I looked with her and it felt like we were staring forever. Then the room no longer looked the same to me. The screams started back and I heard chains all around me. I whipped my head back and forth, a bead of sweat started at my forehead. I stumbled back and bumped into something. I panicked and twisted around, I sighed when I saw that it was only a chain. But as soon as the relief left my mouth, the chain was gone and then it was there again—all around me there were chains, naked people wrapped in them screaming, then just like that, they were gone again. Every time the flash hit my eyes, it happened again and this time, I was the one wrapped in the chain hanging from a ceiling. I was breathing hard—close to hyperventilating. When I blinked, I was standing next to Molly.

I tried to get a grip on myself. I knew the room was playing with me—messing with my head. I didn't know which one was the real one.

"I see you actually managed to bring her here." A very young voice spoke. A voice I knew very well. I squinted my eyes as the footsteps approached and gasped. "You've exceeded my expectations, Molly," he told her.

"Alex?" There was no way the person standing in from of me was my brother.

He tilted his head and smiled up at me. "Yes, Sis?" It looked exactly like my brother, only I knew he wasn't. Alex never smiled in such a sadistic, over-the-top way.

I glared. "You're not my brother."

He arched an eyebrow as he approached me, and the look in his eye seemed to have a certain effect on me—over my heart like he held it in the palm of his hands with a mere stare. He passed me. "On the contrary, I am whoever I say I am." He was behind me, but I was too afraid to turn around. I didn't even want to think his name in my own head. "Melanie, dear." My eyes widened as the hand came down over my shoulder. It wasn't Alex that spoke anymore, but my mom. She turned me around to face her. "Why the look on your face? Don't you recognize your mother?"

I pulled away from her and almost lost my balance. "Stop!" I screamed. I no longer believed it was the room that was psyching me out. "I know who you are—what you are!"

He laughed with my mom's laugh—I loathed him using her voice, her face. "Who I am?" he tested me.

"The Devil," I spat the words out. "Why am I even here? What do you need me for?"

"Need you," he scoffed and slung my mom's head back. "I don't need you, I want to get rid of you before you become a bigger pain in my neck than Grim." I tilted my head at him. "Oh, that's right, you don't even know what you are—no, I mean what you will become." I had to remind myself it wasn't my mom that was looking at me so wickedly. "Right now, you're a pathetic human." He stepped closer to me. "Melanie Rose, you've caused quite the fuss in the Underworld between Grim, Fear, Vengeance—let us not forget Marcus." He snarled at the mention of Marcus. "He started craving too much for a mere incubus. I don't see what Fear saw in the demon to begin with, but you guys did me a favor when you put an end to his life. There was no way he'd ever take my throne from me, but I don't like when any demon or otherwise gets to thinking he should have more power and control than me."

"The way I see it, you guys aren't much different," the words slipped out before I could stop them.

Something dark filtered through his eyes—Mom's eyes. "That's where you're wrong, what he tried so hard to take from you, I can take just… like… that." He snapped his fingers as he said the word 'that' and I jumped.

"But, it's funny that He placed you in a human body. To keep you hidden from me? Or is it something else? But one of my entities found you so easily, and look at us now, standing together like this. Guess His plan didn't work so well after all. I can't have another one of you running around and destroying my evil. Grim's been the biggest pain, ya know, balancing out my evil so that it never gets too out of control—he's infuriatingly good at it, too. I just can't let you be, Melanie, I'd like to make the end of the world happen sooner rather than later so I can crawl out of this place I've been trapped in and reign over the human world."

"What am I then since you seem to know so much?" I asked.

"Human," he answered. "But what's inside you is very far from it." I knew that but for him to be so intent on getting me here... "You're like Grim."

"What?" I just thought I was meant to be with him, I hadn't expected me to be *like* him. I shook my head. "I'm not—"

"You are," he interrupted me. "Grim's been the only one God has ever made. Until you. You're the newer version; the upgrade."

"I'm his—"

"Light?" he finished for me. "What do you think that means? You are his equal in every way. Do you not trust what I say? Believe me, because I plan to take that part of you and hide it since I can't destroy it. You, however... won't be a problem to take care of."

There was a lump in my throat the size of a golf ball. My fingers were numb and tingly, my anxiety was getting the best of me—for good reason. The Devil stood in front of me looking like Mom and my gut told me to fight, but what could I do against him. My life was on the line and those lines were funny even inside my head because how many times had I been in danger before? Killian always reached me in time but for some reason, I didn't think that was the case now.

I was alone.

This isn't being alone... alone is what we'll know soon enough.

Why did my power whisper such an ominous thing at a time like this? I knew the voice could hear my every thought, and I knew it could hear my desperation to understand what she meant, but as always... she only spoke when she wanted and never answered.

Molly coughed and I had completely forgotten she was still here. "We made a deal and I came through, now it's your turn to hold up your end."

The Devil tilted his head at her, almost like he wasn't happy with her. "I don't like being interrupted," he told her, and there was a flicker of fear flash through her eyes before she hid it completely. "But a deal's a deal." He snapped his fingers—Mom's fingers really. I watched in amazement as Molly's body began to rapidly grow. Her dress began to rip and she clung to it. The red of her eyes faded until she was left with brown ones and she was soon taller than me. Her skin lost the pale look it had as a ghost, and I watched her face as she studied herself—a smile touched her lips. I could still see a hint of the girl she once was, so he had only made her body grow instead of giving her a different look altogether.

I couldn't hide my shock as she smiled, holding what was left of the dress against her naked flesh. She brought her hand out and frowned. "Wait… something feels different."

The Devil laughed and she looked up. "Because you're no longer a poltergeist and you no longer have any power Fear gave you." Her face paled and her eyes widened. "Oh, and I added little something special—I made you immortal."

There was a wariness to her voice. "Immortal?"

He nodded and Molly's shoulders stiffened. "Yeah." He laughed again, and it even sent a chill up my spine. "Really, what I've done to you is not much different than what I do to the souls stuck here with me. Let's not forget all the demons you've angered over the years while you were with Fear—imagine what would happen when they find out how powerless you are now. So, I wanted to help you out. I figured you would need all the immortality you could get when your past comes knocking."

"You," she sneered at him. "You tricked me. I wouldn't have made the deal if I had known I would lose what powers I had! How can I protect myself?"

He arched Mom's eyebrow up at her. "Oh, wouldn't you have, though?" He flicked a hand at her. "You can leave here with the portal chip you have, but I wonder how long you can even keep that in your possession? There valuable, especially now that Fear and

Grim went around taking them from any demon that had one."

What was even more surprising was the tears that started to form in Molly's eyes. "What did you expect making a deal with the Devil? You should thank me because no matter what anybody does to you—how much they torture, kill—who knows what other unspeakable things that might do—you will keep coming back to life." She never met my eyes once as she turned around—I couldn't let her leave with the only thing that could get me out of here.

I jumped at her, knocking her to the ground. She punched me in the gut, but my focus was on the portal chip in her left hand. I pressed my weight against her and wrestled to get it out of her hand. I knew I had to be quick, but it wasn't enough. I was yanked up by the cloak I wore.

Molly looked up at me. "Unless you want to stay here with me, I suggest you get a move on. That past is sure to catch up with you." I stopped wiggling against his hold—I stopped breathing at the sound of his voice. Molly stood and took off running without another glance in our direction.

He released his hold on the cloak and walked in front of me. Ryan. He took the face and voice of Ryan now. "What's wrong? Feeling guilty when you look at this face?"

"You must be pretty ugly if you have to use the faces of others to talk to people," I said, not letting him know how I really felt.

"Nice, pretty admirable to be strong when you're actually terrified."

"If you ask me, that's the very definition of strong. Being brave when your feelings are weak."

One last time before we part ways.

I could feel the power coming to life at my fingertips, but all I could think about were the words she said. For some reason, tears were pricking my eyes. My hand was swinging out before the scythe even materialized in my hand. But he was gone before my blade could make contact. "Impressive, even to me, that you manage to wield the power right now." I turned in the direction of his voice. He was grinning, I screamed and swung again. He caught the blade in one hand. "But you're limited as you are now, you're not fully one with the power yet, but I'll be taking it now so that never happens." His hand dug into my chest and I gasped. He touched something that recoiled from him—I sucked in air through my lungs as my head started to shake back and forth. He was pulling at something that didn't want to leave, but there was no stopping him. I realized what the power was trying to tell me now.

Goodbye.

"Please, stop," I cried, tears sliding down my cheeks.

And it seemed fitting that he took the form of Ryan—the boy that lost everything because of me—as he stole something from me. His hand came back out and I fell to my knees. In his hand was a golden silhouette of a woman. Everything about it, the shape, the size, and feel,

I realized was me. That was why she took form as me in the dreams because she and I were the same. Then everything she said to me and the words Prince Cadence had spoken in the woods came back to me: Even though she and I were the same, I wasn't supposed to be her yet. The tiny elf prince had been right all along.

I thought I might understand now how Grim and Killian had felt to be separated from one another. He took something from me that was only meant to be found. Never lost or stolen.

"Now that I have this," he lifted the golden silhouette up, "I have no reason to keep you alive."

I couldn't even feel panic; I was still trying to grasp the reality that he held a part of me in one of his hands. He flicked his wrists and my hands went straight to my neck. I started gasping for air but there was none. I met his eyes as he grinned while he slowly suffocated me.

Lights spotted my vision, I probably wouldn't last much longer. "I don't think that belongs to you," a woman spoke somewhere behind me. My air came rushing back, and all around me, I realized my vision wasn't spotted because the lights were actually people that were engulfed in a beautiful light.

The man next to her walked toward the Devil and took the silhouette from his hand. What was even stranger, the Devil let him without any resistance. Instead, he brought Ryan's face to a smile. "How hard it must be for angels to stand in my realm. How long can you all last here before you're tainted by my darkness?"

These guys were angels? They were two, three… five of them in total. They all wore white clothing that covered most of their skin. The woman that spoke first held a tiny chest in her hand and the dark-skinned male walked over toward her as she opened it up—it sucked in the golden silhouette and my stomach bottomed out as a part of me was closed inside.

The angel that held the box was regal and beautiful as she moved toward me. "Must you use the boy's face?" She looked upset.

"Why? You know I use the faces of others all the time?" He grinned at her. I watched as he changed into a different person before my very eyes. My heart stirred in my chest even though I knew it wasn't Killian. The angel looked even angrier. "What? I thought you would have liked this one more?"

"You knew we wouldn't have let you take what doesn't belong to you. You can't kill the light, nor can you use it in any way, so why did you try?" the male angel asked.

"No, I knew how important she was, but I didn't think she was so important to Him that he'd risk tainting angels to come and get her from me." He was looking at me when he smiled—it was Killian's handsome face staring at me with such cold, heartless eyes. "Besides, it'd be better for me if I could have killed her and hid the power before she became a problem for me later, right?" He shrugged his shoulders. "Can't blame the Devil for trying."

"Let's go. We still have a mess to clean up in the human world," the male angel told the others and they nodded. The female reached her hand out to me and I hesitantly took it.

"Yes, do have fun cleaning up after my demons," he chuckled, and I couldn't even look at him right now, not when he was using my lover's body and voice. "For once, I can say I had no hand in this. Even the Devil has a way he prefers to do things."

When I met the angel's eyes for the first time, I was surprised to see peace in them—even love, maybe. Something about her smile comforted me. But the longer she looked at me, the sadder her smile became. "Let's get you home, Melanie, there's much that needs to be fixed." She pulled me into her arms as her light engulfed us both.

CHAPTER TWENTY-THREE
Melanie

She took us back to my tiny town. It was a mess, but the Reapers were finishing off the last of the demons and there were angels lined up together as they closed the portal. I scanned the faces of everyone there, but I didn't see Killian. But I did see Penny the very moment she saw me as well. She looked relieved to see me as she came running. "Good, you're safe," she said as she looked to the angel next to me.

"Where's Killian?" I asked her.

Penny looked to me and then to the angel again. "He's—"

"You can't see him, Melanie," the angel said before Penny could answer me. I turned around and faced her. "Thank you for everything you've done to protect this town today, but I must speak to Melanie alone," she told Penny. Penny studied her for several seconds before looking to me. For once, I didn't want Penny to leave. For what it was worth, Penny may have been hard to deal with but she was real and Killian was right, she came through more than once as a Reaper. I must have given it away with my facial expression.

"Killian's right—"

"Penny," the angel cut her off again. "She can't see him, and I need you to let me do what I came here to do."

"What did you come here to do?" I asked, my voice coming out harsh. "Killian wouldn't just stand by when he thinks I'm still in danger. Is he looking for me right now? Where is he? Perhaps he doesn't know that you guys saved me yet?"

"Melanie," the angel's voice was full of something I didn't want to hear coming from her.

"He's back!" Penny yelled. I followed her gaze and looked for him. I didn't see him and I could always spot him anywhere.

"I don't see him," I told her. "Where?" My heart was doing a little happy dance at the prospect of being in his arms again and putting this all in the past.

"Melanie, he's right here," Penny said right before her eyes widened. She looked back in another direction. "She's right here!" she yelled to someone, and something in me broke. I couldn't see who she was yelling at. You know when you get a bad feeling about something that you want to ignore, but the truth is right in front of you? That was exactly how I was feeling in that moment.

"I didn't want it to be this way," the angel spoke right before her hand came down over my chest. It was like a huge weight had been lifted off my shoulders the moment her hand touched me, but everything changed after that. I watched as everything right in front of me started chipping away. The library where the angels stood closing the portal started fading from my vision. The

Reapers and the dead demons all around me—gone. I was losing sight of the darkness I've carried for nine years. I jerked away from her but it was too late. I watched as Penny disappeared from my vision just as she said, "Melanie?" Was that the first time she called me by my name? She faded like a mirage.

Everything was back to normal. The library, the town, I saw nothing now. I couldn't even see the other angels... except her. I glared at her. "What did you do to me? Who are you and why are you doing this to us?"

She tried to smile at me, but even to me, she didn't seem happy. "I'm Faye and I just freed you of Fear's mark."

No... I just stared at her. It couldn't have been so easy, not after everything we had been through because of Fear. I didn't believe her. I untied the cloak and let it fall to the ground. I pulled my shirt down and my eyes widened. Fear's mark was gone and so was Grim's.

"I don't understand." I shook my head, trying to fight the turmoil of emotions I was feeling right now. Anger, sadness, even disgust. "If an angel could have erased the mark so easily, then why hadn't any of you done it already. Why wait until now?" My voice was rising. I didn't know whether to thank her or curse her. "Why wait until Grim and Killian almost lost each other? Or how about the moment an innocent life was lost because of this stupid mark!"

Faye lowered her gaze and in her hands, I saw that she had a tight grip on a piece of the white dress she wore. "Because of me. I'm the reason all this has happened." I didn't even know how to respond to her words. I could only stare. "When Fear found you as a child, I saw it as an opportunity and hid it from Heaven until the day you came of age so that I could send Grim to save and protect you." She smiled us at me like it was supposed to make whatever she was saying mean something.

"Why?" I whispered. "When you could have ended it before it even began!"

Tears were in her eyes and it was only making me angrier. "Because I wanted nothing more than the two of you to meet." She took a deep breath and took control of her emotions. I watched as her face hardened to the point that it was frightening. "But now I realize my mistake. The only thing that I've managed to do was mess with fate, and lives were destroyed because of it."

"Everything will be fine, though," I told her. "You just have to save Ryan like you did me, and I need what's inside that chest, it's a part of me." I pointed to the chest in one of her hands. "And I need to find Killian." Even I could hear the hysterical sound in my voice, I was on the verge of falling apart.

"You can't find him, Melanie." My heart was racing, and I felt like I might puke.

"What do you mean?" My tone was filled with anger.

"I mean, he could be right next to you, running around frantically screaming your name, but you wouldn't know because you can no longer see him."

Tears threatened my eyes. Something about her words had me looking all around me… for the man that might so desperately be looking for me as well. "Is it because I no longer have the mark? Or my power?" I asked her, trying to hold back the disaster I was feeling.

"No, we knew that there'd be no way he'd stay away from you even with the mark taken care of. We had you both spelled so that neither of you can ever see one another. No matter how hard he looks—even if he was standing right in front of you—he can't ever see you and neither can you see him."

I took a step away from her, tightening my fists. I never felt so hurt. So angry. So lost as I did right now. "You're lying." I couldn't believe her. "There's no way you guys would do that. Angels are supposed to be good, why would they keep two people that love each other apart?" I snapped.

"I'm sorry." She might have looked genuine—I was too heartbroken to tell or care. "You weren't supposed to meet like this and the fate of everything is demanding to be set right and that means stopping the two of you from being together until you guys are meant to be together!" She tried to take my hand, but I jerked away from her. "Please, understand, I truly am sorry for what I've put you both through and Ryan, I never wanted any of this to happen. But we can't upset the balance anymore, it favors only the evil."

"How could you—it's not our fault this happened."

"I know." She sighed. "But the only ones who will suffer from my mistake will be you and him, and horrible things will continue to happen if you guys are not separated." She met my eyes, trying to make me understand her worry. "You won't be separated forever."

Silence fell between us until I finally asked, "When? When will I see him again? When will we get to be together?"

For the longest time, I was starting to think she wasn't going to answer me. "You will live an entire life, Melanie Rose, and die before you see him again."

I stopped moving. I stopped breathing. I couldn't wrap my head around the words she spoke. "You're not lying, are you?" I was staring at the ground as I spoke. I didn't even want to look at her.

"I'm not," she replied quietly.

A lifetime? I dropped to my knees—they were shaking so hard they could no longer hold my weight up.

"That was the way it was always meant to happen for you two. He would have found you the moment you passed away, and he would have known exactly who you were." There was pride in her voice like somehow knowing was supposed to make everything better. She bent down next to me and touched my shoulder. "The Devil gave you the truth, you are Grim's equal in every way, while he's the Angel of Death, you will become the Angel of Light—which is life itself—the moment your heart stops beating as a human."

I threw my head back and the awfullest sound came out of my throat. It pierced through the empty night. The angel had just ripped my heart open and now she wished to comfort me.

"Do you wish to know more of what you are?" she went on even though I was crying. "You will be able to do things Grim cannot in the future. He's bound by the rules of which God created him of life and death—you, on the other hand, were born from life. You'll have no boundaries or rules. Lives will be saved; evil will fear to cross your path. Demons that deserve better will be able to cross into an afterlife they deserve through you."

I stopped crying, her words brought me back to my conversation with Killian and Grim and how demons couldn't go to Heaven even if they were deserving of doing so. Was this why I was born with the power? "It is," she told me. Did she just read my mind? "I did," she admitted. "But that's not the only reason, I think you know by now how lonely it must be to live as the Grim Reaper. The power was placed inside your mother's womb when we saw that your fate tied into Grim's."

Her hand left my shoulder and moved to my forehead. I watched as the ground shifted below me and when I lifted my head, I was standing on my porch.

The devastation of it all came rushing back. I stood quickly, and she followed. "It was very long time for him to wait for you and although I knew it was wrong of me, the moment I saw the opportunity for you to meet each other, I took it. As an angel, what I've done is unforgivable, but I must make sure I keep you safe. You're too precious to us all and keeping you apart is the only way to do so." She took a step forward, her beautiful face scrunched up with grief. "If you want, I can make it so that you no longer remember. You'll be able to have normal life—"

I couldn't believe the words that left her mouth. I backed away from her. "Don't you dare," I hissed at her. "You've done enough already."

She sighed. "It's going to be a long wait, are you sure you want to remember?" Her words were only making it worse.

"Can we see each other just one more time?" I couldn't swallow down the lump in my throat.

"Do you honestly think he'd let you go if he were to see you again? For you, living to a hundred is nothing compared to the centuries he will have to endure without you." That was right, time was different between our worlds… awful thoughts filtered my mind. How could a month and a half of knowing someone be enough to last several lifetimes without that person? Who could possibly wait that long for one person? The thoughts left as quickly as they came.

Grim would wait for me. He's always been waiting for me and would continue to do so. I was going to be with him again. No stupid amount of time would change how we felt. And even if our time together was short, it was real and I learned more about myself than ever before.

"The spell can't be reversed, there's no way you two can see each other until your death," she said. "And there's no escaping your fate to live out a long life so don't try to cut your life short. We'll always prevent any attempts."

I took a deep breath and gave her a steely expression. "Who knew angels were actually the cruel ones." She didn't let herself react to my words.

"I never expected either of you to forgive me and I never came seeking it, I came to right the wrong I caused."

"Does he know yet?" I asked.

Faye nodded. "I'm sure Gabrielle has spoken to him already, and I will meet him after I part ways with you."

"If I ask you to let him know that this changes nothing, that I'll see him again," I had to look away as I spoke, "and that I loved him, would you even let him know?"

"I would." She nodded. "No one will remember the events that happened this night. No one will even remember you were missing for two weeks." My eyes widened. "There will be no trace of any of it. No one will know except you. I'll ask again, are you sure you want to remember?"

"You know my every thought, so why do you even ask?" She was silent. "Ryan," I started.

"There's nothing that can be done."

"What—" A light came on in the house, I must have woken Mom up.

"Ryan has a completely new fate—his old one was cut off the moment Grim met you."

"What does that mean?" I gave her a dark look.

She ran her hands down her dress and looked unsure as to whether she wanted to answer or not. "Not that it makes a difference now but Ryan had been your fate during your human life, he was to be your husband." I didn't even know how to respond to her words. "You had two different lives to live, one had been with Ryan as a human, and the other was with Grim the moment he found you in death."

Ryan… *I'm so sorry.* But even so, it didn't change my heart. I didn't have to trust fate, but I would trust what my heart felt and it would always lead me to Killian.

"Is he…" I couldn't even say it.

"He's Fear now." I knew that. I just hadn't wanted to hear anyone call him that. Why did I even ask? How did everything get so far from how I imagined this night to end? "He willingly accepted that fate, you saw it yourself. He must find his own way now. Don't doubt what he can be—even as an angel, none of us know. We can't see into the Underworld like we do here on Earth. But, trust in the boy that always trusted in you."

"When—"

"Melanie?" The front door opened and Mom stuck her head out of the window. "What are earth are you doing out here?" she asked, part worry, part lecture in her voice. The angel, Faye, was already gone by the time I looked back to where she stood.

I followed Mom inside and kept looking at her back, expecting her to turn around and yell at me and ask where I've been the past two weeks. "Mom, aren't you going to ask where I've been all this time?"

She turned around holding her neck. "You went to the Halloween dance at school with Tess, didn't you?" They altered her memories? She let out a groan. "I have such an awful cramp in my neck. Alex and I must have fallen asleep watching a movie or something." She paused. "Why didn't I take him trick-or-treating this year?" she wondered to herself.

And it crushed something inside me. It hurt. She truly didn't remember anything. No one knew. I had no one to talk to about what I've been through. Why did I expect things to get better when Fear was no longer in my life? Now my best friend was that very monster, and my boyfriend was lost to me for a very long time. Tess wouldn't remember anything from tonight.

I lost everything and became alone in my own world all over again.

Mom looked back at me, something she saw in me had her eyes creasing with worry. I took a step forward and staggered, my shoulder smacked into the wall. "Melanie." Mom came rushing toward me and her concern broke what was left that held me from falling apart. I sucked in a breath. I couldn't breathe, I *can't* breathe. A gurgling sound came from my throat and my heart hurt so much. I punched my chest over and over trying to regain oxygen into my lungs as I slid down the wall and crumbled to the floor.

"Melanie." Mom was panicking as she bent down next to me.

No matter what I did—how hard I tried, the pain only intensified. I couldn't be cured of what I felt. My heart was broken—torn apart.

I had been ripped apart from Killian in the worst way. I pressed my face into my palms as I continued to cry. Mom gently touched my back trying to soothe me. I kept wishing—praying this was a bad dream, but deep down, I knew that angel hadn't been lying when she said I couldn't see him again.

"Melanie, talk to me. What happened? What's wrong?"

"I can't see him, Mom." Tears, snot, and drool covered my face and palms when I looked up to meet her eyes. "Not for a very long time."

CHAPTER TWENTY-FOUR
Killian

I didn't want to believe the angel's words when he told me they planned to keep Melanie away from me—how could they? As Grim Reaper, I did everything in my power to do what I must as a balancer.

I've been alone, but I accepted it—I took it as my fate until Melanie came along and the thirst for a connection with someone came flooding back. Until I knew she was to be with me and they even admitted that she was born to cross paths with me. Then… they went and hid her from me. Supposedly, our time together wasn't meant to be until the day Melanie died.

I was pissed. I didn't—no, I couldn't control my anger. I attacked every angel in my sight while they were trying to close the portal. They had to bind me with their light and placed me on my knees where they stood and told me the same words I screamed for them not to say over again.

They left me there. I yelled her name over and over, expecting her to magically pop up somewhere with a smile on her face. But she never did.

I opened the portal to Heaven—the very one I ascended people into their afterlife through and tried to go through it. It sent me flying backward every time I tried. I knew how I was starting to look in front of my Reapers as they stood by silently as I screamed and caused a ruckus. My walls were caving in. I had to see the angels again. I had to make them understand I couldn't live without her.

I'd get on my knees and beg if I had to.

I never felt so powerless—I never had a reason to. But that was all I could feel coursing through my veins as I faded into her bedroom. She wasn't there. No, she might be lying on her bed crying right now, but I wouldn't know because they planned to keep her from me in every way. My anger was bitter, a disease crawling up my throat, threatening to spill out.

I could do nothing—nothing. The angels never messed around. I sensed it the moment Molly ported next to Melanie, something was changing. I couldn't reach her in time. Maybe if I hadn't been so thrown off by the change that was taking place, I could have faded to her. There was no way I could have kept her hidden from the angels, but we could have had a few more minutes…

I heard Tina's, Melanie's mom, frantic voice and faded into the hallway downstairs. She was on her knees on the floor, cradling someone I couldn't see in her arms. "Shh, it's okay. It's okay," she chanted over and over. I knew Melanie was right there in her arms. So close, yet… agony ripped my chest right open. In my despair, I understood I wasn't the only one suffering from one angel's mistake.

I bent down next to her mom—her mom couldn't see me because I kept it that way. My hand moved to where I knew she was but as soon as I tried, I was thrown out of the house by the spell. My resolve was crumbling and I stood back up and walked back in the house. I fell to my knees beside her. I couldn't comfort her now; I couldn't tell her I'd wait an eternity to be with her again. I couldn't tell her how much I already wanted that eternity to be over because I didn't think I would make it through the first night. The only thing I could do was wait for the day she was in my arms again.

I didn't even know I was capable of crying until the tears slid down my cheeks, and I found myself screaming out my frustration.

I must be alone one last time so that she'd be mine.

I sensed an angel outside the house and stood. I looked to where Melanie was and wiped my face before walking outside. It was the angel that came to me a long time ago to tell me of Melanie. She had a small brown chest in her hand with gold patterns wrapped around it.

She saw my expression and dared to look sad. "This is a small price to pay to keep her forever… you know that," she told me.

"That time had already started for us."

"Yes, but it wasn't the right time." Time, fate, destiny, I grew tired of the words the angels used to pin everything on. "With her powers being awakened after meeting you, she was nothing but a target. Not just because of the power, but because she was someone you loved. How many demons would have gone after her because of you? You wouldn't have always reached her in time."

"I could protect her." I would have done anything to keep her safe and by my side.

"No, you couldn't have, fate would have ruined you both if the path continued off course." The angel's eyes flickered with a warning. "If we had not arrived when we did, the Devil would have killed her." Her words cut me like a knife because I knew she was telling the truth. I couldn't find her no matter how much I tried—it was like I was being blocked from doing so. The Devil prevented me from sensing her, and he would have succeeded in killing her if it weren't for them.

"Here, this will stay with you." I held out my hand as she placed the chest into it. "Melanie couldn't keep this part of herself after she awakened that part of herself too soon. Your—her light would have been a beacon for more danger. She's too vulnerable as a human. So, you keep it for her and return it to her when it's time."

I held a part of Melanie in my arms—the thought sent another wave of emotion through me. I tightened my jaws to keep from revealing any emotion in front of her.

"When you two are together again, you'll see that this price was small when it meant she was safe and in your arms for eons to come."

Protecting Melanie's soul from Fear was no longer our greatest obstacle.

It was time itself.

CHAPTER TWENTY-FIVE
Melanie

I would have probably slept the day away if Mom hadn't forced me out of bed. The kind and gentle parent who had soothed me the night before was long gone. I was not motivated to go to school or do anything, but the scowl on her face told me I would be. I raised up slowly and peeled my hair from my face that clung to the dried tears.

"I knew this would happen," she began, "I knew he would hurt you. I could tell he was trouble coming from a mile away. What did he do? Did he make stupid promises before he ditched town and left you? Something just wasn't normal about him…"

I gave her a crazy look. Where did she get these crazy assumptions? No wonder my own mind took so many different directions—I inherited it from her. "Mom, just go so I can get ready for school," I told her. It wouldn't matter how hard I tried to defend Killian. She'd only see it through her eyes. He would never get to defend himself either. The damage was done. I shouldn't have let the words spill from my lips when I said that I'd never see him again. It gave her the impression that he was a bad guy.

She dragged out her sigh as she looked at me. "Are you okay now?" she asked.

"I will be when you give me some space. Yelling at me before I'm even up hardly seems like a way to make me feel better." She nodded before stepping out of the room. Once she closed my door, I bunched my knees up and placed my chin on them. I wasn't okay, but I had to be.

Tess was full of life at school that day and at least that gave me something to smile about, but I hated that she remembered nothing. I had been relieved last night when she had finally seen what I've been going through. I had happily thought there would be no more secrets to keep from her, but now my secret would be mine to keep until death.

We walked side by side to fourth period when she randomly said, "I had a strange dream last night."

I stopped and turned to her, something like hope crisscrossed into my heart. "About what?"

"Ryan was in it with us," she started and my hope only grew. Was it possible she could remember what happened subconsciously? "It was crazy. We were right slap-dab in the middle of town and all these monsters were attacking." My eyes widened as she shrugged her shoulders. "And we died." My hope died about the same time my shoulders dropped. Her subconscious was feeding her something, but it wasn't actual truth. "A dragon bit my head off right before I saw what happened to you."

I nodded then smiled. "That was a crazy dream."

She shook her head and muttered, "Tell me about it."

It was funny how I used to think seeing the dead was the absolute worst fate to have. Now as I walked the halls of Campbell High and discovered the absence of not being able to see the things I once could, I realized how wrong I was. It was worse to know they were there and being unable to see them anymore.

After school, I stopped and filled my car up and spotted a bunch of colored notebooks on the counter as I was paying. It gave me an idea. I bought one—blue because it reminded me of Grim—and took it home.

I sat on my bed that night studying the necklace Killian had given me. The only thing the angels hadn't taken from us—the only connection I had left with him. It warmed my chest to know that he was also wearing his around his neck. I let it fall back onto my skin as I picked up my pen and opened the notebook.

Starting this day, until the very last day, I'd write to him what I couldn't say. Even though he wouldn't get them now, he would someday, but it wasn't only for that reason. I needed to get the words out, I needed to find peace in this storm.

CHAPTER TWENTY-SIX
Killian

My hands rested on the desk from where I sat and slid my fingers across the chest that held a part of Melanie inside. I hated that she had to live without it. I knew how it felt to be ripped apart. I felt my anger rising just thinking about it.

I ran my hands through my hair and took a deep breath. I didn't know what I was supposed to do... she was safe and that meant everything to me, but I still wanted her by my side.

My necklace warmed and I lifted my head from my palms. An idea came to me and I hurried to get the necklace off my neck. Our necklaces were connected. What if... my skin was feverish as I sent some of my power through the necklace. It opened a view for me in the center of the necklace. I recognized Melanie's room right away.

My face was hot, even my palms were clammy. I caught myself looking over my shoulder. Bloody hell, I was nervous as hell at the idea of one of the angels coming in and taking the only thing I had left to feel connected to her. I turned my attention back to the view the necklace was giving me. It wasn't Melanie—there was no way I could see her, but it didn't take me long to figure out what the necklace was showing me. It was showing me what her necklace saw, what she was doing. I could tell she was on her bed, probably sitting Indian style. I smiled at the idea of her sitting there. A notebook was open and the pencil was moving—she was moving it, but all I saw was it moving on its own.

I read the words she was writing:

Killian: My Grim Reaper,

I'm calling you "mine" because I feel like that's what you are. If fate led me to be yours then that must make you mine. (listen to how possessive I sound)

I don't want to believe that any of this is happening. One minute, I'm in your arms losing myself to you then the next, we killed Marcus... and Ryan became Fear. I don't want to accept what Fear chose to do to Ryan. How could he? Ryan's strong, though, right? He'll still be the boy I knew, won't he?

A lifetime without you. I won't see you again until death? How do I live a normal life now that I can't see ghosts anymore? What is normal? I've not been normal for a very long time. I don't wish to be normal anymore. The only thing I want is you. We are the only thing that makes sense in my life and now I don't even have you.

I know you won't see this letter, at least not for a very long time, but it's something I must do, even if it's only a piece of paper, these words are for you. I'll keep writing you so I can learn to live without you.

The scariest part of the wait is the thought of you not waiting. I believe in you: us, but this first day has been dark and I'm afraid of future doubts.

I guess this is enough for the first night, surprisingly, I feel better.

Oh, and my mom might sort of… okay, be entirely convinced that you hurt me. Sorry, it's my fault. I cried, a lot and she mistook the reason.

Love, Melanie

And Melanie had just given me the way I'd survive the centuries to come without her.

Killian,

I went to your house today, only it's not yours anymore… A "For Sale" sign was hung up in the window and there was also one on your Corvette. Honestly, I wish I hadn't gone, but I'm drawn to everything that will lead me to you. I guess I was still holding onto the hope that there was a loophole, but there isn't…

Because you would have already come to me if there was.

I'm overwhelmed today as well, maybe it will always feel like this. In time, will I breathe easier?

Love, Melanie

I opened a blank diary up and started writing words that would never reach her after her second letter the next day.

~~Love,~~

Melanie: My Light; My Love,

You are so many things to me. From the moment I met you, I was terrified of breathing the same air you breathe, yet I also wanted your acceptance and I wanted your blue eyes pointed in my direction. You have no idea how much you consume me.

I haven't messed with the house, which means the angels took it out of my hands regardless of what I decided. Not that it matters, I can't see you and you don't need to be protected anymore. If there's one thing good that came out of this mess, it's that I know you're safe. You're free of the mark and you no longer have to worry about demons or ghosts. I'll keep the part of you that you lost with me until you can return to me whole.

I feel bad that I can peek through your necklace and see everything you're doing, yet you see nothing of me, but not bad enough for me to ever stop.

Our time isn't now, Melanie, but that doesn't mean that I don't want it to be. The angels may be slightly sadistic despite their halo. Who cloaks two lovers from each other? I hate the fact that I can walk the same street as you and every single person can see me, but you.

I'll come for you, just wait. Wait, even though we shouldn't have to.

MICHELLE GROSS

'til death,

Killian, Your Grim Reaper.

CHAPTER TWENTY-SEVEN

Killian,

I graduated today. I can't believe it's been seven months since I last saw you—seven months of letters that I've written you. I'm left with a complete notebook and a new diary that gets fuller every day.

My mood is ugly today. While everyone is celebrating with their friends and families, I'm huddled up on a toilet hiding from mine. There's been a distance between Mom and me that I can't break. She thinks my pining over you is pointless and wants me to move on, and I can't make her understand.

So, I'm hiding from her and the stuffy looks she keeps giving me and the pictures she wants to take like the other families in the hall.

I miss you.

Truthfully, I'm scared. I don't know what I'm supposed to do with my life. I'll go to a community college and then what? I don't know. I'm lost. I never let myself think of a future while I saw ghosts, which now seemed rather stupid and pathetic… I just ignored it. I guess it's easy to say I still haven't figured out how to be normal.

Ryan… they reserved a spot for him at graduation today. The seat he would have sat in today was left empty. It was out of respect for him, but it tore my heart right back open. I think about him and where he might be and what he's doing. I'm afraid for him.

I should have asked you at what age was I meant to die, but something tells me you wouldn't have told me anyway.

Sky's been on my mind lately, too. I didn't get to say goodbye to her, either.

Love, Melanie

Melanie,

I used to think your time was short, but now it feels like too many when that time is what's keeping us apart. What's been months for you has already been years here, but I keep myself busy in the human world as much as I can to shorten the time for me. It helps that I always have death to deal with, but here lately, I'm in the Underworld more than I want to be. Demons have been an issue lately and I've been descending more than ever before.

I've been looking for Ryan, but when I get close, he disappears. I get the feeling that he doesn't want to be found, but I also have that sense that he will come on his own soon. I know you'd ask me how I knew and that's why the word "vain" pops up in my head more than I care to admit. I have you to thank for that.

As for what you're going through, I know you'll do fine. You will find your own way. I want to tell you to be strong, but sometimes I don't know even know how. When it gets to be too much, I just remember that I'll have you in my arms again. I keep reminding myself that this is a small price to pay to have you to myself for eternities to come.

Killian

CHAPTER TWENTY-EIGHT
Melanie

"You," I pointed to Tess, "Tessa Jones, the girl who is terrified of needles, want to become a nurse?" I asked for the billionth time as we sat on soft, comfy sofas and filled out applications for the fall at a community college.

She lifted her gaze from the paper and sighed. "That's completely different. I will be the one with the needle."

I snorted. "I still can't imagine it." I shook my head and thought about it again. "I still can't. Why can't I?" I laughed.

She huffed and glared at me. "At least I have an idea. You have no clue."

She had me there. "Sor-ry," I sang the word out nice and slow for a full effect and she smiled.

Something caught Tess's eye. "That dude is totally checking one of us out." She started waving at someone and I froze, not wanting to turn around. She added a whistling sound, and I shushed her quickly. "What? He's hot."

I groaned. "Go talk to him, just don't try any funny business that involves me," I said, squinting my eyes together. She batted her eyes innocently. She was trying too hard to hook me up with someone lately. I stood and walked to the counter, placing my application next to the computer while the administrator spoke to the guy Tess had been whistling at. Tess followed right behind me and the moment we were out the door, she started, "Come on, Melanie. When are you going to get over Killian? He was hot, I'll admit, but he's gone and he's not coming back. The asshole left you. You have to move on."

I turned around and she almost collided into me we were walking so fast. "I don't want to date, Tess. I like myself just fine the way I am." I brought my index finger to my mouth and tilted my head before looking at her again. "Wait, maybe I'll date myself."

She rolled her eyes at me and we continued walking. She was quiet for a while in the car while I drove her home. "Really, though." I sighed, and she went on, "You can't see them anymore. You've finally gotten what you've always wanted, to be normal, and now you don't even want to accept it." I knew I would regret telling her I couldn't see ghosts anymore. "It's almost like you hate that you can't anymore." Her words were close to the truth. Only, it wasn't the ghosts I missed, it was the one they hid from me when he came around.

"It's a lot worse to know they're there and you can't see them. Every time I get a cold chill I think I'm walking through a ghost."

Tess threw her hands in the air. "Now you can imagine how I've felt all these years. You're always saying there's a ghost around and me not seeing anything. I swear, I thought I was going to break out into hives every time." She grabbed her arms and started rubbing them. I couldn't help but smile. "But seriously, what are we going to do with the rest of our lives?"

Wait to die.

"I have no clue."

Killian,

Mom got Alex a puppy for his eighth birthday. A solid white Siberian with blue eyes, and now all I can think about is Sky. I wonder how she's doing and if she finally gave into Rixen?

I really miss you. I miss your home, your world, the colors and sky. What I wouldn't give to be on Sky's back and be there right now... What I wouldn't give to be in your arms.

This fate and destiny thing between us, I've been thinking a lot about it. When we were destined like this to fall in love, it made me question whether we would have fallen for one another without it, but then again, is every relationship, good or bad, decided by fate the same as ours?

We met before we were supposed to, so we kind of made our own fate, right? I can't imagine my feelings being anything but what I decide... I guess what I'm saying is, I don't love you because I'm supposed to, I love you because I want to.

Love, Melanie

Melanie,

Waiting for you—missing you—is hard, but the thought of not knowing you is much worse. It's unbearable to think that I might not have known you already. You're not with me now, but the fact that we're together doesn't change.

You don't know that I'm writing to you every time you write me. I've even tried getting my letters to you. I've placed them in your room before, but the angels have them sent right back to me.

Don't worry, I haven't given up on the idea. I'll find a way to let you know you're not alone—I'm right here, waiting with you, for you.

Sky misses you a lot, but she's a leader now like Rixen. Yes, she finally took her place by his side and you know exactly what that means, Love, the dragons that once made her an outcast, treat her like a queen.

Killian

Killian,

Something life changing happened to me today, well not entirely, but I think I discovered what career I want to do.

I went to the grocery store for Mom today and on the way home, I witnessed a wreck right in front of me. Scared the life out of me! I'd forgotten what it felt like, my heart hadn't pounded against my ribcage in almost a year... I kind of missed the rush of the adrenaline pulsing through my veins.

I pulled off the side of the two-lane road and quickly got out to check on the vehicles. One of the vehicles was an Explorer and I could see the man checking on his family inside. I dialed 9-1-1 as I walked to the other vehicle—small S10 truck. The driver was a woman and she was crying. The first thing I did was asked if she was okay. She was alert and talking to me as she held her stomach. It was easy for me to tell her nose was broken, but I didn't know what else might be wrong.

She was crying, and I couldn't help her. The family in the Explorer were all okay, except for the mom being a little bruised up. The ambulance arrived and I stood there and watched as they took over, reassuring the family and calming the hurt woman as they placed her on a stretcher. Even when they told me to leave, I stayed and even after the police and ambulance left, I was still standing there.

The adrenaline was gone, but the feeling it created in me was there to stay. I had a life moment, Killian. I was standing there on that creepy road and letting the food ruin in the car, but all I could think was, "That's what I want to do. I want to be that person who helped someone, maybe even save a life."

I didn't feel like Melanie; I didn't feel like the girl who feared ghosts all her life. I felt a craving for life and maybe, this was me—the real me, the one that Fear took from me so long ago.

Even as I'm writing this letter hours after it happened, it's all I can think about. I'm excited for something. This feeling... I wish I could tell you in person.

It doesn't matter, though. I'm making the first step in trying to live a life without you, and I know you'd approve.

Love, Melanie

Melanie,

That doesn't surprise me at all. You probably haven't realized it yet, but those feelings probably come naturally for the Angel of Light. It doesn't matter that you don't have that part of yourself right now, you are one and the same.

I find it amazing that you're just like me, only so much more. You were born, unlike me who was created from demon bones. We both possess healing powers, yet yours far surpasses mine... and the way you pulled Marcus out of Fear, unbelievable.

I'm going to have to improve somehow before we meet again. I'd hate to get shown up by you when your powers at full capacity. I can already hear my Reapers laughing now...

I'm lying, I can't wait for you to put me in place because we both know what I plan to do to you once I get my hands on you.

Bloody hell, now I can't stop thinking about it.

Killian

CHAPTER TWENTY-NINE
Killian

I had only just returned to the castle from descending demons when Ryan fell to his knees in front of me. He gripped the portal chip in his hand he must have used to get himself here as he balled himself up. I bent down to him and yelled for Lincoln.

Physically, nothing looked wrong with the boy, but becoming something as wicked as the Devil himself wasn't something any normal human should have been able to handle. But here he was—in bad shape, though—defying all odds that a human ghost shouldn't have survived the merge.

It had been years in the Underworld already since it happened—that was enough time for someone to change. Or no longer be himself at all.

"Ryan?" I said his name, to see if he had control or Fear. Or if he even still existed beneath the surface. "Are you okay?" I asked.

His eyes lifted to meet mine, his tremors stopped only just enough for him to get some words out. "Please, help me. I can hear him. I can't—"

His words gave me everything I needed to know.

CHAPTER THIRTY
Killian

Killian,

I did it, I passed my state exam! I'm a certified paramedic. All that's left for me to do is find a job, but lucky me, a spot opened the very same day I viewed my score. I'm starting to think it's not luck but fate. I think I'm right where I'm supposed to be in this life and it makes me happy.

The only thing I'm missing is you.

It's beautiful out today. I'm writing this letter sitting on a bench by the lake at Barley Drive… I used to come here a lot with my dad when I was little and we would sit here for hours and fish… you know, before ghosts took over my life. Ducks are currently swarming at my feet, I wish I had something to feed them, but I came empty-handed.

It's been over three years… I want to see your handsome face and I really want to kiss you and

I sat underneath a tree at Barley Drive, the very place Melanie was right now. There was an empty bench several feet in front of me, and I was positive that was where she was sitting. The view from her necklace matched the view from that spot… the ducks she wrote about in her letter, I could see them.

She was still writing the letter now and I waited patiently to devour the words she gave me. It was a risk being here, but I was desperate.

I saw a boy fishing with his father and when he began to wander up the hill by himself, an idea came to me. A polaroid camera materialized in my hand and I hollered at him, "Hey, kid." His head snapped around to look at me. I waved him over and he came too easily—I was going to have to warn him about the danger of strangers after he helped me.

He stopped once he stood by my legs. "Is there a pretty blonde sitting on that bench?" I asked, pointing.

He turned his head toward the bench then back to me. His eyebrows were pinched together as if he were confused as to why I ask such an odd question before nodding. "Yeah."

"Can you do me a favor?"

At least he knew to be somewhat wary of strangers because now he was looking at me uncertainly. "What kind of favor?"

"Can you take a quick picture of her without her noticing? I'll get you to take one of me in return to give to her." Now he was looking at me like I was some sort of serial killer. He was too young to hide his accusing stare. "I'm her boyfriend," I added. "I'm trying to do something sweet."

He looked at her sitting on the bench again. "Really?" he asked, still unsure, but I could already tell the idea intrigued him. He would agree just for the idea—

the boy was young and the shine in his eyes told me he was a romantic and would probably make someone happy one day. He would live a long life, that I knew.

I nodded when he looked back at me. "Okay," he agreed, and I handed him the camera. He did a great job at making it look like he was taking a picture of the ducks instead of her. I couldn't help but grin as the picture fell into his hand from the camera. He ran back to me waving it around so that it would develop faster. By the time the picture was in my hand, my heart was pounding. I waited for the picture to fade from black and my heart leaped onto the picture when I saw her. I hadn't expected it to work.

Three years. Almost three hundred in the Underworld. I took a deep breath and fell in love all over again.

She was leaning over a bit, her legs stretched out on the ground with a pen in her mouth and her diary in her lap. She looked deep in thought. She wasn't smiling in the picture, but she was beautiful.

"She's very pretty," the boy told me, and I smiled. "Now, I'll take yours." He took it the same time he spoke, which was probably for the best because I tensed at the thought of trying to pose in front of a camera.

"Here ya go." He handed it to me.

When he started to walk away, I stopped him. "One more thing, Josh."

His eyes widened. "I don't remember telling you my name." I probably shouldn't have said his name.

"I heard your dad say your name," I lied. "Can you give her my picture and a letter?" I asked.

"Sure, where's the letter?" he asked.

I smiled. "Hold on, I'm about to write it."

———————

The moment the boy ran to deliver the letter and picture to Melanie, an angel appeared by my side. I expected one of them to show. I sighed and stood, dusting the dirt from my pants. He shook his head, eyes full of disapproval.

"You risk demons finding her every time you are near her. It doesn't matter that she's completely human right now. They'd have all the motivation they need to harm her if they knew what she's to become and what she means to you. We've not only hidden her from you but the Devil as well."

"She belongs with me. I'd never risk her life, I just want—" *to see her. Hold her. Be with her.*

"It's not just you she's important to," he replied. If he expected a different reaction from me, he wasn't going to get one. It was their fault I met Melanie this soon. He must have been reading my thoughts when he shook his head. "Do you want to be banned from this world?"

I arched an eyebrow and almost snorted. "You can't ban me from the human world, I wouldn't be able to do my job otherwise."

The angel crossed his arms. "Have you forgotten about all the Reapers you've made over the centuries?" Something felt heavy in my chest and my stomach churned. They couldn't—there was no way I'd survive without this world, the world she was in. But I wasn't willing to take the chance either.

"I'm leaving," the words felt bitter and hard to swallow as I said them. I took one last look at the bench and tried to smile, but couldn't. At least my words got to her one last time in this lifetime.

CHAPTER THIRTY-ONE
Melanie

"Here ya go." I looked up from my diary and saw a cute little boy standing in front of me. He held something in his hands. He smiled bashfully and brought his hands out to me. "This is for you." It was an envelope. He kept urging me to take it. I smiled. Did he have a little crush on me?

"What is it?" I asked, taking it from his hands.

"It's from your boyfriend." The boy took off running with a giant grin. My smile vanished as the feeling of hope set in. Could it be…

I tore into the envelope, a letter and a photo fell onto my diary. Killian. The picture was of Killian. My cheeks were hot and the butterflies were coming on strong in my stomach. He sat underneath a tree—wait, I recognized that tree. I turned around, but of course, he wasn't there.

Tears filled my eyes. I sat there for the longest time just looking at his photo until I finally gathered enough nerve to read his letter.

Melanie,

I miss you.

I miss you.

I miss you.

There will never be enough in words to tell you how much I miss you, but I want you to know that my heart is where you are, my body is right here waiting, and my soul is crying to be with you.

I hope that you get this letter before an angel takes it or erases it before you get the chance to see it. I want you to know that I read your letters every day through your necklace. I can't see you, but your words are everything to me. Sorry it took so long for me to find a way to get my words to you at least once until I see you again.

Live life doing what makes you happy because I want you happy and know that I'll be right there to take you back when this life is over for you.

Ryan is staying with me. He's been through a lot, but he finally came. He's still Ryan, but there's more to him now. He had to make changes to survive and live as Fear. I'll help him, I don't want you to worry. I just want you to accept the fact that he's Fear for when you finally meet him again. Not just for your sake but his as well.

You're in my thoughts and dreams every night until I have you in my arms again. By my side is exactly where you belong.

I love you.

Killian, Grim

How could a letter make me feel so much? I wiped my eyes and smiled.

CHAPTER THIRTY-TWO

Killian,

I've never given much thought to my powers until now and don't laugh or even crack a grin while you read this, or so help me… but I'm exhausted since I started working. I knew this job was physically demanding, but I guess I hadn't realized just how much. I'm out of shape…

I didn't think we'd have so many late-night emergency calls in our community, but I was wrong. My first night we got a 9-1-1 call of a man having a heart attack and when we got there, he was a big guy and I only ended up embarrassing myself because I could hardly help Landon—my co-worker with the lifting. He told me I'd get the hang of it, but I'm sure he only said that because I almost burst into tears when I practically dropped our patient.

I was mortified. This job involves lives, and I didn't want to make mistakes. I wanted to help people, not make things worse. I already told you before I almost quit that day, but I didn't. No more living in fear. And since then, I've seen multiple overdoses, two wrecks, and other house calls all within a week.

It would be great to have the strength I had from my power, but I don't, so I bought a membership at the gym. I'm going use my free time to get in shape so that lifting is easier for me. This job isn't what I was expecting, it's a lot more, a lot harder, but I enjoy it.

I hope one day helping people with this job comes as naturally as using my powers had.

Love, Melanie

Melanie,

You're doing great, I'm sure. You'll get the hang of it.

As for Ryan, he's battling his own problems, but he's okay. He's finding ways to keep Fear satisfied. He gets these spells where he needs violence, destruction. He needs to physically do harm. If he doesn't, he risks Fear coming to the surface and doing much worse. He pretends he's okay when he's completely himself, but I see him when he's teetering off the edge and Fear's madness consumes him. He hates himself.

But, he lets it all out often with me—we spend a lot of time fighting the hell out of each other. Sometimes, it's not enough so I started collecting the demons that I'm supposed to kill and delivering them to him so he can be the one to end them. It doesn't matter who kills them, as long as I send their souls to Satan's flames afterward.

Penny has been hanging out with him a lot. I think it helps that that she's not disgusted by him, in fact, I think she cares a lot for him. She won't admit it, but I think she's been secretly going to check on you every now and then. I'd have never thought I'd see her develop feelings for two humans, well, one former one.

Sky doesn't judge Ryan when he's in a bad state, instead, she's there to comfort him when it's over. I think she does what she thinks you would do if you were here.

One day, I hope he can calm the burden he carries. He has a home here now. I won't let him fade away or give up. He's important to you and that makes him important to me.

Killian

———

Killian,

I can't believe I finally moved into my apartment today. In a way, I feel bad that I left Alex and Mom alone, but I couldn't survive another second there, after she brought her co-worker's son home trying to set us up. Our relationship was already rocky but now it's worse.

Alex stays a few nights at our aunt's out of the week since Mom and me both work night shifts. My apartment has two bedrooms so I already promised him that room for when he stays here. He better know how much I love him, I really wanted a room for my bookshelves. It won't be long until he's twelve. How does time manage to feel both fast and slow to me?

I'm never going to be with anyone or start a family like my mom someday wants me to have. As a daughter, I know I scare her. She doesn't want me alone, but I wish she'd just take a good, hard look at me and see how fine I truly am.

I'm happy.

But it's even awkward running into her at the hospital when we bring a patient to the ER. Tess somehow manages to find me every time I'm there—yes, she makes a great nurse and yes, I'm still surprised at how much my best friend's grown over the last four years. Ryan would be proud.

Love, Melanie

Melanie,

Your relationship with your mom is my fault. I swear I'll make it up to you, but I hope you can make amends with her before then.

———

Killian,

Tess met a foreign doctor at the hospital. I don't see her much now that she switched to day shift, but I reckon the two of them are dating now. I think he's Asian—Chinese, maybe. She's totally swooning for this guy, so that means I'll probably be meeting him soon.

———

Killian,

I turned twenty-five today, but you probably remembered. You better have! I spent most of the day sleeping until Alex and his friend came barging into my apartment. The brat wouldn't let me go back to sleep. I made sure to call and yell at Mom for dropping them off, but she only laughed and wished me a happy birthday.

Alex is fourteen now and the little dweeb is already taller than me. His height totally came out of nowhere this year! I think his friend might have a crush on me, though. He's always blushing when I talk to him.

Poor kid—I'm shaking my head and sighing as I write. Nobody knows I have a boyfriend.

I ended up taking them to the movies even though it was my birthday. I mean, does my family have no shame? I need love too… but I suppose my love's in another world missing me, too? See what I did there? I'm totally flirting with you since you're the only lucky one that gets to read my letters.

———

Tess is pregnant. Okay, first I should probably tell you that she's getting married, but a BABY! I can't imagine her as a mother….

———

I want to steal Rylan. I'm holding him in my arms as I write. He's so beautiful, fat, and lovable. Babies smell good. They were going to name him, Rylan, regardless if he was a boy or girl, but I'm glad they named the baby after Ryan. I know he would have spoiled him if he were here, so that's exactly what I'm going to do.

Of course, Tess proves me wrong. She's a great mommy already.

———

It must be all the diapers I'm around lately, but baby-fever has hit me hard. Killian… will we get to have kids of our own one day, and would you want to?

———

Melanie,

We'll repopulate the whole damn Underworld if you want. Bloody hell, why did you have to write that? Now I can't stop imagining what you'd look like with your stomach swelled with my child. You are giving me everything I never thought was possible for me. A family… I never would have dreamed of the possibility until now. I love you so damn much.

———

Killian,

Fifteen years has come and gone faster than I realized. I can't believe I'm already thirty-three. I'm aging, not just in years but in my body, as well. Funny how I didn't really notice until I looked in the mirror this morning. I guess I look the same, just older, but my looks are only going to continue to change. Maybe what I'm feeling is relief—relief that you can't see me as I age while you stay the same handsome man I remember.

Melanie,

317

You're wrong. I have seen a recent picture of you. Every few years I get a new one of you on my desk. I don't know who takes it, but I have a good guess it's Penny because Ryan gets them as well of Tess and her family, and you.

You're beautiful now as you were when I last saw you. Your body is more filled out with age, and I find it a damn shame I can't trace the new curves on your body, but I'll make up for that loss one day.

Age is a beautiful thing to me, maybe because I won't ever experience it. I'm glad you get to experience time and age before you become like me.

——

Killian,

Today was a nightmare. Mom tried to set me up with Alex's friend. I threw a fit and as soon as the poor guy left, Mom and Alex sat me down and asked if maybe I liked women and if so, they were cool with it. They just wanted me to stop hiding it if I was…

So, I told them I was and that I always had a huge crush on Tess, but she was straight and happily married. Of course, they didn't believe me. (Almost time for Rylan's baby sister to get here, but that's getting off the subject… still, I'm so excited!!!)

I know they mean well, but what I'm going through with you is something they'll never know or understand. I hate it and it makes me miss you tonight even more so.

Love, Melanie

318

CHAPTER THIRTY-THREE
Killian

The last few months, Ryan and I have spent building a place on the other side of the woods for him to live. He and I both agreed that it was time for him to leave the castle so that he can have his own place and be who he wants. Penny and him weren't together, but they were spending all their time together—I don't want to be the one to tell them that it was one and the same. They liked what they had, and I wasn't going to ruin it for them.

It had been a long battle—still ongoing—with his relationship with Fear. Not only was it hard for him to keep him satisfied, but Ryan admitted that a part of him—the part that was Fear—hated me. It wasn't easy for him to be around me some days, yet he immediately agreed when I asked if he wanted to live on the other side of the woods. Maybe it was to get back at Fear in some way, or maybe it was to see Melanie again one day, I didn't know and I wouldn't ever ask—, truthfully, I didn't mind his company.

Maybe I was getting fond of him, and it even bothered me the days he couldn't stand to look at me. I've already known him for over a century now.

Unlike me, Ryan wasn't connected, he didn't feel like one person with Fear. He said it felt like a power struggle over his body all the time. He'd hear Fear's voice in his head a lot trying to unsettle him and when Fear managed to take control, he'd disappear for a bit and come back—Ryan was sure that Fear went through the same thing with him—I couldn't imagine a conflict between two very different beings inside one mind. It made me wonder why Fear had chosen to merge with Ryan. They were too different—one good, the other bad. I didn't think he'd ever feel the wholeness I felt with the merge. I was Killian. I was Grim. I was one being that went by many different names all according to who spoke to me.

Ryan disappeared one day and Penny came to me worried. It wasn't the first time and surely wouldn't be the last. It didn't take me long to find him, I just sought out Fear and easily found him. He was at a whore-house in the Underworld, buried deep in a busty brunette he had pinned beneath him. Only it wasn't Ryan, it was Fear. He probably sought out this place because most of these females could handle the kind of violence Fear lived on. This was one of the ways Ryan was keeping Fear satisfied, but I interfered when his tail wrapped around her neck. If it were Ryan, he would do just enough to get high from it, but with Fear, he would probably kill her. Before I interfered, the female's face morphed into a giant mouth with razor sharp teeth—she was determined to protect herself. I yanked him off of her and she hissed when I did. He would survive anything that happened to him, but I'd save him from the pain.

Fear turned back and looked at me, only to change back into Ryan. He laughed, before saying, "I was fine. I had him under control." And I believed him. He looked completely at ease and relaxed.

I arched my eyebrow and shook my head with a smile. "That's not the only place she has teeth." When his smile dropped and the color faded from his face, I laughed.

———

Ryan got himself into bigger trouble a few weeks later. It was becoming another job of mine to hunt him down and stop him from doing something stupid, but he was always doing something before I got the chance to prevent it.

The question I have with him this time: How the bloody hell did one guy get to every wife and concubine in a Demon Lord's harem in a matter of minutes?

The demon was over nine feet tall and was called a lord for a reason: he was beastly. He wasn't an entity, though, but still powerful. The Demon Lord had dark skin and an incredible mass of muscle, and horns way bigger than Fear's. He wore silver cuffs on his wrists and ankles, and only wore something similar to a kilt. His face was that of a giant cat.

When I arrived, the demon had Ryan tied up, hanging by a chain around his neck. All of his wives sat on their knees behind him in amusement. It appeared they enjoyed making their lover upset. I sighed and shook my head. "I think you've punished him enough," I said to the Demon Lord. Ryan looked like he had taken a good beating. He probably came here asking for it. It didn't even look like he tried to put up a fight.

Cat eyes landed on me, and he laughed. "I won't be satisfied until he's dead. He slept with my women!" he yelled in Ryan's face.

"I don't think he's the only one to blame." I looked at the women and they huddled together, playing innocent all the while their eyes held the truth. "Besides, he can't be killed. You know that." Ryan gave him a cocky grin even though his face was blood-red from being choked.

"I don't care."

"I guess we aren't doing this the easy way." I jumped in the air and broke the chain with my scythe. Ryan fell to his knees and quickly removed the chain around his neck.

"They were begging for it. I only gave them what you couldn't." The women all gasped while Ryan grinned. I didn't even get the chance to sigh because the Demon Lord went after him. I faded in between them and pushed him backward and lifted my scythe. I watched him study my blade and I saw the fear. "Do you want to die today?" I asked the Demon Lord. What he didn't know was there was no way I could kill him today since he wasn't meant to die. He didn't know I was bound by my own nature, only Ryan did and he wasn't saying a word. He just wore a cocky expression as he gazed at the other demon.

Once we were back at my castle, I smacked the back of his head. He grabbed his head and glared at me. "What was that for?"

I glared back. "Why are you being so reckless? Yes, you can't be killed, but that doesn't mean you don't feel pain and with the right spell, we know a merge can be broken. Don't piss off the wrong person."

He walked ahead of me. "This is me now. It's my nature—I want to corrupt things; I want to provoke things into feeling fear so that I can feed on it. I want to kill and if I'm not killing, then I need to be the one receiving pain." He turned and looked back at me. "I can't fight it, if I do, then he pushes himself out and we all know the things he'll do is much worse than what I do."

I stepped forward. "I get it, you are Fear now." I sighed and placed my hand on his back. "But we have eternities to figure out how to deal with your burdens."

He was quiet for a long time before he finally said, "Can we not tell Melanie all the things I do now? I can't stand the thought of her knowing the sick things I do…"

"This is Melanie you're talking about; nothing is going to change your friendship with her." I made sure to add the friendship part in there so that he remembered she was *with me.* "And you can't keep it from her. One day, she's going to be here again."

His expression turned dark for a second. "I know the truth, ya know." I arched an eyebrow at him. "That she was meant to be with me first, in her human life."

I sighed. Damn those stupid angels. How the hell did he find out? I didn't think they'd find him just to tell him that… He was one of the Devil's entities, they have no hold over him. "Are you asking for trouble?" I asked him.

He nodded eagerly. I knew what this was about. He still needed relief from Fear's hold. "Let's go. What are you waiting for?" he asked me. I kicked him in the gut and he laughed and coughed, and went at me again. Again. And again.

Until the darkness quietened inside him.

CHAPTER THIRTY-FOUR

Killian,

Alex's wedding day is finally here. I can't believe my kid brother is already twenty-five. His soon-to-be wife is amazing, sweet, and nice—total opposite of my brother. They balance each other out well.

Seeing them so happy puts a smile on my face, but it's also depressing. Tess and now Alex have their own family and we are… well, ours is on pause.

But if there's one thing I've learned from all these years is that, while missing you, I truly understand how much I love you.

Love, Melanie

Melanie,

It must be in the air because Lincoln recently married, too. He moved out of the castle and made a place in the woods with his wife to have privacy. Ryan and Penny won't say they're dating, but I've found them more than once in the woods by mistake in positions that say otherwise. They have a unique relationship. She knows what he does to satisfy Fear and she still goes to him. If it's not love, then it's at least something special.

Dragons are in their mating season right now, so it's not even safe to go outside because you never know what you might see… Maybe Rixen will catch Sky this year. He hasn't yet, she doesn't make it easy on him.

As for me, I'm still waiting for the day I come for you and while missing you, I know how much I will cherish you.

Killian

———

Killian,

I finally bought the house I've been eyeing the past few months. I wasted away a good chunk of years in that tiny apartment and now I'm regretting it, but I guess I just got caught up with work and living… It's a simple three-bedroom house, but it's more than enough for me and I can finally get my things out of storage.

Alex and Sarah are trying for a baby. Rylan is almost ten and his little sister, Hope, is going on three. Tess is bringing them over to spend the night while she helps with unpacking. They love their auntie Mel-Mel, and I could never hate them for calling me by my old childhood nickname that their mother started when it's too cute coming from them.

———

Jed Rose has so much hair and he's a little butterball. Did you see him through the necklace? I hope you saw the picture I took of him with Rylan and Hope, at least. And I've been pretty good about keeping my pictures away from the necklace so that you can't see what I look like now. I look the same, just older… and getting wider (hopefully wiser, too.) LOL. Comes with age, they say…

Hope keeps telling everyone that she's going to marry Jed. He's already taking hearts straight out of the womb. If he's anything like Alex was during his teenage years, Lord help us.

Tess has her hands full with her two already, I don't want to imagine teenage years for her. They've been teaching me Chinese, by the way.

Wo Ai Ni. I love you.

All these babies make me realize I'm aging and that means I'm that much closer to being with you.

———

In life, we knew there was a beginning and an end. People get sick and eventually die, but I spent all these years waiting for my own death, that I had forgotten—or maybe I had never thought of losing someone I loved because I've been wrapped up in wanting my own. I ignored the change in Mom and it never hit me until her test results came back. She had lung cancer. She never smoked a day in her life.

I sat beside her in the doctor's office as the doctor informed her. I didn't move, but I felt her hand latch onto mine. I was scared. I lost many patients on the way to the hospital, I surrounded myself in death—it came naturally to me while waiting for my own to come. So, I knew how it looked. I saw the families panic and grieve, I saw the patients take their last breath… but this was terrifying, and now the fear of death came crawling back. I forgot how scary it was to know you were going to lose someone.

Mom and I had a strange relationship. We loved each other, but we have always been at odds. She never wanted me to live a lonely life. Why did I always picture her nagging about the way I lived my life until the day I died? Why didn't I think that I would lose her first? I loved her. I loved her nagging, I knew it meant she cared even when it crawled through my skin. I was forty and she was sixty-two now, that number seemed too small. It wasn't enough for her.

She hadn't even retired yet. She was still working… she needed to enjoy another twenty years and retire, she earned it…

"I will tell Alex tonight," she said, gripping my hand. We were already walking out the hospital. I didn't remember getting up from the chair. I looked at her— really looked at her. How could I have not noticed it sooner, how much she had aged? Her skin was a yellowish color, and her eyes were sunken in. She was a shell of the woman that raised me. Everything was right there in front of me now that I let myself notice.

She was a grandma now; she couldn't be sick. When she brought her hand to my face, I realized it was because I was crying. "Don't cry. This is a part of life. I knew something wasn't right with all this coughing. I don't feel the same anymore, but there's still time. It's still in the early stages, I have time to see Alex give me another grandchild." She nodded her head with determination. "I'm sure." She smiled with tears in her eyes.

"I'm sorry." I cried. Sorry for not giving her the things she wanted me to have in this life.

She shook her head. "No, I'm sorry." She hugged me quickly and her sorry only made me cry even harder because without saying it aloud, we both knew what we were sorry for.

———

Killian,

You already know the results, don't you? You knew this would happen long before I wrote it in a letter. You know when she will leave us...

Will you promise to be the one who ascends her? Let her see you, Killian, show her what I could never tell her.

I don't want to lose her, I love her.

I can't handle this day.

***

-Killian-

All my Reapers have a day when they'll leave and retire. Demons lived several centuries, but they weren't immortal. They all die one day. I was always recruiting new Reapers; I didn't care what kind of demon they were, if they were willing and decent, I gave them a chance and bestowed my power onto them.

I expected Penny to retire soon, I could see the look in her eyes as she finally started to show age after all these centuries alive. She would leave, but I wondered if leaving meant that she would stop going to Ryan as well. I didn't know what would happen to him if she stopped coming around. I knew they both ran from different things, but I saw comfort between them.

***

-Melanie-

Mom hadn't lied. She sat on the hospital bed holding her second grandchild. Another boy, Allen Rose, who made me an aunt for the fourth time. Tess and I always considered me as Rylan and Hope's aunt, only I knew that I would have been their aunt by marriage if things had been different and Ryan had survived and I never met Killian.

Mom was bald from her treatments, she was pale and super thin, but her smile was bright holding her grandbaby. Cancer had taken a toll on her the past year and a half, but we all knew she was reaching her end. She was in the final stage—the chemo took her as far as she'd let it before she gave up on it—and my heart couldn't stand seeing her in so much pain. She had been determined to see her grandchild, and she did just that.

That must have been all it took because three days later, she became unresponsive. A part of me died that day with her as I watched her breaths grow fainter and fainter until her chest rose for the last time. Alex and I were the only ones in the room with her, Sarah and the babies were in the waiting room. The first thing Alex did when she died was bring me into his arms and hug me. Alex was a grown man now, he no longer needed his big sis to comfort him, instead, he was the one who comforted me.

I watched both our parents die in a hospital bed. This part of life was sad.

But, I knew Grim Reaper was here and he'd take her someplace better than here.

***

Killian

I saw Alex, and I knew he was comforting Melanie in his arms although I couldn't see her. I dreaded this day for a long time for her, but it was something every human went through.

Tina rose from her body as a ghost. The first thing she did was glance toward her kids. She had a mixture of emotions on her face before her eyes fell on me. As a ghost, she already sensed who and what I was, but when I left Grim's state and became Killian, her eyes widened. She still recognized me after all these years. She wouldn't forget the man she thought broke her daughter's heart.

Without words, I walked to her and placed my hands over hers. While I helped her away from her dead body, I fed her my memories and the truth of her daughter. Tears escaped her eyes as they continued to widen as I filled her head with images. When I finished, I dropped her hand and gave her a moment. Her hands went to her mouth. She finally understood her daughter after all these years. She walked over to Melanie and tried touching her as she cried.

"My baby, Melanie, oh, I had no idea," she went on and on. "I'm sorry for never believing you."

"She understands," I spoke for Melanie because her letters were filled with all the reasons why she knew her mom couldn't believe her.

Tina looked back at me. "I'm sorry to you as well. And most of all, I'm sorry that you can't be with my daughter yet." She smiled. "Take care of her for me."

I nodded and became Grim again to open the passage to Heaven. She glanced at her kids one last time before stepping through the portal. There was a smile on her face.

CHAPTER THIRTY-FIVE

Killian,

Age is no longer on my side. I have wrinkles and I'm a little depressed about it, just because I know you are still the same. The kids still tell me I'm beautiful, though. Even at this age, I get asked out occasionally, that should count for something.

———

Jed started pee-wee basketball today. He looks so cute in his jersey.

———

Rylan is graduating high school today. Tess cried the entire time which only made me.

———

I started taking blood pressure pills today. I ache more than anything anymore. The changes I feel in my body remind me I'm that much closer to being with you, but I'll admit, I'm afraid after all these years. How much has changed? How much have I changed?

———

Rylan is a doctor like his dad. Hope is about to graduate now, and Jed is already in his second year. Allen is in middle school. I know I talk about them so much but in this world, they are my world. It's sad, yet bittersweet as I watch them grow up.

***

Melanie,

Penny stopped coming to Ryan altogether after she retired. She was aging, and instead of spending her last years with him, she chose to leave.

Ryan doesn't show if he's bothered by it. He's still getting into trouble and I'm still there to get him out of it.

Sky laid eggs, but it will still be another century before they hatch, though. Dragon eggs take a long time.

***

Killian,

The arthritis in my hands is getting worse. At my age, everything on my body is falling apart. I fear the day when my arthritis gets to the point that I can no longer write to you.

———

The kids had a surprise birthday party on my sixtieth birthday at Alex's. I may have rubbed off on Rylan because even in his thirties, he's still a bachelor and has no plans on settling down. Hope spoke the truth the day Jed was born when she claimed him hers. When he entered college, the two of them started dating and neither cared that she was the older one in the relationship. And Allen's my amazing little painter out of the family.

———

Maybe it's old age or maybe because I've been thinking about it lately, but I no longer hold a grudge against the angel, Faye. She made the wrong choice, but her choice was for our happiness. She had no idea things would turn out the way they had.

Nothing's changed. I still love you as much as I did the last time I saw you. No, even more so. Always more.

———

I stopped writing the letters once I reached eighty. My body was slowly failing me, and with it, I became anxious. Even so, my heart was at peace.

CHAPTER THIRTY-SIX
Alex

I sat beside Melanie's bed as her last breath drew near—no, it was her last. Cancer took her the same way it did our parents, only she managed to outlive the age they both died.

When I looked at my sister, my heart ached. All I could see or feel was loneliness. She never dated, never married, or had kids. All she had was me and my family, Tess and her kids. Thinking back, she always seemed happy, but how could she when she lived her entire life alone. She loved her nieces and nephews like her own, but it was plain to see she wanted her own.

Even in death, I couldn't understand her.

She made me promise not to let Jed or any of them around when we knew it was time for her to go. She refused to stay in a hospital, said she didn't want to die in one like our parents did, so a nurse took care of her in her home.

My head dropped, and I closed my eyes when the nurse stepped out of the room to give me a minute alone with her. I wiped my hands over my face and no matter how hard I tried not to, I couldn't keep my emotions buried. I couldn't stand the way she chose to live her life. Now, I regretted not trying even harder while we were still young to get her to live more. Did she pretend to smile when we were around or was she genuinely happy? I wanted to understand her, but she never tried to help me and Mom understand.

I froze in my chair as something was in front of me, blocking the light from my hands. I looked up slowly, expecting it to be the nurse and I just didn't hear her, but it wasn't. Panic gripped my chest and I grabbed it, I couldn't believe my eyes.

Killian stood before me. I was seven when I last saw him, but I could never forget the face of the man I blamed for my sister's loneliness. How… he looked exactly the same as he did sixty-four years ago.

His eyes were on Melanie as he traced his hand over her frail arm. He uttered one word. "Beautiful." He leaned down and kissed her forehead.

Then he turned back to me. "What—" I began, but when he placed his hand over my forehead, images raced through the back of my eyelids. These memories weren't mine—they were his. Of him and Melanie. All his emotions were rolling over me—he loved her—I knew now. I understood everything.

He gave me back a memory I lost, no, that he took from me. The fear of that night chilled my entire body and I sucked in a breath. It took me several seconds to figure out I wasn't that seven-year-old boy anymore and the monster from the memory wasn't here with us now.

He dropped his hand and I felt the tears rolling down my cheeks. I watched as he pulled a small chest from the inside of his jacket and opened it. A golden silhouette floated up from the chest and he placed it over Melanie's lifeless body.

My eyes widened as her body began to change, reverting back to her younger self. He scooped her up and cradled her to his chest. There was a peaceful smile on her face, like she was only sleeping. He glanced back at me, then to her, and disappeared.

I knew why my sister chose the life she did. I shook my head and started crying again. "I understand you now, Sis. I'm so sorry." I stopped calling her Sis when I was a teenager but felt like calling her that today. My tears turned to laughter.

How was I supposed to explain where her body went?

Maybe I'd just tell them all the truth: Grim Reaper stole her heart a long time ago and all these years later, he came back... and like a thief in the night, he took the rest of her with him.

CHAPTER THIRTY-SIX
Melanie

Opening my eyes was like waking up from a long dream. I was lying on his bed wearing the old gown I died in, only I was young again. Killian lay beside me, propped up on his elbow as he gazed down at me with all the love and affection I missed.

I met his eyes and in my head, I always came up with a billion things I wanted to say to him first when I saw him again, but now that I was right here in his arms, there were no perfect words to give him.

His hand touched my cheek, and I smiled, letting a tear slide down my cheek. So long. So many years. In my darkest nights, I would worry what we had would be gone when I finally got to him again, but the wait was over and the feelings… were piercing my heart. It felt explosive to be next to him again. And right. And forever.

"Hi," I whispered bashfully, and we both laughed quickly, softly.

I felt his body shaking against mine. "Welcome home," he told me, and his voice enveloped my skin. Oh, how much I've missed him.

"I love you."

"I love you."

Nothing else was needed. We grew in our time apart, as we always would as we stayed together. There would always be something new to discover with one another… His hand slid up my thigh, over my hip bone… and I moaned softly. First, we'd start off by rediscovering each other's body.

Then he'd read me letter after letter that he wrote to me while I was away as we lay naked and wrapped in the sheets, then he'd take me again—let me come undone beneath him—again—and again.

Everything was on repeat.

Because there was no stopping us now.

———

We stayed trapped together for days it seemed like before we finally ventured out of the bedroom. I finally took the time to ask, "Where's Ryan?" I matched Killian, decked out head-to-toe in black as we stepped into the ballroom.

"Right here." It was Ryan who answered. I turned my head and smiled when I saw him standing there, arms stretched wide for me, grinning. Only he wasn't the boy I remembered. He looked a lot different. His arms were covered in ink and he was a lot more built.

I hurried to hug him, and he wrapped his arms around me and squeezed tight. "I didn't think I was ever going to see you… he sure kept you trapped in there long enough." I laughed.

When he released me from his hug, I studied him again. "Look at you, Ryan," I told him. "You even have piercings in your ear." The Ryan I knew would have never done that.

"I gotta fit in down here," he stated. I shook my head, and he grinned. "But, look at you." He grabbed my arms and eyed me up and down. "How does my heart still flop out of my chest at the sight of you?" I rolled my eyes.

"Let it continue to flop," Killian said, stepping toward us. "Stop flirting with my woman."

I waved them both away. "Stop, it's weird hearing you guys talk about me like I'm pretty. I spent the last thirty years as an old woman. It's going to take some time before I get used to being young again."

Killian twirled me around to face him. "You were beautiful with age just as you are to me now." I blushed and looked away. He couldn't steal my heart again when he already had it.

"How's my niece and nephew?" Ryan asked right away.

I smiled immediately, reverting to an aunt full of pride. "I was hoping you knew about them!" They listened to me for hours as I spoke about everyone I left behind in the human world.

When Killian took me outside, I searched for Sky. "Melanie…" I looked back and saw their expression and frowned.

"Where's Sky? Rixen?" I asked.

"She passed away a century ago…Rixen died a year before she did." I didn't get to say goodbye… I looked down and Killian grabbed my shoulders so I'd look up. "Sky would have waited forever if she could of, but it was her time and she left a part of herself behind." I arched an eyebrow his way. "She laid eggs, and they're fully grown dragons now."

He laughed at my hopeful expression. "She had more than one?"

"One boy and one girl." He whistled and I glanced up to the sky. My eyes fell over the trees where two white dragons flew toward us. When they landed, I saw that the male had Sky's blue eyes and the girl had red ones like Rixen had.

"What are their names?" I ran my hand over the boy first as he bent his head down for me. He lifted his snout into my hair and I smiled.

"River." He pointed toward the boy, then the girl. "That's Ruby." Killian was rubbing his neck awkwardly as he watched River… it was strange. I squinted my eyes and watched him try to get River's attention. When he finally did, River stepped away from me and started coughing—more like hacking up something. Killian blew out a frustrated breath and slapped his palm over his face. "You weren't supposed to swallow it." Before I could ask what was going on, River threw up a black tiny box and shrugged his shoulders nonchalantly at Killian.

I grabbed my chest because my heart was beating ninety-miles-per-second as Killian bent down and picked up the box. Only he stayed down on one knee and opened the box, revealing a beautiful ring. "Will you be my eternity, Melanie Rose?" He still had to ask after all this time? He knew I wanted my life spent with him a long time ago.

"Our future is already set in stone. There's no getting rid of me," I told him.

"Is that a yes?"

I nodded and smiled. He placed the ring on my finger before scooping me up in his arms.

Our wait was over. *I'm finally home.*

EPILOGUE

It was their big day. All the inhabitants of the woods came out to join them. Killian went all out, turning the woods into a fairy tale—as if he hadn't already created it to be that way, to begin with. The wedding took place in front of the castle where the groom and his two best men—Ryan and River—waited for the bride to arrive. Melanie had made River wear a tie and Ruby a skirt, and every few seconds Ryan would have to nudge River to keep him from trying to bite it off.

Killian had the smile of a man madly in love as he watched the dragons bring Melanie down from the sky in a wagon. As they came to a stop, they helped her out. He lost all thoughts when he saw her, as did everyone else. She wore a golden cloak over her white dress that peeked out underneath. Her blonde curls fell over her shoulders as she smiled at him. She was mesmerizing and deserved to be the center of attention this day.

As she glided down the aisle, she passed many demons and Prince Cadence and the elf clan who took her by surprise when she saw that they weren't tiny, but full-sized people at her wedding. Her attention went back to her soon-to-be husband as she followed slowly behind Ruby as her tail sashayed back and forth—someone liked their skirt.

Xavier was the son of Lincoln who passed away before Melanie returned and he was the one to marry them. Melanie placed her hands in Killian's as they said their vows and as he gazed into her eyes, he found peace and comfort, passion and love, hope for the future. He no longer faced time alone, people would always die around him, but he'd always have her. And she'd have him. He bent her backward and kissed her heavily in front of everyone that watched.

They celebrated the night away where at one point Ryan hooked his arm around Melanie's shoulder and said, "Anytime you want to have an affair, I live right on the other side of the woods." Then before anyone knew what happened, Killian became Grim and pulled the scythe out on Ryan. Of course, Ryan dodged and Grim destroyed the cake and table, and all the food fell to the ground.

"Have you forgotten, Grim… I'm immortal, too. I have all the time in the world to win her over." Ryan continued to bait Grim while Melanie laughed and watched as the two of them wrecked the place.

Looking at them, she realized her best friend wasn't only hers anymore, but she didn't mind at all. It made her happy instead.

Sometime after Killian stopped playing with Ryan, he took his wife to the sky and danced with her there. "Thanks for existing," he whispered into her ear, and she melted into his arms.

The rest of their story was, well… eternal.

And just in case you're wondering, Melanie no longer hears the voice, because she *is* the power. She's whole.

ANOTHER EPILOGUE

Very Bad—Soon-to-be Dead Demon

She screamed. She ran. I smiled.

She couldn't escape, but I would allow her the illusion of getting away for a short while. It made the flesh taste better on humans; fear seasoned them just right. I rubbed my giant belly as I followed her into the alley. She stumbled and looked back, she was getting too close to the road. I pressed the portal chip in my pocket and ported in front of her. She screamed some more, and my eyes rolled back at how delicious she smelled. My favorite thing to eat were humans.

"I don't think you belong in this world." I grabbed the human girl's hair as I turned my attention to the voice behind me. That fear I loved to taste on humans so much, I smelled it on me as I gazed at Grim. "Actually, you don't belong anywhere but one place now."

My eyes widened. "No." I let go of the humans and she took off running.

"Yes," he replied.

I ran my hand over the pocket of my jeans, I only had to press the portal chip and I could buy myself some time to escape. Grim was by my side the next second, twisting my hand, breaking it. I held my mangled hand up and cried out in pain. "Don't kill me," I begged. No demon wanted to die, especially not when it was by Grim. He sent them where no one wanted to go.

"I can't kill you," he told me, and I stopped whimpering long enough to stare him. A ray of hope fluttered in my stomach. "See, I can't kill anything unless it's their time…" I smiled, and a feminine laugh echoed in the distance. I jumped, going on alert again. "But my wife, now, she's completely different."

"What? Wife?" I stuttered. I heard the rumors that Grim had a wife, but he spent so many years alone that nobody believed it.

He nodded. "And she really, really hates demons like you." He stepped forward. "She's got a nasty temper, too."

"I do." I followed the direction of her voice and gasped. She was beautiful. Her skin, hair, clothes were lit up like she was a light; golden as she walked next to Grim. My mouth watered… how good she would taste. Her expression darkened as she looked at me. "Even now, when he knows he's about to die, he licks his lips like he's about to have one last banana split."

Grim placed his hand over her shoulder. "Are you thinking about ice cream at a time like this?" he asked her.

She nodded and tilted her head to smile at him. "Yes, we should get an ice cream cake to take back home."

He laughed. "Some things will never change."

I took off running while they were talking, but she appeared in front of me. When I turned, Grim was behind me. "Please, I don't want to die." Grim's wife flung me against the wall and I dropped to my knees. "Please, please."

"Disgusting," she muttered down at me. "You just became your victims, pleading for your life. Tell me, did you let them live?" My eyes widened with the truth. I was going to die... just like all my food before me.

"Let's go haunt Tess when we are through. Old woman still hasn't keeled over," she spoke to Grim.

He shook his head at her. "Leave her be." She grunted in response and smiled again.

"Fine, then let's go befriend Jed and them. Can't you alter our looks so that we can?"

They started walking down the alleyway side-by-side. "What am I going to do with you?" he asked her.

Wait, what was going on? Were they letting me live? They were clearly walking away from me. I got up slowly and felt a little more confident when I did. "Oh yeah." Grim's wife stopped and looked to Grim. I froze when they both turned back to look at me with the same terrifying grin.

"Told you she had a nasty side to her," Grim said. They gave me false hope?

"Do you know how your victims felt now?" looking me dead in the eyes, she asked. Realization smacked me in the face again. She brought her hand out like she held something, only I saw nothing there. She made a scissor motion with her fingers as she smiled at me.

"Tell the Devil, Melanie says hello."

"No, please!" She closed her pretend scissors down on whatever she was holding.

Lights out.

THE END

Falling for Fear

Ryan.

Centuries spent trying to please the monster he became. A good guy turned wicked.

Molly.

Centuries spent hiding and running. A bad ghost turned immortal.

Could he ever calm his monster? Could she ever find a road of redemption? What happened when fate finally had them cross paths again? What happened when he didn't recognize her now that she was in the body of a woman?

Did redemption come easy, or did it come hard, cruel, and ugly?

COMING SOON!

Falling for Fear will conclude A Grim Awakening series. Don't miss Ryan's chance at a happy ending!

AUTHOR'S NOTE

I hoped you enjoyed the third book! If you would leave a review on Amazon and Goodreads, it would be extremely helpful. I love reading what y'all think!

You can find me on Facebook:

https://www.facebook.com/michellegrossauthor/

Twitter: @AuthorMichelleG

Instagram: michellegrossmg

Made in United States
Troutdale, OR
08/13/2023